Slowly and All at Once

A Coming of Old Age Story

KAREN ANDRUS

Published by
Only Human Books
Sacramento, California

Library of Congress Control Number:
2025913151

ISBN (paperback): 979-8-9992230-0-5
ISBN (eBook): 979-8-9992230-1-2

This is a work of fiction. Unless otherwise indicated, all the names, characters, businesses, places, events, and incidents in this book are either the product of the author's imagination or used in a fictitious manner.

To My Brother
Tak for kaffe, tak for chokolade.

To My Mother
The deep, sinking-into-it hugs are
what I will always remember.

CHAPTER ONE

NINA

According to eighteenth-century playwright Carlo Gozzi, there are only thirty-seven stories told in the world. This one is of a mother and a daughter as they face old age and each other.

⁓

Nina loved teaching her second graders the "Aerial View" art lesson. Before she distributed the pastels, she stood in front of the room and *ahem*ed. A sea of hands filled her view, signaling quiet.

"We need an airport runway," she said, "right smack in the center of the room." She drew a diagram on the whiteboard, which showed the clearing, as well as how the chairs needed to be placed in two columns on both sides of a center aisle. "That's where you passengers will sit on the plane."

"When I count to three, let's see," she raised an eyebrow, "which team can… most *quietly*… and most *carefully*… move the desks to the side?"

The students concentrated on her mouth, and when she reached "three," they scraped the desks over the waxed linoleum.

So much for the "quietly" part. One team swiftly arranged the chairs in the middle. A seven-year-old flight attendant ushered the passengers to their seats. The captain and her co-pilot took their places in the cockpit, backs to their passengers, legs dangling from serious adult swiveling desk chairs.

"Seatbelts on," the captain instructed. "When we get high enough, I'll let you know what we're flying over. Now sit back and relax."

A minute passed in near silence. A minute of silence in a second-grade classroom is a beautiful thing. Most of the seven-year-old travelers were absorbed in the land of make-believe. Maya and Natasha sat together, no surprise. Natasha had the window seat and was looking "out." She gestured to her friend that the window was round. Maya looked over as Natasha described what she saw.

"There are mostly squares," Natasha whispered. "All colors, though. Not just green."

When introducing the lesson, Nina had the class watch video clips showing views of the Earth from 30,000 feet up. Serpentine rivers. Amoeba-shaped Great Lakes. Geologic wonders that looked like skeletal remains. Agricultural geometry—circles and squares. Amazing how imagination obliterated the very real surroundings: the sheen of linoleum, the desks shoved against the particle board built-ins, the line of hooks holding twenty-eight backpacks. The captain was back. "We're passing over more farmland. See the squares under us? See all the colors? And now..." she waited several seconds, "see round shapes, too? That's where the farmers water the crops in circles. Oh, wait!" The captain paused. "We're going through a cloud. It's going to be a little bumpy."

Lucas asked for an air sickness bag. "Ms. Visser, I'm gonna hurl."

The co-pilot calmly inserted himself. "Taking deep breaths is always good. Breathe in," he soothed, "then hold, then breathe out."

When the plane landed, the captain apologized for braking hard. Everyone applauded. The passengers shoved their chairs back over the linoleum to rejoin the desks. Every child found a clearing for the paper they were given and rolled down the rubber bands that held together their pastel crayons.

"Draw and color what you saw from your window on the plane," Nina told them. As she stepped over bent heads and bodies curled in postures of concentration, their aerial views came to life. Beautiful and radiant squares of color, some filled with plum, rose, and deep green, others in tender golds and gritty umber. As the fifty-minute lesson neared its end, students placed their finished art onto the counter by the sink, waiting impatiently to wash their hands of smeary color. One student continued to work with fierce absorption, the only one still on the floor. This was mildly surprising, since when Nina last cast a shadow over her project, the crop circles and squares of agriculture were vivid and completely colored in.

The phone beeped on the wall behind Nina's desk.

"Ms. Visser, it's your mother. She needs you to call her right away."

Nina thanked the secretary and hung up. Five minutes until recess. She focused on keeping her mind clear as she herded the kids into a line, handing out granola bars as they exited.

When Nina walked over to hasten the last artist's efforts, she found the paper saturated in black. "Oh," Nina said. "That's beautiful. Can you tell me why you chose to cover everything over with your black pastel?"

"We flew into a cloud," her student reminded her.

Moments like this made the rigors of teaching worthwhile.

After all the kids headed to the playground, Nina debated whether to race to the bathroom or call her mother first. Ten minutes wasn't long enough to do both. She reached for the phone.

"Mom?"

Lillian started in her usual pragmatic tone. "Dad just loved it when your class sang Happy Birthday to him yesterday."

"Good, good, but why are you calling? I only have a minute."

"He's in the hospital. He fell, and I had to call the EMTs. When they came to get him up, they monitored him and said his oxygen level was low. He's at Kaiser. You need to come down."

"Of course."

Nina hoped her voice sounded calmer than she felt. Remembering the copilot's instruction, she took a deep breath in, held it, and exhaled slowly. In just the last two months, this was the fifth time her mother had called about her father in the middle of class. He was in decline. His falls were more frequent. Now he was in the hospital. Would she be driving the 125 miles to Los Gatos to say goodbye? She couldn't bear the thought. And then her own pragmatism kicked in. She'd be staying late tonight, making plans for the substitute teacher.

"If you can be here tomorrow before 4:00," Lillian continued, "I can still get to the peace vigil downtown."

Nina's jaw tightened.

"I'll let you know when I'm on my way." She dug for the key in her purse, secured the door behind her, and raced to the staff restroom.

Two toilets flushed. Nina nodded to the speech and language pathologist as she exited, and found herself alone. In those seconds of privacy, her thoughts switched to her father, and a sinking sensation rushed over her. He was her anchor. She remembered calling him in despair after a series of interviews for entry-level jobs.

"Dad," she'd started, getting no further before breaking down.

"Honey," he said.

"I don't understand," she whimpered, "what's wrong with me. I'm not applying for a position in physics. I've had… four interviews… at a restaurant! And I still haven't heard back."

"Sweetheart," Cal repeated. "Nothing is wrong with you. You're a wonder, and in time, you'll find what you need. Meanwhile, we are here for you. Always know that."

Somehow, hearing those words cemented her understanding that it was true, he would always be there. Like a brick wall preventing a fall. Suddenly, her face flushed with heat. He wasn't dead, and here she was, feeling behind her for that solid fortification but clawing at air.

The sound of her flush echoed off the beige subway tile. While at the sink, she recognized another of her unrealized fears: without her dad as a buffer, the existing dynamic between her and her mother could only get worse. The bell rang. She rushed out into the hallway to meet her students where they lined up.

After the final bell and crosswalk duty, Nina called to reserve a sub, making a wild guess that she'd need one for four days. She spent the evening in her classroom preparing subplans and un-jamming the copy machine of math worksheets. At 10:00 she headed home.

Nina's phone buzzed. It was her husband, Myles. He'd gotten her text earlier but was asking for an ETA.

She texted back, "Leaving now. Need to leave for Los Gatos early AM."

He called while Nina was driving home. "You doing okay?" Myles' radio-commentator voice provided instant comfort with smooth bass notes. After the past few disrupted months, she knew *he* knew she was going through an intense mix of worry about her father, circling around what they called "Planet Lilly," and the practical pressures of planning for a sub.

"I'll heat up your dinner and get the suitcase out."

"The suitcase is still in the study from last time, and I'm bringing my cart too. I've got a ton to bring to grade and record."

"How clenched is your jaw?"

"Thanks," she said, consciously releasing her molars. "I mean it."

Hands tight on the steering wheel, she shot onto the freeway toward downtown Sacramento, sending her father loving thoughts. Although alone in her car, Nina swore under her breath. Lillian was... *cavalier* about her husband's falls. When Nina and her sister Jenny encouraged Lillian to hire a caregiver for nights, Lillian waved off the suggestion. "I'm right there," she'd said, failing to mention what Nina and Jenny both knew. While sleeping next to Cal each night, she lodged earplugs snuggly into her ears and couldn't hear a damn thing. *And then she calls me when the going gets tough and asks me to time my drive so she can carry on with her life.*

Keeping one hand on the wheel, she hunted for a protein bar in the console while obsessing over her mother's priorities. They were consistent. All of Nina's childhood, Lillian focused on serving greater humanity. Those in need, but on the other side of the earth. When Nina left home at seventeen, her mother's time centered on Bigger World, the non-profit organization she and Cal founded, leading educational tours to developing countries. "So North Americans can open their perceptions. So we can learn from others."

Nina overshot her exit. A horn blasted from the lane to her right.

She vowed to pay closer attention to the road but immediately returned to the importance her mother placed on Bigger World, to the exclusion of her children.

"Siri, call Jenny."

"What's wrong?" Jenny answered right away.

"God, sorry." It was very late in Chicago. "I'll be quick—bottom line, Dad's in the hospital, very low oxygen levels. Mom wants me to come down."

"It's that bad?"

"I don't know, really. But get this, she wants me to get there in time for her to attend the peace vigil."

"Oh, brother."

"Right?"

"So typical," Jenny said. "Why do you think I moved two thousand miles away?"

It was a relief to share the same take with someone who'd grown up with Lillian's mothering.

"Look," Nina added, "I didn't consider your time zone—I was so pissed off I needed to vent to you and only you. I'll let you go—we'll talk again soon."

"It's okay, I get it. Let me know about Dad once you're in Los Gatos."

It wasn't just the time zone that got in the way of Nina's ability to connect with her big sister. Jenny had a lot on her plate. Her wife Sylvana traveled a lot, and now Jenny carved out time from her CPA practice to help raise a grandchild. Her priorities were in Chicago. And, come to think of it, she'd never absorbed childhood the way Nina had. She seemed less impacted by it. Less tethered. Nina thought of the frightening nights as little children, waiting for their parents to come home from ACLU or WILPF meetings, returning later than promised. While Nina tried to distract herself with a book, Jenny shut herself on the other side of the house, watching *Lost in Space*. Lillian praised Jenny and Nina for their maturity; she was proud of them for staying home without a sitter so she and Cal could do important work.

"We're almost finished drafting a resolution for the Central Labor Council to declare our county a nuclear-free zone," Lillian had said, applying lipstick at the entry's mirror. "You big girls are contributing, too."

On that occasion, Nina had just turned seven. She didn't want to let her parents down by expressing how scared she was. Her fear felt small and cowardly. Selfish, even.

In contrast, Cal served as her protector in other circumstances. Like when he guided her across a torrent of rising water in the Narrows of Zion National Park.

"I'll go first," he said, calming her panic. "Then you'll know the footholds. And I'll be on the other side."

Or when she lost her parents in a crowded protest demonstration in San Francisco before he and Lillian surprised her from behind, both singing "I Wanna Hold Your Hand."

"If that happens again, stay in place. We'll always come back for you," Cal assured her.

And more recently, his sincere interest in her teaching challenges and triumphs lightened her adult worries.

"Just talk to your principal," he'd said after Nina received a threatening call from a parent. "She's there to support you. You did the right thing contacting CPS."

Her chest (her heart?) hollowed when she realized how little time she probably had left with him.

Taking 26th Street, she was three minutes from home. Her

mind wouldn't shake its fixation on Lillian's emotional disconnect. And then Nina remembered when Lillian's younger sister Dessa confided in Nina about a phone call she had made to Lillian years before when their own father was in the ICU. Dessa replayed their conversation word-for-word.

"Daddy's had a stroke."

"Oh, no. What's happening?"

"I'm with Mother, and we're visiting him in the hospital in Santa Rosa. When can you come?"

"Oh, Dessa, I'm in the middle of a reservation issue for our flights to Laos," Lillian had said in a rush. "I've got to change it for everyone on the tour. And we're leaving in three days. We'll have to come up after the trip."

"When is that?"

"We're gone three weeks and then Cal and I are spending an additional week after that, snorkeling in Vietnam. You know, decompressing."

"Decompressing."

"Tours are intense."

"Lilly. You did hear me say that Daddy's had a stroke?"

"Keep me posted." Lillian hung up.

CHAPTER TWO

LILLIAN

The Nearings listened to *Democracy Now* every morning on KPFA, Berkeley's alternative news radio station. While Lillian cleared Cal's breakfast dishes from the teak dining table, Amy Goodman's familiar voice provided comfort, even as she reported on alarming threats to democracy.

Lillian returned the yogurt to the fridge, momentarily eyeing the jar of pickled herring. It was a little early for her to eat; her first meal was always lunch. She shut the door on her craving and loaded the dishwasher instead, hitting the button on the side of the kitchen island to heat the water first. She thought of Nina's last visit, when her daughter had complained about the time it took to get hot water this way. She clearly didn't value the trade-offs for conserving energy. Now seated at the island, Lillian separated bills for Cal from the periodicals he'd stacked together on the Mexican tile counter. The previous month's *Nation* caught her attention; soon she was deep into a story about corruption in the upcoming Brazilian Olympics and how, gratifyingly, the contractors responsible would be held accountable. This kind of reporting kept her hopeful.

The window in the dining room opened to the sounds of mourning doves, filling a pause in the radio broadcast. Looking up from the article, Lillian marveled at the birdsong. One of the doves flew from the crimson-leafed branches of the trident maple. She realized she hadn't seen Cal and it was nearing time for them to go to the Y.

"Cal?"

No response over the sound of the radio.

Lillian rose from her seat to circle through the house. Art and baskets from their travels studded the walls, as well as the Navajo rug hand-woven for them when they married over sixty years before. Sixty years. She shook her head. She and Cal were as much in love as ever. She smiled. And then remembered she was looking for him.

Passing through the living room, she winced at the couch stacked with Guatemalan educational materials—reading she wanted to share with members of the tour she and Cal were scheduled to lead.

"Cal?"

She approached the study, a room pleading for help. Sagging shelves lined the walls, shelves dense with binders, paperwork, books, and boxes identified in the various handwriting of numerous volunteers. "South Africa Post-Apartheid," "Guatemala: Agricultural Development," "Cambodia: Mine Fields," among them.

Lillian felt a flutter.

Out the backdoor and past the birdbath, the stepping stones led her to the clothesline around the back. There he was, curled on the ground, all six feet two inches of him.

"Cal!"

"Just get me up, please."

His face was contorted in pain or frustration, Lillian couldn't tell which. Cal struggled as she coached him.

"Roll over on your stomach." She was, after all, only five feet tall and strong, yes, but not strong enough to support Cal's weight. Before his release from his last hospital visit, Nina made sure the Occupational Therapist demonstrated to Cal how to get up on his own. All while Lillian watched.

"You know what to do, Cal."

"I'm trying." He was on his stomach now but immobilized.

"You have to find a way to do this by yourself. I may not be around when you fall another time."

"Lillian, I can't."

"I'll call the firehouse." This would be the third time Cal failed to get up by himself, even after the OT's demonstration.

"I'm sorry for bothering you folks again," Lillian said on the phone, "but my husband fell, and I can't get him up."

"No bother, Mrs. Nearing. This is why we're here. The crew will be out there shortly."

"Remember that we don't want you to use the sirens."

The dispatcher assured her the engines would pull up quietly.

Lillian watched as the EMTs lifted Cal easily, supporting him as they walked him to the bedroom.

"This is why I don't quibble about paying taxes," Cal thanked them.

"Mr. Nearing," the captain said. "Let your tax dollars serve you. Never," his voice was firm, "hesitate to call us. You need to consider Lillian's well-being, too."

Lillian walked the captain to the front door. His build filled it, red hair grazing the frame overhead.

"Mrs. Nearing," the captain repeated, "never worry about calling us. We want you to. But listen, your husband shouldn't be walking outside in the back. At all. Your yard is like the deep woods. Branches impeding the way, roots to trip over, piles of leaves making things slippery. And," he pointed, "those stepping stones? Very uneven, very unstable."

"But Cal helps hang the laundry." She stepped outside and lowered her voice. "He needs to feel like he's contributing."

"Things have changed, Mrs. Nearing.

"Lillian."

"I see this a lot, Lillian, and it's hard to accept, I know. But it is clear that it's time for your husband to have a walker."

Lillian shook her head, feeling a little unbalanced herself and aware of numbness in two of the fingers on her left hand. "I don't like to think he needs help."

"We've been out here… four times? And listen, we don't mind that at all. But since he's falling so often, have his doctor order a walker." It was a directive.

Lillian's eyes blurred. "I don't see how he can travel if he needs a walker."

"For your peace of mind, Lillian, and," he looked at her pointedly, "for his safety."

Lillian bit her lip. "I hear you."

"Things have changed," the captain said.

The team left. Cal lay safe in bed, so she came into their bedroom quietly. His eyes were closed, his breath steady.

"Darling," she whispered. "I'm going to the Y."

He nodded; eyes still closed.

Her need to swim felt urgent. Her meditation in motion. A way to stay strong. She longed for the water. The cleansing.

She needed to forget that things were changing.

"**F**ucking fuck." That was Nina's answer to Myles when he asked about dinner.

It had been a day. At first recess, Maddy had asked to stay in the classroom; then mutely showed Nina the tender pucker of a fresh burn on her inner thigh.

"Oh, sweetheart." Nina looked into her student's deadened eyes. Maddy shared that her grandfather babysat the night before. Sickened by Maddy's distress and the awareness a family's life would be turned inside out, Nina called CPS. The calls to Child Protective Services were one of the most painful aspects of her job. In her twenty-five years of teaching, this was the fourth time she'd had to report.

When she picked up the class from recess, Aria hastened to her side to explain she had a stomachache "up here," pointing to her forehead. And Xavier W's notable head-scratching likely meant he had lice. After sending Xavier W to the office, Nina received a call from the secretary saying his mother was picking him up for a thorough delousing at home. This meant Nina needed to make copies to her classroom's families to alert them to lice being present in the classroom, along with directions on how to detect nits and get rid of them.

Working in the copy room, Nina received a call from Lillian.

"Nina, please come down as soon as you can."

"What happened?"

"Dad fell and hit his head. We're in the ER."

Nina assured Lillian she'd get things in order as quickly as possible and drive to Los Gatos first thing in the morning.

Even before she opened her front door, deep bass notes of Oscar Peterson's stride piano reached her ears. This meant Myles was done after his own long day. From the foyer she saw his long frame settled onto the living room couch, his hands behind his head, eyes closed.

He stirred. "Hi, darlink," he offered, "welcome home. Can you believe those flat ninths?"

"Flat ninths? Right, yes. Hon, can you turn it down for a second?"

Nina updated her husband on the abrupt need for her to drive to Los Gatos, then stepped away to déjà vu the routine for a substitute and subplans. She'd received an emergency call from her mother now every three weeks since January. She put a pause on her finance project for her parents, which was to set up online billing for them. Autopay would make everything easier, but the time-consuming part wasn't entering the simple list of household bills but adding from the endless canon of organizations to which her parents contributed. Starting at letter C (*Center for Constitutional Rights*) and ending at W (*Women's Empowerment Network*) it occupied eight two-sided pages. And she still had to pack. But first, she needed to call parents who volunteered to chaperone on the class field trip next week. She had just swiveled to face the corner of her office with her phone on speaker when Myles showed up in the doorway to ask about dinner. As in, "what are *you* going to make for dinner?"

Those were some of the reasons for her "fucking fuck" response to an innocent question. But really? Should dinner be added to her list?

Myles quickly rephrased. "I'll figure out dinner. But first…" he came over to kiss her on the top of her head. "…was there anything good that happened today?"

This was what her husband did. He'd ask that question when she was out of bandwidth and snapped his head off. Nina heard him say that to his cello and violin students as soon as they entered the house for their lesson. It was a good tactic.

She wasn't ready to shake her frustrations; there was just too much to do. But her reptile brain receded ever so slightly. She let out a sigh and made a small smile.

Myles stood with Nina's bulletin board of photographs and postcards on his left and his grandparents' oak-encased mirror hanging on the wall to his right. He stroked his beard, expectant.

Nina swiveled to face him.

"One of my former second graders came by after school to show me how beautiful her cursive is."

"Cursive? That's still taught?" Myles stopped. "That's gratifying isn't it, when they come back to see you?"

"I know, right? Well, she had a page of vocabulary and one of the words was 'religion,' which she had to use correctly in a sentence."

"Uh-huh."

"So Alyssa had written in, yes, magnificent cursive, '*religion: my family belongs to the Moron religion.*'"

Myles laughed, then turned to go defrost dinner.

With the phone calls finished and the sub plans sent off successfully (crossing fingers that she'd be assigned a reliable substitute teacher), Myles returned and set a dinner tray next to her open laptop.

She rubbed her eyes, yawned, and closed her computer. Was she imagining an itch on her scalp? She knew she wasn't imagining the headache pulsing in her right temple. She swallowed a Naratriptan, laid out clothes for the morning, and then stood in the shower, trying to empty her brain while washing the day out of her hair and body. Three-minute showers fared better for drought-conditions in California but were insufficient for the kind of emotional clearing she really needed. She stood under the showerhead, got wet, turned off the water, lathered, and turned the water back on to rinse. Under the warm, clear water, she paid close attention to her hands, using the soft washcloth to massage between her fingers. Her hands needed some love and rest.

Joining Myles in bed, she landed with a sigh. His Kindle illuminated his face as he turned to her.

"Hon," he said, squeezing her hand. "If you hadn't had such a late night I'd have asked for a duet."

Playing duets on the piano served as decompression for them both.

"I had Satie out, ready to play."

"Sweet thought, honey." She knew he'd picked Satie's "Gymnopédies" because it was one of her favorites. Soothing. Restful. "Like you said, it got late."

Myles squeezed her hand again, then brought it up to kiss. "I know it's inadvisable to bring big stuff up before we sleep, but after these last few crazy months, I've been thinking, and I have to ask... have you ever considered retiring early?"

She closed her eyes, finding relief in darkness. Retiring was not in the plan. But neither was stretching between two poles of need: the rigors of teaching and the demands of her parents. Her life was so crowded with challenges that she wasn't doing *anything* optimally, including being a marriage partner.

Two hours later, Nina was still wide awake, thinking back to the last time she'd been to Los Gatos. It was almost always by herself since Myles was working. Walking the neighborhood with Cal and pushing him in his wheelchair was a way for both of them to get out and allowed Lillian a little time alone, too. Nina loved the walks, especially because Cal did. He'd remarked on the emergent leaves on the Gingkoes planted decades before, the young pink buds on crepe myrtles, and the truncated elms struggling with age. "Like me," he'd said. They'd returned to the house to discover the washer in the laundry room had flooded into the kitchen. Lillian plugged away on her computer, unaware until Nina, after turning off the machine and throwing down a shelf-full of towels onto the tile, ran into the study. Nina called her parents' go-to handyman, only to discover he'd retired. The plumber he recommended miraculously made himself available.

What was it the time before? Right, the apartment unit the Nearings converted from their old garage. Freda, the tenant, had reported a leak from the ceiling of her kitchenette. Nina had scrambled to find someone to detect and repair the leak, more out of concern about potential mold than further leaks.

What would it be next time? Whether it was a health emergency, a house emergency, or a car emergency (Lillian had taken over driving and recently rear-ended a new Mercedes, to which her first words to the Mercedes driver were, "It's just a car."). What would happen if

Nina learned about it in the middle of a lesson, leading a field trip, or presenting to her union's health care insurance committee?

Nina felt the tell-tale sign in her right temple. Dread deepened as she got up as quietly as possible and padded, slow motion, to the freezer for an ice pack. *Maybe I'll knock it out before it turns into a migraine.* Back in bed, Myles snored next to her. Her eyes were wide open to the dark.

CHAPTER FOUR

NINA

Nina couldn't keep lurching from crisis to crisis.

Over the weekend, she sat out on the deck, facing tender green leaves on the fig tree by the budding old-growth camelia. It felt good to be outside without wearing winter layers. Mingus was lying in a spot of sun. When the Vissers brought their Scottie home twelve years before, his tortured moan sounded like an alarm until they understood it was his expression of happy excitement. Charles Mingus wrote "Moanin" and was one of Myles' favorite stand-up bassists, so the name "Mingus" stuck. He hadn't moved or even looked up when she'd pulled her chair from the patio table.

For a moment, Nina fantasized about giving up her profession. The space that would create. She could hear Myles in her head: "You *need* an opening. That's why I brought it up." She'd have room for her parents' emergencies. She'd also have room for her own dreams. Yoga. Bicycling. Reading. Local politics. Climate change activism. Calligraphy. *Oh my god, calligraphy.* She collected herself. She could not indulge in fantasies. *I'm only fifty-seven.* Education was her second career; she'd been teaching for twenty-five years, so not much of a pension would be forthcoming. *Can we afford it?*

No surprise, but they'd be hit financially. She'd have to sit down with Myles to find ways to cut back. Whenever Nina thought about big decisions, her go-to strategy was learning from others on the road ahead of her.

After adjusting the umbrella, she brushed dried leaves from her chair. Scrolling on her phone, she began calling teachers who'd recently retired. All women. Would they have done things differently? Any advice? Did they regret it?

The responses she got depended on each person's specific conditions. Some were already well off; retirement was a painless decision.

"Oh, Nina, retirement is a dream," Kathleen Plover said. Her partner was ten years younger and fully invested in a lucrative law practice. "She's what makes this possible," Kathleen said. "I'm grateful."

That's not me, Nina thought. When Myles stepped away from teaching at the community college, his pension allowed him to pursue private practice. Was it enough to support them both?

One widowed teacher retired and moved in with her adult daughter's family. In turn, she provided daycare for her grandchildren. She was conflicted about retirement because of the money, but at sixty-six, she no longer had the stamina for the workload.

For others, retirement was feasible because their pension was enough to augment their spouses' income. They'd reprioritized their expenses, but they'd made it work. Most important, not a single one of these women had regrets.

That resonated. Strains of Bach floated through the screen door. Myles loved being a private music teacher and had no interest in giving that up. And, she reminded herself, he's the one who confidently suggested she retire.

The common theme she heard from each retiree? They all experienced an enormous weight lifted when they gave up teaching. Budgeting might be an issue, but time was abundant. Blissfully abundant.

Most teachers Nina knew started working at the crack of dawn, in their classrooms at five or six so they could leave by four or five in the afternoon. Nina opted to stay late instead so everything was ready when she got to school at 7:30. Kate Chiosso was a stay-late compadre. When Nina was newly hired, Kate had introduced herself as "not the young skinny Kate who teaches fifth grade, I'm the old fat Kate. I teach kindergarten." They'd repeatedly run into each other in the copy room after dark, both preparing for the next day. Soon they were "late night buddies" calling each other from their classrooms to coordinate departure times. It was safer walking together to the poorly lit parking lot. Kate had been retired for two years when Nina called. Even though Kate and her husband had less income now, she laughed about it.

"We have time! We feel rich."

"How do you spend it?"

"I sleep 'til ten!" Kate had taken up pottery, throwing pots on an electric wheel at a co-op studio. She was experimenting with white porcelain clay that week. "I don't get there 'til 3:00. It takes me fifteen minutes to bicycle over. It's a wonder," she marveled, "to schedule things around my natural rhythm."

"That sounds delicious."

She and Myles would have to reconsider some of the luxuries they enjoyed. Escaping to blissfully foggy Bodega in the summer for a week. Winter break in southern Utah. Maybe they'd have to give up the once-a-week mow-and-blow guy. The house cleaner had always been a luxury. Keep patching the roof until they had serious reason to replace it. Maybe not expand their pet family. Mingus was on seven medications. He was an expensive dog, and further, he showed no appreciation for all they did for him.

But the gift of time. The bliss of time. Nina wanted *that*.

"I think it can happen," she told Myles that evening as they walked Mingus. "Retirement."

They rounded a corner with three dogwoods in full blossom against the twilight. White, like the moon.

"You had some time to think about it?"

She nodded. "Just as you'd already figured out, we can make it work. It will mean cutting back a little, though."

"I know that. But by having less, we'll have more." He switched the leash to his other hand and wrapped his arm around her. "More breathing room for you, and more joy. I really believe that."

"You're the best."

"We've been through this before, you know, when I stepped away from the college. Now it's your turn."

Nina stopped and turned in for a full hug. "Thank you."

She made an appointment with the district office and set the transition in motion.

A thrilling chill traveled down her back, loosening her shoulders. All would be well. She could hardly wait.

Chapter Five

Nina

The closing of her classroom. The great give-away of teaching treasures. The vow not to bring any of it home, Nina free floated into her new life. She could not remember ever feeling this light. Not during summer vacations or high school graduation; not even college graduation. Retirement was a unique "ending." For the first time in her life, she had no pressure to work on any next steps. No job to research; no interviews to prepare for. The world felt wide open. She called Kate, waiting until after lunchtime to avoid waking her up.

"And how do you feel?"

"Like I've been born again."

Kate laughed. "Let's have lunch."

"Soon!" Nina agreed, then said, "How about just a cup of coffee? Somewhere we can sit outside before it's full-on summer."

They made a date.

The prospect of extra time was lovely but she also had to commit to the primary reason for retiring early. She could now be more devoted to her parents. Her father. But the expectation of visiting them once a month or so, and even getting the occasional urgent call from her mother, would now be manageable. She had space for it. And she also had room for so much she'd been unable to fit in as a teacher. Reconnecting with friends, like her chosen sister, Cori.

She hit Cori's number.

"Cori!"

"Ninja Turtle!"

Nina listed off her wish list of ways to fill her newfound time. "I feel so free! I don't know where to start!"

"New world, isn't it? I can hear the smile in your voice."

Nina's smile broadened.

"I have an idea," Cori ventured, "for sorting out a way to land in retirement."

"I don't need to sort anything out. I'm going to fill each day with all these things that have been out of reach."

Cori paused. "This is just my observation, but one of the things that's been out of your reach is a processing deep dive. A chance to reflect on your life up to now."

"I'm not sure I really want to relive all of that."

"Well… you don't have to get granular about your professional past, but writing can be a great way to clear the way for new beginnings."

"I'm listening."

"A structured setting can really be beneficial. Have you heard of the Amherst Writers and Artists Method? There's probably a group in Sacramento."

"Is it… a therapy method?"

"No, no," Cori laughed. "It's a safe place for writing whatever comes up. No judgments. No obligation to share."

"What's it called?" Nina scribbled. "Amherst…?"

After repeating the name, Cori urged Nina to look it up. "I recommend it to clients who are retiring. I would do it now myself if I had the time."

Nina found an Amherst Writers and Artists group that met at a Quaker's Friends Meeting House just a bicycle ride from home. It was facilitated by Meredith, a copywriter turned poet. Light flooded the meeting space through tall casement windows. The second week, Meredith opened as she had the first time with a meditation, a shared poem, and then an offering of five single word prompts for quick warm-up writing:

1. euphoria
2. rebirth
3. renaissance
4. phoenix
5. wide open

How did she dig into my unconscious? Nina asked herself.

After the warm-up, the group launched into a longer twenty-minute write, responding to new, longer prompts, or, as Meredith would say, "write what needs to be written."

So much needed to be written.

Nina's past rose to the surface—things she hadn't thought about in decades. That was what needed to be written. Nina chose the prompt "write something focused on color."

Yellow

I was about to turn eighteen in East Africa. It was 1975.

I woke up the morning before my birthday, the whites of my eyes as yellow as fading marigolds. I could barely stand, and in the bathroom of the guest house on Kenyatta Road, my stools were white as ash. I clutched at the pain between my sternum and my belly. I felt the shape of it from inside, the first time I'd ever been consciously aware of an internal organ. The doctor at the Nairobi hospital wasted no time with the diagnosis. I had Hepatitis A. It was highly contagious, he said. I would need isolated bed rest for at least a month. The diseased liver couldn't process any medication; there was no help for this condition beyond serious rest. And my diet? White rice, he advised. Nothing else. I had no appetite, so it hardly mattered.

A friend helped me telegram my parents in California, conveying my condition and the doctor's explanation of the liver's inability to absorb medication. Three days later, I received an upbeat telegram in response. "Darling, love you. Hope for quick recovery. Sending herbal supplements. Soon to leave for China. Great group. A first! Wish us luck! L and C." Not "Mom and Dad." The casual tone flattened me.

I slept day after day. I couldn't read. Couldn't talk. A friend brought steaming boxes of white basmati rice from an Indian tea shop. I forced myself to choke it down. After three weeks, I was finally capable of standing, and a week later, I determined I was strong enough to take the stairs to pick up the rice myself.

Until now, Nina had forgotten about that telegram and the cheerful dismissiveness in the "wish us luck!" Had her parents not understood that she was seriously ill? Or had they not wanted to be inconvenienced? Lost in her thoughts, a gentle gong signaled the end of twenty minutes when she was mid-paragraph.

At the break, Nina cupped a mug of herbal tea to warm her hands. The fragrance of almonds rewarded her nostrils.

"You were a teacher?" asked Randy, a story-telling Teamster who'd been writing with the group for a couple of years.

Nina nodded.

"Miss it?"

She took a sip as she considered the question. "Well… I taught for twenty-five years. I was never bored!"

"But?"

It was always hard for her to sum up her teaching experience. Her work was purposeful. She got to laugh every day, to sing, to make art, to love her students, to help them learn and grow. But it came at a cost.

"It swallowed my life. Twenty-five years is a solid chunk of a life. I'm thankful for that career, but… I don't need to look back." Nina drained the remaining tea, adding the teabag to the compost container. "I'm wide open now to… doing whatever I want." She paused. "Sort of." After another beat, she was back on point. "Things I thought I'd be able to do as a teacher during summers, spring breaks, all that."

Judy, another writer and retired teacher, interrupted. "Summers! Ha! The Great Summer Myth."

Judy and Nina looked at each other in kinship. Summers for elementary school teachers meant in-service trainings, preparing for the next year, reserving field trips for the grade level, learning new curriculum, sometimes changing grade levels and classrooms too.

"This," Nina swept open her arms, indicating the adjoining room's tables and chairs, all highlighted by the ceiling's skylight, "is a big part of the next chapter. It feels so good, I can't believe it." She grinned.

He grinned back. The Buddha bowl sang its deep, muted signal for the second long write.

New life. She couldn't stop smiling.

Her phone buzzed. Lillian's name appeared on the screen, and Nina's smile hardened to a resigned line. As she stepped away to answer, the thought crossed her mind, as fleeting as a moth's wing, *How much new life would there really be?* Was she crazy to hope for an opening that was finally all her own?

Her finger hovered between the red and the green before it landed on red. She'd return the call on the way home.

CHAPTER SIX

LILLIAN

Lillian paced. It was Monday. She'd already tried calling twice. Since Nina wasn't picking up, she tried Myles, in case he'd be taking a break. Conversations with him soothed her and made her giggle. He entertained her by dropping his favorite names in baseball.

"Buster Posey," he'd said last time. "How iconically baseball is that?"

"Not as notable as Van Lingle Mungo."

"Very nice."

She knew it was unlikely he'd answer the phone, but what could Nina be doing? She was retired, for god's sake. Just before lunch, she punched Nina's number again. As the phone rang on speaker, she separated the bills from the growing stack on the kitchen island and culled through letters asking for money. Even though Nina arranged for everything to be on autopay, Lillian kept getting pleas in the mail. It didn't bother her to send an additional twenty-five dollars each time. It was a small way to help the planet and correct inequities. So much work to do. Checks to write. Phone calls to return. Dessa left, what, two messages? Lillian didn't have time for casual conversation, even with her sister. Urgently needing to get Bigger World plans in place, Nina's negligence about returning her calls was extremely frustrating.

"Finally!" Lillian said, a little breathless when Nina picked up. "I've been trying to reach you." Nina started in on how, after reading *The Life Changing Magic of Tidying Up*, she was on a tear getting rid of stuff and didn't want to lose momentum. When she'd climbed into the attic to tackle some boxes, she'd left her phone downstairs.

"I understand, dear," Lillian soothed, shaking her head. Nina was aggressively organized to the point that her visits made Lillian self-conscious about the "excess stuff" in their home. Nina wanted them to get rid of perfectly serviceable things, and without asking, she added little white wire baskets and mini shelves to make more space in their kitchen cupboards. Lillian caught herself and returned to the subject at hand. "Dad isn't up to co-leading the Guatemala tour. I need you to stay with him while I lead it myself."

Nina didn't respond.

"Are you there? I can't hear you. You there?"

The voice one-hundred-twenty-five miles away was clear and cold. "Have you considered canceling the tour?"

"Oh, I can't cancel. The group—there are twelve folks on the tour. Everyone's made final arrangements… two couples are flying in from out of state. We'll all meet in Houston for the flight to Guatemala City."

More silence on the other end.

"Dear, cancellation is not an option. Isn't the timing perfect, though? You're retired now!"

More silence.

Lillian jumped to the time frame, starting in a month. "It'll be lovely for you both," she said to her daughter. "Dad is looking forward to spending a stretch of time with just you."

She paused to listen to Nina, feeling her chest tighten. Why was it always so hard with this daughter?

"Mom, did you consider calling Jenny?"

"Dear, your big sister has so many responsibilities. And she's in Chicago."

"Have you spoken with her recently?"

Lillian thought back. "No, but you know she's like me. We don't chit-chat."

"Is that what this is? Chit-chat?"

Lillian waited quietly.

"I'll have to switch my facilitation date with my writing group," Nina said. "And Mingus is scheduled for a Lepto shot. That's just off the top of my head."

She waited while Nina checked her calendar for what she would have to cancel to spend two weeks with Cal.

"I appreciate that," Lillian said. Her tightness loosened. "Thank you, dear. And look, I'll email the itinerary. I know I don't usually, but you'll want to know the dates and when to pick me up from SFO when I get back."

Lillian hit "end" and exhaled. With Nina on board, she could clean up for an outreach group she'd volunteered to host. So many papers to sort. That could wait. She needed to vacuum and bring in some folding chairs from the garage. These days, without Cal's help, everything took longer. At least he wasn't falling as often. The walker really did make a difference. Less worrying and one less distraction.

She checked in with Cal, who was sitting at the dining table she'd recently refinished. "Darling, ready for lunch?" She kissed him on the top of his head.

Cal smiled and nodded as he continued reading the most recent issue of *Mother Jones*. Lilly swept aside the papers on his placemat. He had started categorizing materials they'd brought back from their South African tour. What to save for future presentations at fundraisers, and what to recycle.

As she cut cantaloupe to add to the plain yogurt, she remembered when lunch was Cal's job. He always sprinkled flax seed on top; she did the same. Bringing over two bowls, they ate together, listening to KPFA. Their habit.

"Thank you, darling," Cal smiled as she stacked the bowls to take to the sink. She had less than an hour before the group showed up.

The women in Venn Way were spending the summer preparing for a change in the program they brought to local elementary schools. The vision remained the same: to heighten awareness of unconscious bias involving race, gender, and age. That afternoon, they were learning how to use PowerPoint for their presentations. The thought had crossed Lillian's mind before Nina retired that she might be interested in Venn Way for her school district, but Nina repeated she didn't need more ideas. What she needed as a teacher, she said, was more time.

Lillian sighed. She needed more time, too. So much work to do. She was tired. Guatemala couldn't come soon enough.

CHAPTER SEVEN

NINA

Summer 2016 came in hot. June burned into July. When Nina brought her coffee to a place shaded from the earnest morning sun, Mingus was already stretched out on the deck, warming his flanks. His head rested on his front paws; his eyes closed into the warmth.

Lillian would be away for fourteen days; Nina would stay with Cal. Her mother's needs pressed against Nina's own better wishes for herself, but the rancor started to fade.

Nina slowly began to glimpse a glimmer of the very benefits Lillian had suggested when she first brought up the idea that Nina would have her father to herself. Images of special Saturdays of her childhood returned to her, filled with the smell of summer.

Pulling our bikes out to ride to the apricot orchard, I pedaled the ice blue and silver Royce Union I got for Christmas when I was eight; you rode a tall dusty Huffy inherited from neighbors who were moving. We ignored the "No Trespassing" signs, giggling as we picked through the already ripe, already felled fruit, filling the brown paper bags we brought with us.

Another long-forgotten memory scratched at her.

How about the notes I packed in your lunches every day? Different quotes I'd copied from Bartlett's Familiar Quotations *in my best penmanship.*

"Hold fast to your dreams, for without them life is like a broken winged bird that cannot fly." You loved Langston Hughes. And decades later I assigned that poem every year for my students to memorize. We both loved Mark Twain: "Politicians and diapers must be changed often, and for the same reason." "Continuous improvement is better than delayed perfection."

Half the time, her nine-year-old self hadn't fully understood the quotes, but the other half cultivated a bond between her and her father. She delighted Cal in recent years with stories from her classroom. When she taught fifth grade, one of the assignments she gave out asked students to write a biography about an important figure in U.S. history. One student chose Mark Twain. Standing in front of the classroom, she opened by saying, "Samuel Clemens was born in Missouri in 1839. He became a famous writer by using a pen named Mark Twain."

Nina sipped the last of the coffee, smiling to herself. She stood and tilted her face back to take in the rays, feeling a soft tenderness about the stretch ahead with her father.

The alchemy of devotion takes time. She went inside to pack.

CHAPTER EIGHT

LILLIAN

"Ladies and Gentlemen, we are forty minutes from landing at the San Francisco International Airport. We ask that you find your seats and secure your seatbelts as we descend."

The view below glittered in city clusters. Lillian's seatbelt was already buckled; the airline's sanitizing wipes and unopened pretzels tucked away in her bag for another time. Closing her eyes, she tried to keep the last two weeks alive in her visual and emotional memory before it became a dream. Before she was truly back.

Guatemala, as always, had been amazing. Staying on Lake Atitlan felt transformative and relaxing—one of the few places she could take a breath. She allowed it, which was uncharacteristic and not something she surrendered to at home. And usually, when she and Cal led tours, they booked spartan lodging. She thought of their Bigger World trips to Johannesburg, where they stayed at a YWCA in Soweto. Men and women were relegated to separate quarters there, and they slept on mats on top of concrete blocks. She felt different about Hotel Toliman. The decadence was… justified. Her friend Reyna managed the hotel, which meant her staff was well-paid and enjoyed benefits… highly unusual in Guatemalan resorts. Reyna made sure Lillian's groups were accommodated in simple luxury. The rooms overlooked gardens lush with giant ginger blossoms and mango trees. Hammocks hung from sturdy limbs for sublime afternoon reading. The staff knew Señor and Señora Nearing from multiple trips over the years, and they honored Lillian like a returning elder sage. The picture-perfect lake was a mile high, surrounded by three dramatic volcanoes. Its serene beauty offered a perfect balance to the frenetic Bigger World schedule. Reyna arranged for boats to take the group to visit Mayan villages around the lake, stopping at non-governmental organizations established for disabled artisans and weaving and coffee growers' cooperatives. This time, they toured a music school and a women's shelter, both new developments. Most striking, Lillian thought, were the shelters. Domestic violence was once a terror left unspoken. Now, it was talked about, and abused women had a safe place to go. Reyna also arranged a lunch at the hotel's restaurant with a human rights activist. Everyone sat facing the pristine lake while the guest speaker lectured about Guatemalan history. Lillian watched her group absorb the disabling effect of five centuries of Spanish colonialism in Central America. Context made such a difference in the way these North Americans viewed the country they were visiting. The socio-economics hadn't changed since the Conquistadores plundered the region in the sixteenth century. The indigenous poor stayed poor, and the same few Ladino families held the wealth and power. And, Lillian grimaced, U.S. policy had kept it this way. Knowing this made it easy to get discouraged, Lillian acknowledged how so many marvelous Guatemalans stepped up to serve those in need. Risked their lives, in fact. And, she reflected, our wonderful contacts—Jesuit priests, peace activists, Mayan restorative justice panels, organic farmers, cofradías—all of them brought a new awareness to the folks on this trip. And hope. Always hope.

The 747 lurched as it hit the tarmac, and Lillian opened her eyes. *So much to share!*

Some in the group had caught other flights home from the Houston airport; three stayed with Lillian to land in San Francisco. Kirti was a Bigger World scholarship recipient whose enthusiasm for Lillian spilled into her every conversation.

"Oh, Lillian, I'm not ready for re-entry!" Kirti said as they gathered at baggage claim. "It was so incredible. How could that be just fourteen days? It feels like I've been gone a year. How can we adjust to our old normal?"

This was exactly the point of Bigger World: bringing a broader focus back to the States and, hopefully, an impetus for new peace and social justice activists. Especially young ones like Kirti. Ambassadors of peace spreading their new knowledge about how U.S. policy affects the lives of those in other countries.

"Make a new normal!" responded Mark, who'd traveled with his fourteen-year-old daughter. He winked at Lillian before spotting his backpack on the belt. "Do you see your bag?"

Lillian motioned to the turquoise carry-on by her side. "This is it. All I ever need comes with me on the plane. Kirti, ready?"

In an earlier conversation, Lillian suggested that Kirti take advantage of Nina's pick-up and delivery. No need for her to bother her father to drive forty-five minutes to the airport. Kirti lived with her family in a duplex near the Apple campus in Cupertino; it wasn't that far out of the way from Los Gatos.

The smell of car exhaust met them at the arrivals curb. When Nina pulled up, flashers on, Lillian silently noted for the hundredth time that Nina and Myles still didn't drive a hybrid. She swallowed what she wanted to say and opened the front passenger door.

"Mom!" Nina smiled, but the smile was tight.

Lillian steeled herself. *Now what?* With Nina there was usually something unpleasant in the offing. Bending so she could see Nina's face, she gestured behind her. "This is Kirti. She added so much to our group!" Lillian saw Kirti smile at Nina, shrugging her shoulders. "We need to drop her off on our way home."

Nina got out to open the hatchback and helped Kirti load the luggage. Lillian heard them exchange hellos, and Kirti said, "Your mother is amazing." She savored the familiar satisfaction that followed every trip. Kirti would never be the same; neither would any of the other travelers on this tour.

"Oh, darling, what a marvelous trip! And what a wonderful group. One of the best. So enthusiastic. Mark's daughter wants to come back with me the next time as our translator!"

Nina concentrated on pulling from the pickup lane to merge between a Tesla and a Range Rover. "Mom," she said. "I'm glad you had a good trip. And Kirti, I apologize ahead of time for what I need to talk about with Mom. Unfortunately, I'm leaving first thing in the morning, so I won't have another chance. I thought we'd be alone, and this is, in fact… quite personal."

"Oh," Kirti looked serious now. "Please pretend I'm not here. I'll just close my eyes. I'm pretty wiped out as it is, so please, don't worry."

Lillian looked over at her daughter. "What?"

"Mom," Nina said, her eyes focused on the entrance ramp to 101 South. "Dad needs so much help. He needs eyes on him at all times. I haven't slept a full night for two weeks. Do you even…?"

Lillian interrupted, trying to control her frustration. "I'm home now, so you'll have plenty of chance to sleep again." Nina's judgmental inferences were so predictable.

Nina kept going. "Mom, that's not the point. My point is that it is *because* I didn't sleep that Dad didn't fall. He didn't fall once. Do you hear me?"

"I will be with him now," she reiterated, her voice clipped. "You don't need to worry." This is how Nina was welcoming her home? Already accusing her of a transgression?

Nina's voice escalated. "YOU DON'T STAY AWAKE. He falls when he tries to get to the bathroom on his own. You need to get someone to watch over him at night."

"Dear, let's talk about this later."

"There is no later. I'm leaving early tomorrow, and we can't talk about this in front of Dad."

"Certainly not." Lillian noticed her stomach constricting. This was not the homecoming she had hoped for.

They were both quiet.

"We were able to meet with the Mayan Restorative Justice panel. We can learn so much from their approach to…"

"MOM! Do you even hear me?" Nina was not interested in Guatemala; that was clear. "I just don't see you fully grasping Dad's level of need. *Our* need. *We* need help. To help Dad."

Lillian heard Kirti shift in the backseat.

"I hear you, dear." Lillian got quiet. A familiar tension filled her chest. She knew her words were blunt, but frankly, she did not appreciate being lectured, especially in front of Kirti. Her daughter's chiding punctured the euphoric high from the trip, and her neck flushed with heat from the public nature of Nina's confrontation.

The bright lights of Stevens Creek Boulevard glared as Nina's Mazda passed dealerships on both sides of the wide street. Kirti leaned over Lillian's seat to point out the next turn, which led to her family's cul-de-sac.

After heart-felt goodbyes between Kirti and Lillian ("I'll call you with the date of our reunion potluck," Lillian sang), mother and daughter drove to Los Gatos in silence.

CHAPTER NINE

NINA

"I didn't know this!" Nina rushed from her study, following a trail of popcorn ending where Myles sat at his computer. "Hansel!"

Myles looked up, then down at the kernels by his feet. "Oops."

She shoved the letter she'd just gotten from the Social Security Office in front of his face. "How could I not know this!?"

There were several aspects of retirement Nina was learning about after the fact. She was prepared for the high cost of health care. She and Myles had planned for that long ago with the health savings account through her district. The premium was almost as high as their mortgage payment. It was enough for them to wish they were both already sixty-five, when Medicare would kick in. But this? This was a surprise.

"What are you showing me?" Myles kept his hands suspended over his laptop's keyboard. Thelonious Monk played through the speaker. The sour notes held a particular beauty for him, calming to him while he attended to business.

"This letter says I won't qualify for survivor benefits from your Social Security. And it's because I have a teacher's pension."

Myles took a moment, then said, "I thought… that meant, you know, you'd get no Social Security benefits for retirement… that's no surprise." His eyes stayed on his monitor. "But you're saying even survivor benefits? You don't get those? What about the twenty years you worked in the private sector? You paid into it all those years."

"Right, yes, I did, but…" Nina shook her head. "No survivor benefits. I get it about my pension. I can't have both Social Security and my pension. But now this! If you survive me, you're set up to receive survivor benefits through my pension until the day you die. Me? If I survive you? I get nothin'."

"That sucks, indeed."

"You know, I expect I'll be okay. But how many other women are affected by this?" She bristled. "Women get slammed because they lose earning years on both ends of the life cycle. They leave their professions to raise kids, return to work, and leave again to take care of aging family members. Look what that does to their pensions. And then they get no survivor benefits!?"

Myles swiveled around to where Nina had taken a seat on the daybed. "I didn't know this, honey. It's kind of amazing in its wrongness."

"Not a word," she said, "but I agree. I mean, women who've never worked in a profession, who've stayed home to raise their family but never paid into the system, they get their spouse's Social Security benefit. How is this unfairness so unacknowledged?" Nina blood boiled as she continued getting worked up.

"You kind of sound like your mom."

Not the thing to say. "What?"

"Sometimes you and your mother get agitated in the same way about things that are beyond your control."

"First," Nina paced her words, "when you compare me to my mother, you are dismissing me. Some things are worth agitation. It's not some genetic reflex." Her voice became quieter. "There is definitely unfairness to have to discover this *after* the fact."

"Got it."

But Nina wasn't done. "And second, why do you assume this is out of my control? That nothing can be done about it? I could address it. California Retired Teachers Association must be involved with this. That's the first place I'll check."

"Let's take a walk," Myles said, standing up quickly. "You get Mingus. I'll get the poop bags."

Walking always helped. Limbs in motion, senses catching up with the world, the two of them facing outward. It was cold, leaves long gone from the Modesto ash and linden trees on their street, but the air would be clear and sweet. She wrestled into her down jacket and grabbed her gloves, shaking off Myles's statement about her resembling her mother. The ranting. She admitted that part was true. But like her mother, she also understood that righteous indignation was often justified and that there was usually a course of action out there if you looked hard enough.

And really!? She yanked the leash off the hook in the mudroom. At first, her decision to retire early felt like a choice; now, it felt like a sacrifice. Wait, who was she kidding? It was never a choice. She couldn't teach, be a good daughter, and a wife. It was a sacrifice, but a loving one. And now, this Social Security development? This felt like punishment.[*]

---

[*] The Social Security Fairness Act was finally signed into law by President Biden in January 2025. It took decades of advocacy by the California Retired Teachers Association to muster the strong bipartisan support required in Congress for this to happen. The WEP and GPO penalties no longer reduce retired teachers' earned benefits.

Myles led the way with Mingus at his side. As he opened the back gate, Myles looked up at the Chinese Elm craning over their backyard. Nina knew what he was thinking. During Sacramento winters, the hundred-year-old trees in the neighborhood stood like specters, bare twisted limbs and branches reminding their human stewards that this was the time to prune, which brought her thoughts to her parents' out-of-control "forest" on their corner in Los Gatos. Nina's temple pulsed as she made a mental note to schedule a pruner. Which house first?

"Earth to Nina." Myles wrapped his arm around her. "Where'd you go?"

"Sorry. I'm back."

As they walked to the park at the center of their neighborhood, the sun made a feeble attempt to bring light to the last part of the day.

Nina's phone buzzed. Or *klonked*. It was her mother.

"Dad fell. We're at the ER."

"The ER? Did he hit his head?"

"The EMTs checked everything and were alarmed by his low oxygen level."

"Because he hit his head?" she asked again. "When was this?"

"Yesterday—I didn't see the need to alarm you. He was admitted to the hospital. And they've determined he has pneumonia."

Nina's heart quickened. She coached herself to inhale, to collect herself, to stay clear. "So, that can be treated…?"

"It's bacterial, so they're treating him with antibiotics, and they're giving him oxygen therapy."

"I'll come down," Nina said, looking over at Myles. "I'll get to your house late. We can go to Kaiser in the morning."

"Thank you, dear," Lillian said, ending the call.

Nina hated to think of her father suffering. The sinking feeling traveled to her belly. She needed to be with him.

"I wish I could come," Myles said. More than before, they relied on his income to stay steady.

"I know."

By the time they were home again, her rant had ended. Minutes later, she loaded her to-go suitcase into the Mazda.

CHAPTER TEN

NINA

J ust as Cori had suggested, the weekly writing group served as a clearing space for Nina's retired life, but she was also exploring a way to generate some income. The teacher's pension wasn't enough to finance her "born again" interests. Her calligraphy skills served her well as a teacher, adding some largely unappreciated elegance to various school projects and posters, and now she reckoned she could put up a shingle to market her art form. It wouldn't bring in big bucks, but it'd be something. But mostly, she loved doing it. The pleasure of dipping a virgin square nib into India ink. The woody smell of heavy paper stock. Yum. Experimenting with sweeps and flourishes? It was just fun. She attributed her mastery in large part to her mother, who came to rely on Nina's sign-making skills for protests and demonstrations over the years. She remembered her mother correcting her when she was nine years old, sprawled on the floor, gripping a giant, flat-tipped marker as she filled in balloon letters "NO NAYPOM."

"Napalm," Lillian enunciated slowly, "is spelled with a silent 'L'. N-A-P-A-L-M."

After addressing envelopes to a friend's wedding she'd gotten more requests from two of their guests. A serious restructuring of her office demanded purging so she could organize space around calligraphy. This meant vacating shelves to hold reams of handmade paper she'd collected over the years, for spools of grosgrain ribbon and tule, for the bottles of pigmented ink and wax seals, and for volumes of instructional books on calligraphy and fonts and style. Just as she emptied a second shelf, her phone vibrated. It was her sister from Chicago, who rarely called.

"Everything okay?" Nina asked as she turned her ringer on.

"Mom said she's been trying to reach you. Did you hear from her?" Jenny's voice was guarded.

Nina's heart beat faster. "What's going on?"

"Dad's back in the hospital with pneumonia. But this time…" her voice trailed off.

"What, Jenny?" A chill flooded the back of her neck.

"This time, the doctors are saying that he's… no longer thriving."

The chill deepened. Nina wanted to stop time.

"What does that mean, 'no longer thriving'?"

"It means," explained her older sister, "that there's nothing more… to be done."

Again, Nina couldn't speak.

"They said he's not going to get better," Jenny said. Her words were weighted and slow. "It's time for hospice."

"What!?" Nina swallowed. She was not ready for this. "Oh, god."

Jenny waited, likely unable to speak herself.

"Isn't there time to think about this? So we can be… more confident about what to do?"

"No. There's no easing in," Jenny said. "This is happening. Now."

"What about Mom?"

"She knows…" Jenny stopped.

"She knows what?"

"She understands what hospice means."

Nina heard Jenny swallow.

"How does she seem?"

"She's getting help setting it up," Jenny said. "She… opened… to the idea of it once she realized it was covered by Medicare and that it meant she'd be able to continue leading the Venn Way meetings and visiting classrooms. It *will* make life easier for her as…"

"Oh, Jenny!" Nina's compassion dropped abruptly. "Mom's always so fucking self-serving. Now she can get to the peace vigil on time! Maybe she'll even lead another Bigger World tour while Dad's dying!"

"Right?" Jenny knew what Nina meant. "At least she's not in her 'if I push him hard, he'll get better' mode. Poor Dad. All that water-walking."

Nina's eyes refilled. This conversation was both settling and careening. Settling because she wasn't alone. Her sister shared her experience living with a mother so lacking in emotional intelligence. She understood. Careening because of the clear trajectory of her father's decline. He was dying. Jenny's loss was equal to hers. They both adored their dad. Sobbing again, she couldn't talk.

"She's not in denial anymore," Jenny said. Nina heard her blow her nose. "I'm arranging my flight. I'll text you the details. See you soon. And…" she choked it out, "I love you."

"Soon," Nina swallowed again. "I love you, too." Had they ever used those words with each other? She was sure they hadn't. Walking from her study to the hall's charging station for her phone, she considered how amazing it was to think she and Jenny loved each other. That they were friends. Their childhood, after all, was like a time of war. She'd mocked Nina's enthusiasms, like her foray into poetry "Oh, you're *so sincere*," she'd say before ripping up her sister's Haiku and punching her in the gut. Nina schemed to one day punish her for her big sister's tortures, and when she turned twelve, her growth spurt bypassed Jenny's. She felt secure for the first time. She knew that if she needed to, she could kill her sister. Would she have done it? No, but just knowing it was possible? That was a powerful thing. The following year, when Jenny turned fifteen, she grew half a foot, but that single truce year built a bulwark for Nina. Things remained a little more peaceful after that. She started to pay attention to Jenny's relationship with their mother. It was taut. That wasn't new; tension was the norm. However, Nina became aware that while she willingly went with her mother's programs, Jenny resisted. Nina came to understand that her sister's anger came from that. From feeling like her own interests were disregarded. Jenny took it out on her little sister mainly because, well, it was convenient, but Nina also woke up to the way her dynamic with her parents affected *her* way of operating in the world. She was a pleaser. She got the head nods, the praise, the approval. Jenny was the difficult one. No wonder she was mean to her little sister.

After Jenny started college, her world expanded and she sweetened. The friends she made brought out the best of her. And it was then, when they were almost adults, that they shared their experiences growing up.

"You always say 'yes' to Mom," Jenny once said to her sister during one of Nina's visits to her dorm in Santa Cruz. "I've always said 'no.'"

"And I had it easier because of it," Nina said.

"You were the good girl. I was the oppositional daughter." Jenny had unfolded her five-foot-nine-inch frame from a worn beanbag to reach for a down vest for Nina. She'd inherited Cal's height. As she'd led them down the long hall to the exit door, other students waved in passing or stopped to introduce themselves to the little sister. Nina shook hands shyly, feeling very young, wanting to be older. Outside, a circle of redwoods dripped morning fog.

"I remember your oboe lessons," Nina had laughed, staying on the subject as they headed outside, "how they were never your idea. How Mom would have the car running, but you'd climb the plum tree by the driveway and refuse to come down."

"I liked making her mad," Jenny said. She led them up a pine-needle soft trail to show the ocean view she'd discovered. "It was payback for the way she pissed me off all of the time. How she demanded that I think like her. And signed me up for things that didn't interest me in the least. I mean, look at me. Civil disobedience? C'mon."

While they hiked in silence, Nina reflected on her own lack of courage when it came to her mother. Easier to please her than to face her wrath. Simple things set Lillian off. Anyone disagreeing with her triggered her fury. One of Jenny's acts of power was displayed when she used the Trick-or-Treat for UNICEF money to buy a cap gun. And another, later, when she stuck a "Reagan for President" sign on her bedroom door.

"Ronald Reagan single-handedly took down the mental health services system!" Lillian had raged.

"He's my hero," Jenny had gushed and when she sang, "It's Morning in America!" Lillian had burst into tears. It was so satisfying, Jenny said, to upset their mother. "It was the only way to get her to show real feelings."

But both Jenny and Nina cringed as they relived scenes their pacifist mother made at return counters in department stores, hardware stores, shoe stores, even grocery stores. How she ramped up before the clerks even turned in her direction. Planting a pair of velvet oxfords, a carton of canned olives, a box of yellowed envelopes onto the counter—whatever the items were, she rose up in attack mode, demanding to see the manager while Jenny and Nina pretended to belong to someone else behind them.

"I am *incensed* to have to take the time out of my day to return such shoddy merchandise!" her voice shrilled. "This is... *unacceptable!*"

While breathing in the cool mist that hugged the coastal range, Nina found herself appreciating how self-aware her older sister was. She knew what she needed.

Jenny became a CPA and took a job in the middle of America. She was insistently apolitical. Her parents shook their heads at their older daughter's conservatism. ("How can Jenny be gay and conservative?" Lillian was apoplectic.) While Jenny had always tuned in to her own needs, Nina gave in to what would appease Lillian—agreement. Agreement guaranteed peace. The visit with Jenny at UC Santa Cruz planted a seed she needed to cultivate: to pay more attention to what she herself needed and to have the guts to express this to her mother. Now in late middle age, she still needed reminding of this. A lot of reminding. Wait a minute. Late middle age? She was almost sixty.

Where was this flood of memories coming from? Nina repositioned herself in her office chair. The sounds of Myles's piano student working on a jazz variation of Chopin filled her ears, the hesitant bright notes jarring her. Invitation samples taunted from her open portfolio. Facing a wall covered with framed watercolors, oils, and photographs, her gaze landed on her favorite black and white portrait of Myles, taken while he played standup bass. Her eyes moved to their framed wedding invitation she had calligraphed thirty years before.

She placed a call to the bridal couple whose "save the date" card she had just started working on.

"A family emergency has come up. I can't take the job. I'm sorry." She heard herself as if she were eavesdropping on a stranger—a polite officious stranger. She suggested the couple call a local stationery store. "They might have a calligrapher to recommend. And I sincerely wish you all the best."

Next, she called the eager couple counting on her for their invitation design.

"But you knew exactly what we wanted!"

Nina apologized again, this time explaining that her father did not have much time left.

"Of course, of course," the bride said. "I'm sorry."

Still opposite the wall of art, she forgot where she was. The only picture in her mind was of her father, his face a visage of kindness. The "welcome" he always projected. And then came an image of her mother, and with it, a rush of sorrow and foreseen emptiness in Lillian's final days with her beloved.

Nina knew Jenny understood, even with all they were losing themselves, the importance of offering any mustered strength and tenderness toward their mother.

Chapter Eleven

LILLIAN

Cal rested in a hospital bed, which now dominated their bedroom, a room designed to open to the dining room and living room.

Cuban timbales reverberated through the house. Peelings from freshly squeezed limes filled the space with a bright scent and the compost container to nearly overflowing. Kirti and Mark each balanced trays of mojitos as they wound their way through the living room crowded with friends who'd been on the Guatemalan tour together the summer before. This wasn't just a reunion; it was also an opportunity for Lillian to pitch the next tour, a Bigger World trip to Cuba. She cleared the kitchen island for new potluck contributions, and after folding the foil back from a tray of steaming tamales, she made her way to check in on Cal. "Darling?"

Lillian rested a cool hand on his forehead. He was no longer talking much but he could smile, which he did. "Friends want to sit with you to say goodbye. Are you up for that?"

Cal, eyes kept closed, nodded. "I just don't know why I'm still here."

"You'll find out in a minute, darling." One by one, Lillian ushered in friends they'd known for decades, as well as those who were relatively new in their Bigger World lives.

The music played so loudly that from the bedroom Lillian didn't hear the knocking on the front door. She looked up in happy surprise to see Nina and Jenny walk into the bedroom. Both hesitated when they saw visitors sitting by their father's bed.

"Girls!" Lillian exclaimed. "I'm so glad you're here!" She had to raise her voice to be heard. "Look, Cal. Nina just picked up Jenny from the airport!"

"Mom?" Nina gestured over the exuberant noise. "Who… what…?"

"Everyone wants to say goodbye to Dad."

Cal's eyes were closed, but a gentle smile was discernible.

"What about the music, Mom? All of this…?" Nina motioned "action" with her hands.

"Isn't it lovely?" Lillian laughed. "Just five minutes ago, do you know what Dad said?"

She saw Jenny and Nina look at each other and then back at her. They both shook their heads.

"He said, 'I just love this house.' It's because of these gatherings. I'm just so grateful. It's perfect."

"Mom," Nina said, both hands on Lillian's shoulders. "Can we talk outside for a minute?"

Before they walked out the backdoor, someone's eight-year-old daughter confidently stepped through the door's open frame.

"What happened to the screen?" Nina asked. A corner of mesh hung, listless, from the doorframe. The jacaranda's new lavender blossoms brushed against it.

Lillian laughed. "One of our volunteers' Australian shepherd walked right through it just before you got here. Now, what did you want to talk about?"

"Mom. It's been ten days since he last ate something. He's in hospice. He's dying."

Lillian's neck stiffened. "Darling, I'm aware."

Lillian led the way so they were just a few feet outside. The birdbath, scummy and full, sat within view of Cal's bed. Until recent days it had served as a source of his pleasure, mourning doves cooing and splashing from its rim.

"Mom, is this what he wants?" Nina pointed to the house, filled with salsa dancers and the vibrant sounds of the Buena Vista Social Club.

"Nina, I told you, Dad loves this. He said so. He hasn't said much of anything in five days, but today, he said, 'I love this house!' This makes him happy."

Why was Nina always so distrustful of Lillian's decisions? Tension rose in her chest. This was a beautiful moment; everyone was feeling good, and everyone felt Cuban simpatico. Hopefully, this would lead to a few tour sign-ups. Lillian was thinking of a Cuba trip in the fall. It would be their, let's see… she caught herself. It would be *her* eighth trip there.

"And Nina?" her smile was gone. "Don't question me about your father." She lowered her voice but made sure she would be heard. "That goes for you, Jenny, too. Your last phone call implied that I didn't have Dad's best interests in mind." She looked hard at one daughter, then the other. "I want him to be happy. And," she pointedly pushed, "I know better than anyone what is best for him."

Lillian looked over Jenny and Nina's shoulders at the view opposite Cal. The view he'd see if his eyes were still open. The sunset shone an unsettling, muddy red. She tried to shake off her anger at Nina, at both of her daughters, deciding that while she didn't need them there, Cal did.

CHAPTER TWELVE

NINA

"Myles! I'm so relieved you picked up!" Myles had been teaching. As soon as the words came out, Nina choked. For privacy, she had left the brightness of her parents' house for the lanai just outside the back door, its screen still hanging from the frame. This was once an inviting place for family dinners in the summer—rare times when her parents didn't have on the five o'clock KPFA news. But now layers of dust obscured the lanai's past function. As Nina tripped across an overlay of worn rugs, her face and neck were enveloped by sticky strands of a spider web.

"Honey, what's going on?" Myles had heard all about the Cuban party the week before. "Dad keeps saying he's ready to go, but Mom keeps bringing all of these people in to see him—"

"You're not surprised, are you?" Myles asked. "I mean, that's her."

"I'm not surprised at all!" Nina bristled. "But that's what's wrong here! For whose benefit is she keeping him so... much in the world? So engaged? Not Dad's!"

Myles sighed. "That's a tough one."

Nina shared that now Cal's dying process seemed slowed by a combination of body and mind. "He hasn't eaten for eighteen days. Eighteen days! Wait," she stopped as she remembered that Myles was working. "How long before your next student?"

"It's fine, I've got…" he checked his planner, "ten minutes."

"The hospice nurse says this is a long time to go without food but not completely unusual. The whole thing is," her voice shook again, "you know, he hasn't been talking at all, but the last two days he's asked me why it's taking so long. He's so ready."

"So what are his days like?"

"What do you mean?"

"How engaged is he in the world? Is the radio on? Is he listening to music? Are you reading to him?"

"All of the above. Jenny reads him the sports pages."

"Right. The Giants. There's a lot going on." Myles was following his favorite team, too. He segued to his own father's final days and how fully he and his sisters raucously occupied the space of his deathbed, singing and telling stories. "But everyone is different, and every death is, too. Maybe he needs less stimulation."

"Maybe…"

"Listen, I have to go in a minute, but you'll be interested in this. You know my viola student who was once a nun?"

"Yes, the Vivaldi enthusiast."

"Yes, that nun. Like I have so many nuns," he said, then shifted. "She told me that in the convent, when a nun is near death, she is given a bed in a blacked-out dark room, and sisters take turns sitting with her, but in silence."

As she looked around her surroundings, the lanai seemed like a struggling cousin of the dark space of quiet Myles described. The beams hung low, the screen walls sagged, and an inch of dust covered shelves of not-now-needed items: used mailing envelopes, an old stationary bike, a backless chair, once-elegant baskets now missing handles, entire sides springing strands of jute. A spider skittered over the futon armrest. Nina brushed the back of her neck, her arms, her leggings. *I wouldn't want to die in this dark place*, she thought. But she got it. "That resonates," she said.

"I'm sorry, I need to go." Myles rushed. "I love you. Call me when you want me to drive down. I'll cancel my lessons."

Her heart swelled. Myles made all of this… *easier* was not the right word, but she was lucky, she knew. She could lean into him. It made all the difference.

Chapter Thirteen

LILLIAN

Cal was in the final stages, nearing death. The hospice nurse matter-of-factly stated that more changes were coming, but Lillian was informed most by her hollow feeling. She hadn't voiced any of this to the girls; they were clearly sensitive to the transformations in their father. Jenny was the one who suggested that the hospice chaplain talk directly to Cal and ask questions about what would come next.

Ever since Jenny came things have been easier. Who knew she would ever think this about her oldest? When she overheard Jenny on the phone with her wife in Chicago, the expressions of love were clear. Jenny and Sylvana had made a beautiful family, adopting identical twin boys from Ghana who were now—could it be?—approaching forty? Alessandro and Matteo. One a tattoo artist, and one who'd dropped out of med school to open a successful tattoo-removal practice. She smiled at the irony of their choices, but more than anything, her heart warmed for the supportive parent—and now, grandparent—Jenny had become. The ease of her relationships with her sons. Her strong marriage.

Jenny had been such a difficult child. Conversely, who could have predicted Nina would be so hard as an adult? At least she'd married a marvelous man. Myles had come down and extended his weekend to say goodbye to Cal. He brought such warm energy. Playing piano for Cal, he chose songs they all enjoyed from the 1940s; during "Ain't Misbehavin'," Cal's lips moved. It was one of his favorite songs to sing with his octet. So like her son-in-love, Lillian thought, to bring music into the space. But Cal's timeline was unpredictable, and Myles finally had to return to Sacramento while the rest stayed. It was hard for everyone.

I wouldn't have thought to bring in a chaplain. Lillian tried to ignore the fluttering in her chest. A slight dizziness.

It was Jenny who sat down with the chaplain beforehand to explain Cal's ambivalence about God.

Suzanne was a middle-aged woman with soft, knowing eyes. Jenny had offered her a seat facing a wall covered with Guatemalan weavings. Nina sat, already perched stiffly on the turquoise couch.

"Dad might describe himself as agnostic—maybe he even identifies as an atheist," Jenny offered.

Nina interjected. "He's a humanist."

Lillian nodded. Cal was that. She felt again the flutter in her chest.

"He is certainly a humanist," Jenny agreed. "His parents took him to a Unitarian church, but that was only so he could sing in the choir. Beyond that, he's had nothing to do with an organized church." She paused. "Well, Quakers, yes, but not as a spiritual practice."

"More to enact legislation for peace and justice," Lillian softly interjected.

"I understand," Suzanne met Lillian's eyes, then Jenny's, then Nina's. "It's not something I often share," she said, "but I am actually most comfortable with people who don't have a fixed idea of what comes after this life." She smiled gently. "It's easier to spend time with dying people who embrace the mystery."

She is perfect, Lillian thought. *Oh, Cal, she's perfect for you.*

Suzanne led the women back to the bedroom and reached for a chair to pull close to Cal's bed. He lay face up, eyes closed. An afghan crocheted by his mother decades before stretched over his long, ever-thinning form. The chevron pattern alternated turquoise and sage, colors Lillian knew her mother-in-law had chosen to please her. Lillian had the hospital bed positioned so Cal could see the black squirrels scrambling the jacaranda's trunk. That was when his eyes were still open.

"Cal," she said, "I'm Suzanne, the chaplain."

"Welcome," Cal whispered.

Lillian swabbed his dry lips, then kissed his forehead.

Suzanne asked if Cal knew he had entered the stages of dying.

"Yes."

"Well, Cal…" she smiled softly, "I have all the answers to every mystery in the universe. Do you have any questions?"

Cal managed a discernable grin. Lillian, Nina, and Jenny audibly exhaled. *Suzanne was the right choice.*

"I understand that you know you are dying and that you're ready. And you're wondering why it's taking so long."

"Yes."

"Are you at peace?"

"I am."

Cal's hands rested on his chest. Suzanne brought her hands over to cover his. "That's everything, Cal," she said. "That's all you need."

Lillian's eyes blurred. She felt Jenny's arm around her and Nina's eyes on her. She knew they were wet like her own.

Jenny walked Suzanne to the door. When she returned, she and Nina each took one of Cal's hands while Lillian massaged his head. *He loves this*, she thought. She saw his lips move; his voice barely audible.

"I wish you could all be with me when it happens," he said.

Lillian's eyes stung. She kissed the top of his head, lingering there. Jenny and Nina were in tears—Jenny's silent and Nina's accompanied by lots of nose blowing.

"We want to be here, too, darling. And we will be. You won't be alone."

Unfortunately, she knew the timing was out of their control. She held her hand to her chest to calm the flutter.

That night, after tucking Cal into the hospital bed at the foot of the queen they used to share, she folded back the West African coverlet and climbed in on her side, pulling all the other blankets to her chin. It wasn't enough to get warm. As she curled her shivering body toward Cal's empty side, she longed to lose herself in a dream in which he was sleeping next to her, but she was intensely wide awake.

What was going to happen? Would he just "slip away?" Would she be there with him the way she promised? Now that his death was imminent, how could she help? With no experience being at anyone's deathbed, her mind grasped for a memory to help guide her now.

What happened when Daddy died? And Mother? When Daddy suffered a stroke and died soon after, we were out of the country. Dessa took care of the cremation, but what about before? Had Dessa spent time at Daddy's bedside? How do I not know any of this? Did I even ask her?

Lillian's memories climbed to the surface. Her father's memorial was held after she and Cal got back from Vietnam. She helped get the word out for friends and family to assemble at the big Sebastopol house, built for gatherings of scale, overlooking soft hills studded with apple orchards. The smell of the Gravenstein apples. The mineral taste of the well water. The memorial was a potluck, as always, just like any other political fundraiser Mother and Daddy had hosted.

Mother looked radiant. Odd that she would look so radiant at her husband's memorial, and odd that that's coming to me. What was even said about Daddy? He was such a force… but all I remember was shock at the absence of that force, which ultimately, and bluntly, left no buffer between me and Mother.

And Mother's death? It happened after Nina spent a weekend in Sebastopol. One of the things she did was share a list of emergency contacts with the gardener. A couple of days later, the gardener called Nina.

"Su abuela," he'd said to her. "She's at the hospital. Kaiser. Santa Rosa."

When Nina phoned the information desk to check in, a nurse answered.

"Hello? I'm trying to reach Clara Abram."

The nurse hesitated. "May I ask who is calling?"

"Her granddaughter. Nina Visser."

A pause, then a muffled one-sided exchange. One stark phrase was clearly audible:

"Next-of-kin?"

"I'm her granddaughter," Nina repeated while the nurse kept her phone receiver covered.

"I'm sorry to ask you, who is Clara's most direct next-of-kin?"

Next of kin. Death vocabulary. Nina gave the nurse my phone number, then Dessa's. And that is how I learned Mother was dead. After I spoke with the nurse, I immediately called Dessa. While I felt, what, a chill of shock, Dessa broke down.

"She was alone, Lillian. Alone. If I'd known, I would've been there with her."

It hadn't occurred to Lillian that their mother would have wanted either of her daughters there, for any sort of comfort. She hadn't asked for them, after all. Mother was demanding when she wanted attention and matters attended to—which was often—but she never sought solace from her girls. Her comfort gathered in the glow of an audience. Conversely, Lillian and Dessa learned in early childhood, through Mother's absence, to find their own comfort elsewhere. At first, they found it in each other; in adulthood, Dessa found it in her husband and children, civic responsibilities, and local activism. Lillian had Cal, their peace and justice activities, and Bigger World.

Lillian steeped in her reminiscence of the aftermath of her formidable mother's death. *I suggested to Dessa,* she recalled, *that we drive together to Santa Rosa to make arrangements. Mother wanted her body donated to UCSF "to advance science." I didn't want to be alone to view the body. I never had that chance when Daddy died. Never witnessed the evidence of his death. This time, along with my sister, I'd have closure. A chance for it, at least.*

With a shudder under the coverlet, Lillian realized something. After each of her parents' deaths, she hadn't cried. Had. Not. Cried.

This was different. Being with Cal in his last moments, their last moments… being with Cal before he was forever gone…? At this very moment, seven feet away from her, he was breathing the same air she was, taking in her cells as she took in his. In days, hours, or minutes, this would cease.

Chapter Fourteen

Nina

The hospice nurse let the family know Cal would likely die in the next twenty-four hours. Nina felt a faint buzzing inside and a weird girding numbness spreading under her skin. She kept reminding herself death was universally human, indiscriminatingly human. All of us face this in our lives. The deaths of the ones we love. And all of us carry on. It was her turn. She was, incredibly, going to survive it.

That night, after Nina and Jenny kissed their father good night, Lillian administered Cal's methadone. She kissed him, too.

"Darling, this is your last night. Sleep well." She softly kissed him again and lingered, her cheek on his. Nina felt the intimacy to be more than she should witness.

They all went to bed.

As soon as she woke up, Nina rushed to Cal's side. The turquoise and sage afghan rested in place just as it had been the night before, but his chest moved as he breathed. Her mother was still asleep, but clearly, Jenny had gotten up earlier, evident by the opened bedroom window.

Jenny walked in, phone to her ear. "Thank you," she said, then fit the phone into her back pocket. "That was Suzanne." She was whispering.

"Oh?" Nina whispered back.

"I called to ask if she had any ideas to help Dad move to the next... place. She told me something Buddhists whisper into the person's ear: 'You are moving into the light, you are moving into the light.'"

"Let's go," Nina said.

She held Cal's right hand while Jenny held his left. She whispered the words into her father's ear, repeating, "You are moving into the light, Dad, you are going into the light."

Jenny added into Cal's other ear, "And it's beautiful, Dad, it's beautiful."

Suddenly, abruptly, Cal sat up. His eyes opened full and wide.

Nina and Jenny both jumped.

"Get Mom!" Jenny said.

Nina rushed to her mother, who was sleeping just feet away.

"Mom, Mom!"

Lillian woke up at once, snatching at her earplugs. "Is he dead?"

"Mom, he sat up. His eyes are open. Mom, hurry."

In one swift motion, she was at Cal's side.

Cal lay back again, face to the ceiling, eyes open but not seeing.

"Darling. Cal. I'm here, darling."

Lillian felt for his pulse. Her nod indicated he was breathing. She caressed his head; the three of them sat together for another half an hour, each of them massaging his hands and arms.

Nina left to get dressed. When she returned to the bed, Cal's skin was the color of wet cement. Lillian and Jenny's eyes found hers. He was gone.

Lillian's voice was calm. "Hospice explained that when there is no longer a pulse, respiration continues. I am to keep my hands on him for ten minutes."

Even though they knew, they each searched for his pulse, detecting nothing. As a measure, Nina felt for Lillian's pulse, and she felt for Nina's. Neither of them discerned a beat. They laughed softly at themselves and returned to massaging Cal. All three of them stayed with him, still holding his hand, rubbing his head, talking quietly together. They didn't hurry. All was calm, peaceful, even relaxed.

Nina got up to call Myles. When she came back, Jenny was talking.

"Remember," she said, "Dad may still hear us at some level; just be careful what you say."

"What bad thing could we say about Dad?" Nina asked, with Lillian nodding in agreement.

Jenny gave a quiet smile. "True that."

A sound of birdsong filtered in from outside the open window. They turned to see a finch alight on the birdbath, then looked at each other, wiping their eyes but smiling.

Lillian left for the kitchen to call hospice. When she returned, she reached for Cal's left hand, sliding the wedding ring from his finger. She slipped the ring through a silver chain she retrieved from her pocket. When she placed it around her neck, Nina helped secure the clasp.

It was at that moment Nina recalled a Danish tradition she'd recently learned about: loved ones attending the dying are directed to open the nearest window "so the soul may easily exit the body."

As if Lillian read her mind, she said, "Let's keep the window open."

The muted call of mourning doves matched the moment.

CHAPTER FIFTEEN

NINA

A celebration of life is a lot to orchestrate.

The day of Cal's memorial, Nina felt like a machine. One foot in front of the other. A last-minute phone call to instruct the Nearing's swim friends how to direct parking. A quick run to the top of the amphitheater with the audio guy to locate electric outlets for the sound system. The hours she spent earlier lettering captions for the memory boards Jenny had assembled, along with brushing calligraphy on directional signage, had served as a sort of meditation for the sisters; now they hauled placards and easels from a borrowed van to point people to the amphitheater behind the library. Myles, along with Matteo, one of Jenny's twins, stayed on hand to help other elders as they were dropped off near the library's entrance. The other twin, Alessandro, was throwing a frisbee on the expanse of lawn in front, attempting to tire out his five-year-old before taking their seats designated for the family. It would be a long day for little Theo.

Nina wasn't surprised she was putting her grief on hold. Her only feeling was a necessary dullness to stay focused. Locating a venue had taken concentration. Myles had drawn up a diagram projecting the number of attendees—two hundred? Three hundred?

Cal was beloved by many, so while Los Gatos's Institute for Non-violence—the locus of Cal and Lillian's community—would have been perfect, its cramped space and dead acoustics wouldn't work for the event.

"I know a Unitarian Church," her closest friend Cori shared. Churches had the space, of course, but Cal's spirit in a church did not feel at all right.

Jenny wondered about renting a theater. "We need a big space and good sound."

"Sounds expensive."

Thinking it would be for naught on a Sunday, Nina called the library on Main Street where Cal and Lillian stood on the curb every Friday for the peace vigil. She was surprised when a librarian picked up, and further surprised when the librarian forwarded a promising idea.

"We can offer the amphitheater behind the library. Even though it's open to the public, it *is* secluded and hidden from the street. And it seats two hundred."

"We may have closer to three hundred. It's hard to predict."

"That shouldn't be a problem. If you provide your own folding chairs, there is space for them at the top. Close to a hundred can circle the top of the amphitheater."

Where would people park? The Institute for Nonviolence had no space, and on Sundays, the curbs were crowded with cars un-loading Los Gatos brunchers and shoppers and hikers. Jenny dele-gated friends to reach out to others who'd loved Cal as their mentor; a friend from the YMCA would let swim friends and staff, too, know about the celebration details. Folks were encouraged to car-pool. Word spread from activist friend to activist friend. Food was easy since Cal and Lillian's gatherings were always potluck; friends confirmed they'd bring something. Nina made sure there would be plenty of ice and beverages and that a sound system could be arranged for sharing stories and music. The sisters decided not to print a program… Lillian told them she would speak first, followed by dignitaries, then the family. In that order. Anyone else moved to speak could do so after that. It would be loose, in the spirit of Cal and Lillian's get-togethers.

The afternoon of the celebration, a crowd loosened into a steady processional from the packed parking lot and street. Heritage oaks shaded the amphitheater; the sweet, dusty fragrance of oak wafted up as feet crunched leaves on the path leading to the concrete steps. Some attendees sang along to the Pete Seeger recording of "Turn, Turn, Turn" as they took in the view. Lillian's customary turquoise was hard to miss in the bottom front row. She sat between several men and women wearing suits, many of whom were checking their phones.

"Who are those people?" Myles asked. He was next to Nina, one row behind Lillian.

"Labor leaders, heads of non-profits, civil rights and environmental figures… they flew in from all over the country."

"And… *they're* in the front row."

"You're surprised?"

Lillian rose to speak first, which signaled the music to end. Before moving to the podium, she stood in place, looking up and around. Clustered in the terraced rows were gray-haired women in flowy caftans, hand-embroidered peasant blouses, leggings, and loom-woven tunics. Men, bearded, clean-shaven, old and young, appeared to have pulled from the same REI sale rack: cargo pants, pullovers, athletic shoes, and Birkenstocks. A group of frizzy white-haired union activists came wearing pastel guayaberas, shirts brought back from Labor Day celebrations in Cuba, fitting for a summer day like this one. There was not an empty seat.

She turned around to find her daughters. "Your dad would have adored this."

At the lectern, everyone's eyes were on hers.

"Thank all of you for coming. Cal would have loved being here today. That you are here means you were meaningful to him." She was clear-eyed as she recounted first meeting Cal at UC Berkeley. "We both sang in the Glee Club. Like almost all of the guys at school, he was there because of the GI Bill. He said the war changed him not just because it confirmed his conviction to fight against fascism, but also because of the Army's hypocrisy in values, segregating Black and white battalions. While he was legally forbidden to mix with Black Americans, the War still broadened his social circles. He served with other folks he'd never have met otherwise. Jews, Italians, Irish. So when he learned I was Jewish, it moved him profoundly."

Nina and Jenny turned toward each other. "Really?" Jenny mouthed. This was new information for both.

"Cal's anger about racial segregation resonated with me, along with his observation that wars ravage the innocent. We both wanted to actively work on civil rights for all Americans, and for non-violent solutions in the world."

Lillian spoke of their decades working for peace and justice and the founding of Bigger World. "He was my partner." She struggled for a moment. "In all things, in every way, he was my partner. We were both moved to change our planet for the better, and to work for justice for humanity."

The crowd stirred as a dozen people rose and hoisted signs Nina recognized from the peace vigil. "NO WAR. NO JUSTICE,

NO PEACE." Another placard, this one festooned with flowers: "TO EVERYTHING, THERE IS A SEASON." She warmed to the softness in the words in one of Cal's much-loved Pete Seeger ballads.

Lillian turned to the man who offered his arm to take her to her seat. Another man, gray-suited with a "Huelga" lapel pin, stepped to the dais. His admiration for Cal's leadership in the labor movement ended with "¡Sí se puede!" The crowd roared. One after another, Cal's peers rallied his causes until, "Finally," Nina whispered to her sister, "our turn."

Jenny gripped the podium, gathering courage to recount her most vivid memory. "When I told my parents I was gay, Dad wrapped his arms around me and whispered that he was so glad I could," she choked back a sob, "...I could move forward in the world into my true happiness." She rushed to step down and take a seat between Sylvana, who pulled her close, and her two sons and Theo, who was under his father's chair.

After Myles gently elbowed her to take her sister's place at the dais, Nina lifted her face in time to see Cori across from her, making the ASL sign for "I love you." There were neighbors from childhood, her parents' Tai Chi teacher, Aunt Dessa smiling encouragement.

Nina sang the song Cal offered every morning of her childhood:

Good morning to you! Good morning to you!
We're all in our places, with bright sun-shining faces,
and that is the way we start out each day!

She recalled his breakfasts. How he cut the grapefruit so each segment spooned out easily for his daughters. How when she was afraid of something dark in her closet, he never denied its existence; instead, he told her he'd handle it, and promised it wouldn't hurt her. He did that by announcing to the closet door that he was coming, and when he opened the door it was to signal the darkness to spend time in someone else's closet. Nina slept well after that.

A hawk swooped low over the amphitheater, so low that she stopped to watch. Everyone followed her gaze.

"Hi, Dad," Nina smiled into the microphone as she waved to the bird. "We're all here, loving you." She shared their mutual appreciation for quotations and continued with some more of his rich biography, conscious that she was going on too long, but how could she leave anything out? This was her last chance, and it felt like she was searching for Cal among the friends and family shaded by the grand oak trees, some fanning themselves, all rapt, searching for *him* to hear her stories of him, her affection and respect for him, the deep shock of his absence. She wanted *him* to know the special place in her heart only he could fill. This time at the microphone broadcast her eulogy wide across the amphitheater, but for Nina, it was all for *him*.

"It's your turn," she said, gesturing to the crowd. "If you wish."

She took care to step down from the podium. Her plum tiered skirt was long enough to catch on the splintered platform.

Alessandro handed Theo off to squirm on his mother's lap. He and Matteo approached the podium together. The tattooed grandson spoke first.

"Our grandfather listened. He withheld judgment. He loved us. Even when our choices didn't exactly match up with his ideas, he supported us."

"My brother and I," added Matteo, "are both entrepreneurial. We each have our own business. Grandpa always called us 'his favorite capitalists,' which was saying a lot."

"Since he was obviously not a fan of capitalism," Alessandro added, managing a smile as he faced the circle of filled seats. "He didn't let his opinions get in the way of love. He encouraged us to make our mark in the world in some way that leaves it a better place." Alessandro paused. "I don't think he'd envisioned our marks to be as literal as tattoos, but I see my business as a way for people to have their stories heard. Seen. I think he applauded that."

Matteo leaned into the mike. "A few of you may know that while my brother is the tattoo artist, my business is tattoo removal. I've never… been a fan of ink." He rolled up one of his sleeves and raised his unmarked arm to the sky. "I've been tat-free in my life so far, but—before we left Chicago, I shocked Alessandro when I asked him to tattoo this in my grandfather's honor." He rolled up his other sleeve and held that arm up. "If it's too far away for you to read it, it says 'Man of Peace.'" Matteo looked down at Nina. "My Aunt Nina's calligraphy is here to stay."

Nina brushed tears away. When Matteo had asked her to calligraph that phrase, she hadn't known where it was going to land.

One of Cal's long-ago volunteers, short wiry hair now streaked silver, explained how Cal had taken her sixteen-year-old combative self to an ACLU meeting, which inspired her to go to law school, practice law, and eventually become a superior court judge.

"Most adults I knew focused on my argumentative nature like it was a liability," she said, stopping to blow her nose. "Cal saw it as a strength. He encouraged me to join the speech and debate team, which taught me how to channel an argument."

The peace vigilers came up as a body, carrying their "NO WAR" signs, and led a rendition of the civil rights anthem, "We Shall Overcome."

Bearded and bereted, Nat stepped forward. "Cal was the Patriarch of the weekly vigil," he began, using his sleeve to wipe his nose, "and a helluva labor organizer. Once, after maybe one too many beers, he told us he planned to continue his work for peace and justice long after he shed his body. He joked he'd been meeting with other elders to map out a way to assemble purposefully in the afterlife. You know, to keep helping the world." He paused at a wave of chuckles from the crowd. "Like me, Cal didn't think anything happens after we die… but his future plans sure make me wish I believed in God."

Next up was Cal's octet, founded at UC Berkeley sixty-five years before. Next-generation baritones, basses, tenors, and leads climbed to the base of the amphitheater to solemnly sing "Shenandoah." Their mournful harmonies captured the melancholy of loss.

She glanced at Lillian, who had lost so much. But instead of listening closely to the octet, Lillian occupied herself by foraging for something in the Tanzanian basket at her feet. *Really, Mom?* Sure enough, Lillian was stacking flyers for the trip she was hawking to Cuba in the fall. For a split second, Nina realized Cal wouldn't have minded.

Myles squeezed her hand and whispered, "Look."

Nina sensed a flurry of movement overhead. The giant hawk returned to circle over the crowd, silhouetted darkly against the light blue of the sky. *Dad? Are you here? This, after all, is where you spent so much of your devotion to peace on earth. And here, today, is where your devotees are gathered to let you know how much you've contributed to their wholeness. Their peace.*

CHAPTER SIXTEEN

THE SWIM GROUP

"It was the most beautiful death," Lillian said after the server left the table with the orders of pad thai and tom yum soup.

Along with Siti, the two other women, all of them swim friends and white-haired, clung to the words Lillian shared. Besides the memorial, it was their first time together after Cal's death and the first time she had anything personal to say. It wasn't a customary recap from the most recent edition of the Nation. Lillian realized, oddly and uncomfortably, that she was revealing something personal. Siti pulled her chair closer to the round table and leaned in to hear better.

"A homecoming, really," Lillian continued. "We always taught the kids about the cycle of life—how it starts and ends on a cellular level. How energy just changes form. Cal's gone back to the earth. Home. Well," she paused, "after UCSF is finished with his body." She felt for Cal's wedding ring on the silver chain around her neck.

Siti appeared to shake from a chill. "Lilly," she said, sweetening her friend's name and slowing her usual rapid-fire conversational style. "You don't think something else happens, that we go somewhere else?" She often referred to herself as a born-again Buddhist-Christian. "Don't you expect to see Cal again?"

The sounds of cutlery scraping porcelain accompanied their conversation and soothed Lillian. The fragrance of star anise and cardamom, familiar from her many trips with Cal to Southeast Asia, comforted her. Her smile was soft. "We had sixty-two years together. Good, good years. We were so lucky."

Siti had been married and divorced three times. Rita and Lien had both lost their spouses to death, but their marriages had been troubled. They had talked before about their shared widow experience of new openings, trying things unavailable during their lives as wives, less fixated on the loss of husbands than they were on the loss of time. Swimming at the Y was one of the wishes they manifested, which was largely how this group of friends coalesced.

"So now what?" Rita asked. "What do you see as you look into the future, Lillian? Or is it too soon?"

Lillian's eyes brightened. "Cuba! We're leading our eighth tour to Cuba in January, and I'm working on the itinerary with the facilitator now. You're all welcome to sign up!"

At Lillian's reference to "we," the others shifted in their rattan chairs. She didn't miss a beat.

"It will be spectacular," Lillian continued. "We'll stay with the same families as before. It's so informing and enlightening when we have years-long contacts to visit." She sighed. "Relationships are everything. We get first-hand accounts from families as they live under changing conditions, year after year. We watch children grow up to become doctors. We see literacy programs flourish. And music programs provided with more funding. And we'll visit the same farmers we got to know in the '80s, still implementing organic farming practices." She paused, thinking aloud. "We can learn so much from Cubans about sustainability."

Siti leaned in; this time, it seemed, so she could be heard better. "What about human rights there?"

Lillian was about to respond with a litany of human rights violations right here at home when the server arrived, not a moment too soon. She placed the ornately decorative soup tureen and soup bowls on the table. All watched as Lien ladled out the fragrant, steaming tom yum soup. Everyone's favorite; something, Lillian knew, they all agreed on.

Chapter Seventeen

Lillian

The morning sun woke her from a dream about Thai food. The shoji screens lining Lillian's bedroom cast a blue light like the tint of the powdered skim milk she used to mix up for the kids. That milk, she recently learned, had contributed to the robust growth of pampas grass just outside the back door.

"We hated it, Mom." Jenny laughed. She was uncharacteristically talkative when she called the day before.

"I had no idea," Lillian said in wonder. What else had she missed?

The streaming light shone just enough to slide her into the slow morning rituals she needed to start her days.

On the way to the bathroom, she passed the kitchen island and turned on the radio, dialed to KPFA. Amy Goodman's familiar voice came across mid-sentence with its usual authority: "…women's conference in Ghana, sponsored by Women's International League for Peace and Freedom. Much of the focus will be on micro-lending for women, appropriate technology in agriculture, and higher education for girls."

Lillian didn't want to miss any part of the story, so she left the bathroom door ajar. Women's conference? Sponsored by WILPF?

She had attended several over the decades in various countries. Denmark, China, Columbia, Belgium. They'd been drivers of inspiration for her, and she'd met amazing people, many of whom ended up figuring into their Bigger World trips. Many of whom became lifelong friends. But for all of the trips she and Cal led to African countries, she'd never attended a WILPF conference there.

She needed this.

By the time she was dressed, she'd already stepped it out in her head who she needed to call to make this happen. First call, Lisa Macananey, president of the local chapter.

"Lisa, Lillian here. I just heard about the Women's Conference in Ghana. Are you going?"

"Oh! And how are you, Lillian?" Lisa was a chit-chatterer.

"Fine," Lillian attempted patience, "but I'm in a hurry. Are you going to Ghana?"

"I wish I could, but I can't. I'm on the Friends Committee for Legislation. Our bill is coming up."

"Do you know the details of the conference?" Lillian asked. "The dates?" Coming in the middle of the story on the radio, she had missed that.

There was a pause as Lisa checked. "Ten days from now," she said, following with, "but even if you *are* interested, it's likely too late to get a visa."

"We'll see."

Back at her desk, she moved a stack of *Mother Jones* magazines to unearth her laptop. She looked online for the Embassy of Ghana. It was located in Washington, D.C. The only other consulates were in New York City and Little Rock, Arkansas, of all places. Nothing on the West Coast.

Adjusting her reading glasses, she checked the time before carefully tapping out the number for the D.C. office, grateful she'd made it before closing time.

After waiting between robotic prompts, she finally got a human. She warmed her voice, having learned over the years that her chances of getting what she wanted improved by sounding appreciative and even interested in the people working in bureaucracy.

"Oh, hello," she smiled into the phone, "I so hope you can help me. My name is Lillian. How is your family?" Lillian and Cal had learned on one of their trips to West Africa that this is how strangers greeted each other, at least in some regions.

The voice on the other end responded, sounding somewhat surprised but pleased to be asked. "My name is Mawuli. My family is together," he said, "and how is yours?"

Lillian didn't really know how her family was but echoed back. "My family is together, too, although we are missing my husband, whom we recently lost."

Sympathy sounded on the other end. *Good,* Lillian thought. *That could help.* And it did. She was able to persuade Mawuli to expedite the visa process. "I only just learned about the conference, and it is very important I attend. I'm almost ninety," she paused and, as she expected, heard Mawuli exclaim.

"Truly? That is most impressive, Lillian!" He asked for her email address, and seconds later, she could hear the smile in his voice as he announced, "I am emailing an application this very moment."

After a fair amount of effort, she printed the application from the link he shared, filled it out, stuffed it in a pre-used envelope, and then climbed into the Prius to drive to FedEx. Mawuli had explained using FedEx was the most expedient way to get the application to D.C. As she approached the counter, Lillian noted the nametag on the FedEx employee's golf shirt. "Cross your fingers, Nyala!" she declared as she placed the envelope on the counter.

Nyala looked up. "Cross my fingers, ma'am?"

"I'm not ma'am, I'm Lillian. And I need a visa in less than ten days. For a conference," she paused, "in *Ghana*."

"Okay… Lillian." Nyala picked up the envelope, shaking her head. "This envelope won't work." She pulled a virgin FedEx priority express envelope from under her side of the counter.

"Don't waste resources. Look," Lillian chided as she pointed to the address she'd already crossed out and covered with an adhesive-challenged label with the embassy's address she'd written on it. "This is ready to go."

"You want this to get there in a hurry? It's urgent?" Nyala gave Lillian a tired stare. Nyala was not impressed with her charm or enthusiasm, Lillian realized.

Lillian sighed. "I can't waste time. I can't miss my chance to get to the Women's Conference," she looked pointedly at Nyala, "in *Ghana*."

Nyala clearly didn't care about the Women's Conference or Ghana. "If you use our envelope," she said flatly, "we can guarantee it will get to Washington, D.C., in two days. If you use yours?" Nyala picked at the already loose label. "It may never get there."

Lillian surrendered. She charged the mailing to her credit card, thanked Nyala for her assistance, and drove home. Maybe Nyala wouldn't cross her fingers, but Lillian had great confidence that all would be well. She'd get the application approved and receive her visa in time. This, of course, was the way she approached everything; her optimism served her successfully almost all the time. Back at her desk, she pulled the file with her frequent flyer miles with Turkish Air. She Googled the flight dates from San Francisco to Accra.

While she parked herself on hold with the airline, she leafed through a *YES* magazine. Full of stories of progressive change, these were the kinds of stories she knew she'd encounter at the conference. It's what she enjoyed most, learning from other women.

Her success filled her with warmth and excitement. Lillian reflected on the progression of her actions and the wonderful result. It all started with Amy Goodman on *Democracy Now*, which led to her warm conversation with a Ghanian bureaucrat. A further outcome from the phone call with Wawuli was his promise to arrange for a cousin to meet her at the airport. That cousin would likely know a place Lillian could stay near the convention center. Maybe even with the cousin's family, who knew?

CHAPTER EIGHTEEN

NINA

It was Nina's turn to facilitate the AWA writing group, which meant she led the opening meditation and chose the poem to share. Ten writers attended that morning, laptops and notepads at the ready.

At 9:30, with everyone seated, Nina rang the Buddha bowl.

After the meditation, Nina passed out a copy of the poem ahead of time; now she read it aloud while the others read along:

North Star

By Nina Visser

It's fixed in the dark.
You can depend on it.

Sometimes haze obscures it
but patient waiting
and patient watching
eventually find a clearer sky.
And there it is, in steady residence,

the North Star.

Concealed in the illumination of day,
it hides in beams of earth's closer starlight,
shows up when the earth turns

like a secret you feel for in your pocket.
Your fingers brush it, yes, it's there.

A secret that rests in the velvet dark,
there to guide you,
offer comfort.

It's known by desert travelers,
refugees on the sea,
children wide awake
who search their hearts,
search the sky,
finger the lining of their pockets
knowing that even if it takes
a lifetime, a generation, an epoch,
they are never lost for good.
The star has been there all along.

When she had typed up her poem, she thought of her own North Star. Her star was the opening to the ever-present voice she always had available at all times, that is, when she consciously made the space for it. The Guide-In-Residence, as it were. The voice she yearned for when she needed clarity. To her great wonder, the challenges of her father's final year seemed to have widened the opening for that guidance.

Mornings came more easily now, sometimes with a bike ride to the meditation center where she could sit with a dozen others for forty-five minutes. Books catching dust on the bookshelves were books she was finally able to read in the middle of the day. McClatchy Library posted free oil painting classes she bicycled to once a week for two months. She met friends in leafy Curtis Park where they sat on facing benches near the basketball court, Nina with a thermos of homebrewed coffee, others with Peet's takeaway cups. Occasionally she would glance at her watch to remember what she would be doing if she were still teaching.

8:10 AM:

THEN: meeting kids as they lined up for the morning sing in the school's amphitheater, turning in attendance and lunch count as soon as she got to her desk.

NOW: walking Mingus around the neighborhood, taking in the scarlet leaves of the Chinese pistache trees and vivid gold of liquid maples, smelling the damp earth.

10:40 AM:

THEN: making a mad dash to the restroom before yard duty by the bark-covered play structure, citations in hand, wondering why tether ball was legal, trailed by the kids who clung by her side until the bell rang.

NOW: pouring a second cup of Italian roast while she read the *New York Times* in the shade of the old-growth camelia in the backyard.

3:10 PM:

THEN: Choosing the quietest group to calmly exit the class-room first, following the last straggler out so she could tackle grading and recording the assessments of the day in time for the grade-level meeting with her team.

NOW: Taking a nap.

Speaking of now, back at the Friends Meeting House, she felt a giddy chill for her good fortune. After she finished reading the poem aloud, it suddenly registered as a statement about her *mother's* North Star. *What is it Mom holds on to for guidance? What directs her as time unfolds? What grounds her after she's lost her beloved? And now, as she ages, how does she process the sadness and tragedies of the planet?* It came to Nina swiftly: her mother's North Star is the point of light penetrating the sadness and tragedy of the bigger world. Her North Star is hope. Hope made real by her actions. *I'm grateful she has that,* Nina thought. *And she has her health. Her home. I don't have to worry about her,* she thought in an exhale. *At least for now.*

In the sunbeam from the skylight, the seated writers looked at Nina in concentrated readiness.

"Remember," she said, "the next prompts are simply suggestions; the important thing is to write what needs to be written."

When she facilitated, her mind was seldom sufficiently empty for her own writing. But that was the gig. Looking through the large windows framing the garden outside, she took in the kumquat tree branches hanging over the neighboring fence and primroses climbing the pergola. *Okay, Muse, come on in,* she thought, fixing on the first twenty-minute prompt she'd suggested: "Write about a tradition from childhood." After a minute passed, she began typing. She didn't think; she just wrote:

Tradition

Once a year, my mother's side of the family bought tickets for Pete Seeger concerts, which were followed by dinner at the same restaurant in San Francisco's Chinatown.

Steep shadowy steps led us to Yee Jun's basement where the waiters, old men, would greet my grandparents, each time noting with apparent amazement that my aunt and mother were both married with children.

"Dessa! Not a little girl! Lillian! Your own daughters!"

Along with our cousins, my sister and I would scramble for first dibs to sit in the big booth with the wood swinging shutters. The restaurant was steamy and warm, filled with sizzling from the open kitchen, smells of fragrant garlic and peppers and tangy honey sauces mingling with the clatter of silverware and the sound of my family ordering, family-style. While waiters brought hot tea to steep and set down cups for everyone, my father pulled a pen from inside his jacket to write on a napkin:

Broccoli Beef
Dai Bao
Won Ton
Five-spice Chicken
Crispy Onion Cakes
Sweet and Sour Pork
Green Beans
Rice

After ordering, the adults launched into politics. We kids scooted under the table to climb the stairs up to the street. We played red light green light in the alley with the dumpsters until our uncle came to tell us the food was on the table. By then, the conversation had grown animated, goaded by my grandfather's penchant to challenge opinions even slightly divergent from his own.

"McCarthyism may appear to be in the past, but don't you see how 'Communism' is thrown around by people who have no idea what it means?"

My uncle would counter, "Our civil liberties are stronger now," after which the adult daughters spoke over each other about Vietnam, the Gulf of Tonkin, and the next protest march.

Jenny and I spooned up the sweet and sour sauce and fought over the last of the chicken, and when the fortune cookies showed up, we all took turns around the booth to read our fortunes out loud:

"Perfect," my grandmother said. She read hers aloud: "Self-absorption in the superficial abandons the greater good." She eyed me. Was that because sitting behind her in the car after the concert I told her I liked the Beatles?

"*Listen, ooh, ooh, ooh,*" I sang, "*Do you want to know a secret, ooh, ooh, ooh, do you promise not to tell?*"

"Such personal indulgence," she'd sniffed. "Bourgeois."

"This one should be yours," my dad said to my grandfather. He read: "Courage is not simply a virtue, but the form of virtue at the testing point." He meant it respectfully. My grandfather's immigration story was studded with bravery.

"And this one should be yours, Cal," my grandfather responded: "Don't just think, act."

My mother warmed her hands around her tea cup. "They go together, don't they?"

The waiter arrived with the bill on a plastic tray. "Good to see you and your family. Your grandchildren," he said to my grandparents. My grandmother rose, imperious, while her husband peeled large bills from his wallet.

The vibration of the timer shocked Nina back to the Friends Meeting House.

"We're coming near the end of our twenty minutes," she said abruptly, then softened her delivery. "Give yourself three more minutes to find the words to end for now."

When it was time, she gently rang the meditation bowl. Nina invited writers to share what they'd written if they wished. *Kind of like the Quakers who meet here on Sunday*, she realized. *Breaking the silence only if they are moved to do so.*

"Let's remember that this is the first time each writer is hearing their words out loud. Let's limit our comments to stating what was strong or memorable—what stayed with you." She scanned the writers at the table. "And even if it stirs something in you that is from your experience, let's keep it to how the writing itself resonated… remember, too, that what's written here stays here."

Randy nodded. "Las Vegas writing."

Nina felt warmth and gratitude for this expansive and safe place for them to tell their stories. The surprise of it. That was the beauty of the AWA writing method. Unpremeditated. All new. Or newly seen, by both writers and listeners. And, as was the case for Nina that day, witnessing the surfacing of an unexpected memory. A past family tradition. Reading fortunes out loud and matching them up to the right person. Affirming the value placed on courage and action while dismissing self-indulgences. This is how her mother grew up, and it is how she mothered her daughters.

CHAPTER NINETEEN

THE FRIDAY PEACE VIGILERS

Time moves on, Lillian thought, *but war stays constant*. Standing in front of the Los Gatos Community Library, she adjusted the sign to hold it a bit more comfortably. It was nearly the same size she was; all five feet of her mostly concealed behind it. Her white hair brought historical context above the message in bold caps: "**NO MORE WAR.**" Would this ever be true of the world? She was twelve when the United States entered World War II. Then Korea. Vietnam. Iraq. Afghanistan. Not to mention covert wars in Central America. It was overwhelmingly tragic. Tragic and avoidable.

This is why she stood here, year after year, with like-minded friends every Friday afternoon, as she had, with Cal, for decades, to remind people driving on their way home from work that while they went about their day-to-day lives, war was raging somewhere on the planet, all while plenty of peaceful solutions existed to resolve the root of world conflicts. Fear of the Other. Income disparity. Systemic racism. Hierarchies of power.

"That's twenty-two!" Nat, his gray dreads covered by an Oakland A's baseball cap, always tallied the number of honks they elicited from his "Honk for Peace" sign. He and Elaine were other regulars at the vigil during rush hour, along with several other couples and a rotating group of friends from the Institute for Nonviolence.

"More honks last week," Lien noted. "Maybe people are already on vacation now?" Lien had only participated in the weekly vigil half a dozen times. She first met Lillian and Cal while swimming at the Y and for years came to potlucks at the Nearings' home. It was during a Pete Seeger sing-along that she learned about peace vigils.

The intersection was as crowded as ever, Lillian disagreed. Just fewer honks than usual. A line of cars ploughed through the yellow light. Since Cal's death, she'd missed only a few Fridays, largely because of the conference in Ghana. This time, she'd had a harder time than usual parking. It was so tight she'd backed into the car parked behind her (but that's what bumpers were *for*) and then had to walk a block to join her friends in front of the library. A block wasn't what it used to be.

"Lillian, you look resplendent in all that turquoise!" Elaine had greeted her as Lillian pulled her sign from the depths of the Prius' back seat.

"I got this in Accra," Lillian smiled down at the vibrantly patterned Kente-style dress she wore. "I brought more textiles like this—but other colors, too, to sell at the peace fair at the Institute. It's in the fall. You should make a point to get there. I always sell Fair Trade chocolate and coffee, too."

Lillian and Cal established the Institute for Nonviolence in 1957 to provide a place for peace and justice activists to gather and plan educational and activist events. After renting various office spaces over the decades, a concerted effort to raise funds successfully financed the purchase of an aged house located close to the library. It served as the peace community's permanent resting spot.

Another car honked.

"Peace!" Lillian shouted, smiling. The temperature dipped; it was almost dusk.

"We're up to eighty-three honks," Nat said, looking at his watch. "It's 6:00. Time for Benia's. Who's coming?"

The restaurant's menu dominated the wall on a giant chalkboard behind the counter, but the group walked directly to their customary table, where Martina, their favorite server, met them. Lillian still hadn't shared the news with Martina about Cal. Why was she taking so long? Was she waiting for Martina to ask about Cal? *Still too soon*, she thought. *I don't think I can say the words—*

"Lilly!" Martina made a beeline for the elder dressed in her signature color. She pulled out her pad. "Clam chowder as usual?"

Lillian worked on studying her menu. "Martina, can you come back to me at the end?"

As Sam ordered his standard BLT and beer, and the others made their choices, the server returned to Lillian.

"So, Lilly—what'd you decide?"

"I think I'll have clam chowder," she smiled, handing Martina the menu. "So many choices."

"Clam chowder, it is! Extra lemon on the side!"

As others peeled off their windbreakers and sweaters, Lillian kept herself wrapped in her ruana. She was glad she'd brought it. June was unpredictable in Santa Clara Valley. It was more a preview of summer than an announcement. And when it got dark, the temperature dip could be dramatic.

John and Riva had been vigiling with Cal and Lillian on Fridays for a dozen years. "Lillian, how're you doing?" John gently asked. Cal's memorial had been a year ago, and with every Friday, they had been keenly reminded of Cal's absence and Lillian's loss—a loss of more than a husband; it was the loss of a partner in existential purpose.

"I'm a little cold," she said, wrapping her ruana a little closer, "so I'm looking forward to the soup."

"How are you holding up?" Riva gently prodded. "You know, with Cal..."

Lillian sat frozen for a moment, feeling unsteady even though she was seated. Martina showed up balancing a tray of filled water glasses, one of which came without ice. She set that one down in front of Lillian, who sat straighter in her chair, trying to relax her tensed shoulders.

"I can't believe he's been gone a year," she said after Martina left. Her fingers followed the silver chain around her neck to Cal's ring. "I've been so busy with the next tour and the presentations about restorative justice... time has flown, really. It's hard to believe..." now she trailed off. "It's hard to believe I'm alone." Had she actually said that out loud? She had always felt that together, they were a singular force. It had always been thus. It was what drew them to each other from the beginning. She thought of the quote they'd included in their wedding vows, a quote from Antoine de Saint-Exupéry: "Love does not consist in gazing at each other but in looking outward in the same direction." Being alone, doing this work without him... required a great adjustment. "But I know Cal would want me to be doing what I'm doing," she said, turning to Riva. "I'm continuing our work."

The friends around her listened solemnly. One pulled a tissue from a fanny pack.

"It's a way to feel he's with me," she added.

"I miss him, Lilly," John said.

"Oh," she responded, "oh, *I* miss him *so* much. I find myself looking for him after I've read something. Something I want to share with him. That happens a lot."

"Your kids? Does that help? Do you see them?"

"Well, you know that Jenny is in Chicago with her wife and two sons. And now I have a great-grandson, too. Theo," she smiled. "And Nina lives in Sacramento. They call me, but," she shrugged, "I'm not a phone person, you know."

The clam chowder arrived, along with the other entrees. Lillian squeezed two lemon wedges over the steaming soup, then stirred the tart juice into the cream, bits of clam, and potatoes. She blew on it before taking a sip.

Even with her friends around her, even with the hot chowder, it was hard to get warm without Cal.

Driving home in the dark, more an effort than ever, Lillian found herself thinking back to the time she and Cal almost perished together. The memory made her fingers feel fragile around the steering wheel. Would that have been better? She wouldn't have been left so empty. So cold. So alone.

Back then, still robust in their seventies, snorkeling was their favorite activity for relaxation and renewal after leading Bigger World tours in Vietnam. There was nothing like that sensory immersion. In the clear aqua ocean, weeds undulated far below the surface. Breathtaking surprises thrilled them, like the time schools of shimmering damselfish crowd-danced above nudibranchs, and another time they spied those marvelous sea slugs. Kodachrome-colored beings, purple and cobalt blue, waving soft stalks of brilliant orange with pinpoints of yellow.

That particular day, they'd elected to take a snorkeling excursion boat to a reef known to host clown fish, a favorite of Cal's. The swim package included fins and masks. Sitting in the shaded awning of the tourist vessel, Lillian and Cal felt a familiar anticipation as the boat anchored near the reef and gently rocked in place. A group of young vacationing Europeans crowded on the deck as the masks and flippers got distributed. As years passed, Cal and Lillian became accustomed to being the oldest customers aboard these commercial enterprises. That day, though, the party atmosphere was jarring. "Who wants a beer?" was asked more often than "Who needs help defogging their mask?" The music blasting over their voices was decidedly not Vietnamese, but strains of "Wasting Away in Margaritaville" would fade as soon as they kicked away from the boat's ladder, so really, what did it matter? Cal slid into the clear water first, grinning through his mask and giving Lillian a thumbs up. As Lillian approached the rope ladder, she kept Cal in her sights.

Suddenly, her playful excitement wrenched to a stop. Gripping the rope ladder, she watched, horrified, as a fierce competing current swiftly pulled Cal away. As he drifted further from safe proximity of the vessel, she could see him struggling to change direction. He was distancing from the boat fast. Very fast.

"Help!" Lillian screamed. She turned fully around as she screamed again. No crew member heard her. She bit into her snorkel, disregarded the ladder, jumped in, and swam hard toward Cal. By then, he was thirty feet from her. With alarming speed, he was pulled further away. Lillian's resolve to reach Cal fueled her swimming skills and likely revived a muscle memory from lifesaving training when she was a teen. Finally, finally, through her mask, she saw his tall frame struggling underwater, his legs kicking against the strong tide, one foot fin-less. Lillian darted the last few feet until she grasped his shoulder. She pulled her mask from her mouth.

"Cal," her breathlessness limited her. "Stop fighting." They were both drifting. Fifty feet from the boat. Fifty-five feet. Sixty feet. "Relax," she said, "I'm bringing you in." Cal could only sputter, but he understood. Lillian secured her mask and reached around his neck from behind; his body surrendered. Lillian began towing Cal slowly but doggedly toward the vessel. The current held its opposition and challenged her, but she shut out fear, willing her whole being to get them both to safety.

Two life preservers bobbed twenty feet from the boat, secured by a rope to the ladder. Someone had noticed their absence. With her last ounce of strength, Lillian snatched at the first preserver. "Hold on, darling. Hold on." Only then, two crew members dove into the water to help her to safety. One threw another preserver toward Cal and pulled him, at last, to the boat.

They were intact, but Lillian was enraged. She was too spent to raise her voice, but her adrenaline pumped high. "I screamed for help," she gasped to the crewman who helped hoist her hundred pounds back onto the boat. By now, other tourists were watching. "That music?" she said to him, as Jimmy Buffet continued to sing about Miami Nights from the bar's speaker. "You couldn't hear me scream because of that music!" Here, she sobbed. "Your job is to keep us safe!" Now, she and Cal were sitting on a wooden bench in a sheltered part of the boat, towels tight around their shivering bodies. She shifted her body into his. "Darling," she said, turning to kiss him.

"Lilly, I lost my flipper, I couldn't…"

"It doesn't matter now, we're safe."

"Lilly, you saved my life," his voice barely audible. He reached to put his arms around her.

Wrapped against Cal's chest, Lillian whispered in his ear: "When I saw you drifting away, I knew you were in trouble. And I knew," and here she caught her breath, "if you were going to… to go… I was going with you."

As Lillian relived that day, she understood something. If they'd both died that day, they'd have missed almost twenty more years together. The only thing to do, now that she was without Cal, was to live life as he would have wanted her to live—with the same purpose and meaning as when they were alive together.

She pulled into the driveway and hit the remote to enter the garage. The headlights shone onto the back wall where she stored boxed pharmaceutical donations for the next tour. She sighed.

There was always so much to do.

N I N A

The Visser's credenza held a framed photograph of Nina's parents wearing South African election monitors' vests, laughing together. They looked refreshed and youthful in their late sixties. Nina focused on the image as she called her mother.

Lillian answered on the first ring.

"Mom, you know what day it is?"

"Of course, dear. It would have been our wedding anniversary."

Nina was now in the kitchen to pour her first coffee of that late morning. Without thinking, she opened the door to the back garden. The smell of smoke hit her like a wall, and the dark day abruptly reminded her about the fires. This was a summer of fires.

"How is it for you today?" Nina asked the question gently. She closed the door against the smoke and walked back into the library adjacent to Myles's study. Mournful sounds of his first cello student reverberated through the wall. She sank into the Craftsman rocker Myles inherited from his grandparents in upstate New York. The arms were scarred from decades of his grandfather knocking the bowl of his pipe on them, adding warmth to the well-loved chair.

"Dear," Lillian sighed over the iPhone's speaker, "today is another reminder how lucky we were to have each other for sixty-three years."

"So lucky," Nina echoed, not bothering to correct the math. Even a year later, her mother hadn't yet acknowledged Cal's death. Maybe, Nina wondered, if Lillian addressed it out loud, would the pain lessen? If she allowed herself to feel it, would it eventually go away? Would her mother even bring up Cal's death without being prompted? Her teeth clenched. Why did she make it her job to make sure her mother was giving voice to grief? She wished her mother would cry more easily, cry so her pain could start cycling through. She worried that Lillian's restraint, holding back her emotions, would result in more intense pain. Even physical ailments. She thought of one of the most resonant sympathy cards she'd received after Cal's death, which quoted Shakespeare: "To weep is to make less the depth of grief."

But Lillian didn't cry. "I'm on my way to the Y, so I'm glad you caught me. Give my love to my son-in-love."

"I miss Dad," Nina said more quietly, still hoping to hear her mother's voice break. "I just wanted to… check in with you."

"Thank you, dear. Today's swim will be my meditation in motion. It always helps."

Lillian had described her swimming this way for years. Today, Nina was somberly thankful that her mother had at least this outlet.

Dad? Are you with her while she swims?

After the call ended, the sound of the front door opened for one student to exit and another to enter. She heard Myles's warm greeting and customary opening question: "So, what was the best thing about your week?"

The response was delivered with the high pitch of a seven-year-old.

"Mommy had the baby, and I got to name him!"

Nina walked back through the back side of the house to the bedroom. In an effort to shake her malaise, she made the bed and wiggled out of her robe and nightgown for her summer standbys of lightweight cargo skimmers and a Lucky brand T. *Does everything I wear now come from Costco?* She headed to her office, which doubled as a guest room. It was filled with all of her choices and tastes. The walls were painted a muted mossy green with art displayed in frames she'd acquired at estate sales: watercolors by friends, small oil paintings by local artists, photographs of riverscapes, and one of Margaret Mead's most resonant quotes in elegantly simple type from a hand-applied letterpress: "Never doubt that a small group of thoughtful, committed citizens can change the world. Indeed, it is the only thing that has." It occurred to her that if her mother went to Alessandro for a tattoo, this statement would be perfect around her neck.

Her task that morning was to, yet again, update her mother's bill pay page. After Lillian's trip to the Women's Conference in Accra (still unbelievable, Nina thought), she'd asked Nina to add two organizations for regular contributions. One, Lillian thought, may have changed addresses.

"I've gotten two checks returned," she'd said. "I appreciate your help, dear."

Before Nina opened her laptop, she swiveled to face the small altar she'd arranged to honor her father. A photo of him in Havana sat next to a small bronze Buddha she could fit in her hand. Beside that was a Doonesbury cartoon Cal mailed to her years before. It showed one of the characters with his daughter, whose last line was a whiny, "Why did I have to inherit your nose?" Cal included a sticky note: "Will you ever forgive me?" These days, she could care less about her face's most prominent feature, which had been a source of distress in middle school. Cal acknowledged her misery then, and later, it had become a shared joke between them. Once in a long while, they'd rub noses and laugh.

She struck a match to light the candle Cori sent just after Cal died. A full calendar year had passed since the first lighting. The smell of its warmed wax invited her daily meditation, but now it had melted down to the wick. Her parents' wedding anniversary, poetically, would be its final illumination. Nina rolled out a soft pad and placed her bench on it. Checking in with her posture, she closed her eyes and breathed in the freesia scent, welcoming deep, inviting thoughts to come and go, come and go. A place of peace, a landing for a North Star. In that place, she relaxed into a warm and reassuring presence. Her father was with her, and he was just fine. *Dad*, she trembled. *Help Mom open to your presence, too.*

Opening her eyes, she made a wish for Cal and blew out Cori's candle for the last time.

CHAPTER TWENTY-ONE

NINA

"Coriander, call me." Nina left a voicemail for her best friend.

Cori and Nina had become close—sister close—while they both waitressed their way through college three decades before. Cori completed a PhD in Psychotherapy, and Nina earned her teaching credential, all while taking orders and balancing steaming walnut mushroom casseroles at The Good Earth across from the University of Santa Clara.

One of their first get-togethers came on a rare day. They both were off from the restaurant, and neither had classes. Cori drove to the house Nina was co-renting in the Santa Cruz Mountains.

An outsized deck hugged a massive live oak facing west towards a ridge of dense forest. It was hard to believe they were just a twenty-minute drive from work. They'd pulled out rusted chaise lounges to relax in the shade. Cori wore a flouncy summer skirt while Nina was still in the shorts from her morning creek run at the base of her hill. She handed her new friend a tall glass of iced tea. They'd been talking since Cori emerged from her VW bug, precariously perched on the steep driveway. Mountain parking wasn't easy.

"You *choose* to go to these retreats with your mother?" Nina interrupted in disbelief. Cori had been describing the Jungian retreat she'd attended with her mother every year since she turned eight. One of the rituals was painting from the unconscious. They enjoyed it so much they continued it together at home.

Cori had turned to face Nina. "I call her Lulu. She's my best friend." She paused. "I told you that, right? I take it that that's not the case for you and *your* mother?"

"Oh," Nina flushed, her skin's color axiomatic to almost any reference to her mother. "How much time do you have?" She looked through the deck railing at the ridge while attempting a description of her parents' life in peace and justice. "My sister and I... we were like children of preachers. Instead of bowing our heads in prayer every night, we ate dinner to the sermon of left-wing liberals on KPFA news." Cori's face looked blank. "On the radio. The public radio station out of Berkeley. Progressive."

"I've never heard of it."

"Most people have never heard of it. But it dominated our dinners. We never talked about our day. We didn't talk at all. Hang on," Nina got up to retrieve a framed picture of her parents.

"This is Lillian and Cal."

"Your mother is stunning. What is she wearing?"

"That's a Guatemalan huipile. She brought it back from a trip they took to learn about agricultural development in Guatemala, and it was after that they decided to start their non-profit organization, Bigger World. They wanted to invite other North Americans to spend time in less traveled countries—to broaden their global awareness."

Cori focused on Cal. "Nice dashiki," she noted. "And quite a beard."

"This was taken after they led their first reality tour to Southern Africa."

"Well, they sound fascinating. Very open to the things beyond their experience. I'd guess you were pretty lucky."

"It's complicated," Nina responded. "I admire them and appreciate their curiosity and respect for how others live around the world. I just…" Nina was exposed. "I just wish for the same degree of interest in their own children. Especially from my mother."

"Well," Cori started, "what about your father? You seem to blame your mother for the… dysfunction."

Such a therapist, Nina thought, but it was good. Had she noticed before how readily she criticized her mother for every ill, yet readily forgave her father?

"Dad's imperfections—I mean, he's human—don't rub me the wrong way in any sort of deep sense." She thought some more. Was there anything that he did that really bugged her?

"I guess, I don't know, I guess it bothers me that he asserts himself aggressively against some political entity, you know, but is completely non-confrontational around his own wife. But on the other hand, that doesn't seem surprising. I mean, it's his marriage. I suppose it's a way for him to keep the peace at home."

Nina looked out over the mountain. The sun crowned; from their place on the deck, there were no shadows.

"They share the same values and actively work to make the world a better place. They're a perfect match. But Mom is extremely driven and… doesn't seem to be able to connect emotionally—personally. Dad, on the other hand, is a good listener. We have fun. He makes me laugh. Me and my sister. My mother… I sometimes wonder," Nina's said, "why she had children. We are so often an inconvenience to her. She doesn't ever ask us what we want or need or care about. She praises us… when it serves her."

"Tell me more," said the psychology student, taking a sip as ice cubes hit the insides of her glass.

Nina rose to reposition the chaise, following the shade. "When Jenny and I were small, Mom would sign us up for all kinds of things, not asking if we were interested. It was like we were being parked somewhere so, you know, she could do her thing. We attended International Folk Dancing Camp. Civil Disobedience training. Basket weaving… literally."

Cori laughed, then got up to reposition her chaise, too. "What else?"

Nina sipped from her sweating glass. "She decided our interests for us. She signed Jenny up for Modern Dance. She hated it. It didn't matter. Oh, and get this one: I begged her, but Mom wouldn't let me join Brownies. She said it was a paramilitary organization."

Cori was grinning. "Really?"

"I shit you not. And Barbies were banned because—she told me when I was seven or eight—they were misogynistic."

Cori shook her head. "What did you *get* to do?"

Nina thought for a minute. "We traveled most of every summer. All over the world. Sounds great, but Jenny and I both missed out on being with our friends at home." Suddenly self-conscious, Nina continued, "I sound so spoiled. But it was always awkward on the first day of school, knowing that while we were, for instance, camping in Romania or hiking up to a hostel in the middle of a Chilean shanty town, my classmates had spent time playing together and swimming in each other's doughboys. I wanted to be them."

"Doughboys!" Cori laughed as she stood to pull her chaise ever closer. "I remember those. But I'm jealous! Didn't you enjoy *any* of those trips?"

"Not at that age. I mean, it was good, but some of it was just wasted on my youth. You know, being in Florence to see the statue of David felt like an obligation on the way to get an ice cream cone. But sure, it broadened my world. We spent time with people who weren't like us, many who lived in poverty, which gave me an appreciation for what I had." Nina corrected herself. "How much I have. We met families whose parents totally risked their lives for their beliefs, working for human rights. That's not lost on me."

"What else did you get to do?"

Nina leaned all the way back, taking in the cloudless sky framed between the limbs of the statuesque oak. "When our friends spent the weekend at the beach, we marched in peace demonstrations in San Francisco. When the Brownies sold cookies, we trick-or-treated for UNICEF. We went to Pete Seeger concerts and harmonized to "The Internationale" and "Lift Every Voice and Sing" on the way home.

"What?" Cori straightened.

"What?"

"*You* were singing the Negro National Anthem? I don't know any white people who know that song. That's *our* song." Cori's voice had risen an octave.

"That's who my parents are," Nina responded. "We sang it in marches and at meetings, and yes, there you have it. That song is part of my childhood, too."

Cori shook her head. "Wait 'til I tell Lulu." She stretched out again. "Okay, keep going."

"I'm dominating this conversation," Nina said apologetically.

"I'll have my turn. This gets more interesting as we go."

"Well, starting when I was eight, Jenny and I were dropped off at Quaker summer camp for three weeks in the summers."

"Lulu would have missed me too much to send me to summer camp."

Nina heard that with wonder. And sadness. It taxed her imagination to think of her mother ever missing her too much. Or missing her at all. Cori's description of Lulu's maternal affections evoked an unfamiliar stirring in her, something she couldn't name at first.

Nina and Cori learned each other's family dynamics. Nina taught her friend about non-violent civil disobedience and the Spanish Civil War against Franco's fascism, while Cori described growing up relating through the language of psychological archetypes and the unconscious.

"Lulu got her graduate degree in Experimental Psychology at Spelman. It opened her to a Jungian way of seeing the world. That's how she raised me. By herself, by the way. And in all of that, I learned that everyone has an ego they present as their best self to the world, and everyone has a shadow. A shadow that includes an ugliness or weakness in the self. It's part of being human. I believe it's healthy to acknowledge that."

Nina had been listening. "That's what your paintings are for, then?"

"Exactly."

They were both quiet.

When Cori spoke, her eyes were closed. "So you've shared your mother's shadow with me. How would you describe the *best* of your mother's self?"

Nina felt something simmer. This was a hard ask. "The best of my mother's self..." she drained her iced tea. "The best of my mother is what shows visibly in the world. What she *does* in the world. This is what draws so much admiration to her. She is viewed as heroic by so many. A warrior of compassion. She *fearlessly* addresses injustices. And that's how I've seen her, too. I have great respect for that side of her. But," she struggled to find a way to explain the conflict, "it's made it hard for me to acknowledge any need I've had for her attention. It feels very wrong. Petty. Small. Selfish." Nina paused. "And she just doesn't let anything get in her way, either. Ever."

"Which," Cori chimed in, "can be hard on those in her immediate circle. Those who see her attention not predominantly on them but instead on people outside of it."

"Exactly." Nina felt an inner tremor. This made sense.

That conversation happened almost forty years ago. They remained so connected that a few years after Nina and Myles moved from the Bay Area to Sacramento, Cori and her husband Gordy followed. The move wasn't just because of their friendship, though. Lulu had moved back to her Sacramento childhood home several years before, and this was a way for Cori to be close to her mother as she grew older and her needs changed.

When Nina retired from teaching, Cori continued her work as a therapist. But after hearing Nina's enthusiasm about the local AWA group, she arranged her schedule so she could follow her own advice and join the weekly writing sessions. Along with her insightful writing voice, which often manifested the shadow, she reliably contributed toasted almonds for the brief break between twenty-minute writing prompts.

One week, Cori invited everyone to a writing conference held in September at the college where she taught Psych classes in the summer.

"We can ride together," she said during a break at the Friends Meeting House. "It's great—you don't need to fly anywhere or pay for a hotel. It's right here in Sacramento!"

Nina looked online at the conference offerings. Nothing grabbed her. Writing with her AWA group had grown to serve as an organizing principle for her weeks and a welcome ritual for reflection, but did she want more? And if she wasn't compelled to commit to a writing conference, what was it she *really* longed for? The answer came in a rush. She wanted more of the visual satisfaction that flowed through her pen. She wanted to ink flourishes and shapes between lines, lettering and type fonts and serifs. She wanted more calligraphy.

When she googled calligraphy conferences, the closest she found was a Hand Lettering Festival in Berkeley. The offerings made her salivate:

- An Italic Journey from Classical to Modern
- A Geometric Analysis of Contemporary Capitals
- Brush Letterforms
- Arabic Calligraphic Poem Structure

So enticing, as tempting as dark chocolate-covered almonds. She hit Cori's number.

"Corian Backsplash?"

"Nincompoop!"

"Did you look at the website? So many workshops. It's hard to choose, right?"

"It looks great, but…"

"What?"

"It made something clear for me. I love our writing group, and I love the AWA process, but right now that's enough writing for me."

"Really."

"I want to be doing calligraphy again. The idea of it excites me—so much that I registered for a lettering event. It lasts two days, and it's got scribes from the UK and Jordan and Japan who will be teaching. I just can't wait!"

"You know what, that's great. Sometimes, one idea creates an opening to another—I know how much you love your calligraphy. I'll bet you'll be in heaven."

———

The night before the festival, a text pinged. It was Freda, Lillian's tenant. "Yr mom's car has new dents. Plus her bumper is hanging and dragging on the ground. When u coming to Los Gatos?"

"Damn." From where Nina stood in the living room, she noted a dead fly, legs up, on the window sill. While she sprayed cleaner onto a fiber cloth, she noticed how she'd made a concerted effort to avoid thinking about her mother's hit-and-run driving pattern. She attacked the sill, clearing the bug carcass with a damp sweep. So now, with Freda's message about another scrape, more avoidance was… unavoidable. Rubbing the fiber cloth under hot water, she rinsed it until the water ran clear. Would Lillian hurt herself? Hurt someone else? Worse, kill someone?

Should she cancel Berkeley? Nina caught herself. The conference would last two days. She'd been looking forward to it for weeks. But what if, during those two days, her mother pulled a hit-and-run? She couldn't live with herself. If she drove down to Los Gatos instead, she could take a stab at convincing her mother to give up the car. She pictured saying, "Being car-free is a gift to the planet!" Not to mention it would be a gift to Nina. Maybe then, for one goddam stretch of time, she'd be able to focus on her own retirement. Her rebirth. Her joy. Like this lettering festival.

"Fuck."

As she'd furiously wiped the sills clean, she couldn't avoid noticing streaks on the glass, so it was only after all the front-facing windows were spotless that she realized it was past time for dinner. Summer had unquestionably sweated into September, so she pulled on two ceiling fans on her way to the kitchen. Myles stood at the counter opening boxed Vietnamese vermicelli. She'd forgotten he'd volunteered to make dinner that night. The kitchen smelled fragrant with pork and lemongrass.

She wrapped her arms around Myles' waist from behind.

"You okay?" he asked.

"I'm disappointed."

"Did I do something?"

"No, no, no, it has to do with Mom, and the Berkeley festival this weekend."

"What hap…?"

Her phone buzzed. She recognized Cori's chime.

"Corinthian!" Nina put the phone on speaker and motioned to Myles with her forefinger, tapping her watch: one minute! Walking swiftly from the kitchen back to her office, she lifted the stack of calligraphy conference materials from her chair to her desk and fell into a swivel chair, twirling with her legs straight out.

"Nintendo! You all packed for Berkeley?"

"Well, yes, but… I'm not going, after all."

"Because?"

Nina repeated Freda's message about Lillian's car.

"BFF, listen. You are spending a disproportionate amount of time supporting your mom. Agreed?"

"Agreed. But a crisis never happens at a convenient time, and I feel like I'd be holding my breath, knowing I should be in Los Gatos."

"Some crisis cannot wait, but in this case…"

"Cori, she could kill someone."

"How much driving will she be doing the next few days?"

"Who knows? She drives when she's moved to get some-where—like anyone."

"Look, beloved friend, I speak from experience. When I began taking care of Lulu, everything felt like a crisis. After a while, I accepted I couldn't control everything. I still anticipated problems and tried to be proactive, but I gave myself some slack. I needed the slack to keep resentment out of the equation."

Nina listened.

"Nina, *you* need some slack. You need to feed your creativity, your art. It makes you a better human, and a better daughter."

Nina took this in. "You realize I have been doing calligraphy and loving it since I was twelve years old?"

"Probably earlier than that, Ninny. You were doing all of the protest signage when you were eight? Nine? So this is a lifelong passion, my friend. It's been fifty years."

Fifty years. She hadn't really considered that her devotion to the pen had never ebbed.

"Gotta go in a minute," Cori said, "but I just flashed to that day on the deck when we were just getting started on who we were. FORTY years ago, Nina, we talked about our futures, how we wanted to live rich lives the way our mothers did. So it's our turn now. Loving your mother is part of your living fully, but not all of it."

"Just as my sister and me were not… everything… to Mom."

"Right. And… this lettering festival is about enriching your life in a way that's unique to you. And," she continued pointedly, "you are more than your mother's caregiver."

Nina quieted for a moment. "I might be better at it if she's not my only devotion."

"It's a privilege to have some long-view perspective, isn't it?"

"Forty years! Love you, Corpus Christi."

"Back at you, Ninja Warrior."

Full circle, Nina thought. Almost. Cori helped her remember what she'd lost sight of: her own full life.

"Nina, you coming?" Myles' question was loud.

How long had he been waiting?

She walked into the dining room to the table set with large bowls of steaming noodles.

"I've reheated everything."

"Sorry, hon." She pulled her chair out. "Cori and I have been playing tag. I had to pick up, even just to say we could talk later."

"Clearly you talked more than that."

"Well, yes, and I'm relieved. She helped me avoid a mistake I was about to make."

"Does this have to do with Lillian's car?"

"Freda's text about Mom's car set me off. I was about to cancel the festival."

"Nina," Myles eyes softened, "you're still going, right?"

Nina nodded as she closed her chopsticks around a curly piece of pork.

"I'm glad Cori helped you get clear about your priorities."

"I've been seeing my own interests as selfish. That I should be available twenty-four seven for Mom. So… I'm realizing… I can do both. I'll have a wonderful weekend, and Monday I can head to Los Gatos."

"You'll be better for it."

Nina foisted a chopstick into the air. "Point taken."

"You do realize that Cori is not the only one with spectacular insights about you," Myles stabbed a spring roll as he spoke. "Text or call me anytime to discuss further."

Nina blew him a kiss and secured a water chestnut. "I know. And hon? So delicious. I truly appreciate when you toil for hours so we can enjoy fine dining."

"I toil for hours, I wait for hours, and I reheat for hours. All in the name of love. And seriously, honey, I support your original plan. You'll have a great time in Berkeley."

CHAPTER TWENTY-TWO

LILLIAN

Pulling her unwashed Prius alongside several gleaming luxury cars already parked on the sweeping driveway, Lillian was reminded again that this book club was not her usual gig. No other cars sported bumper stickers. Like Lillian, these women were all Jewish. Unlike her, they lived in a rarified world of wealth. Opinions were not made public. Rather, supporting particular philanthropic organizations made plain their points of view. Showing up at the apropos gala. Being in contact with like-minded people. Keeping up appearances. Sharing personal shoppers at Nieman Marcus.

While Lillian had no material wants, she did share in the enjoyment of shopping. Her shopping habit, however, was not exercised at Nieman Marcus or Nordstrom, as she'd overheard others casually mention when recounting their weekends. Her retail interests were exclusive to local thrift stores. Big spending for her was paying more than ten dollars for any piece of clothing. Make that five. And the Jewish angle? While she was *technically* Jewish, she'd never practiced. Neither had her folks, who had, however, acknowledged that Judaic principles guided their values. Belief in the common good. Humanitarianism. Justice for all. It was still a surprise to be included in such well-heeled gatherings every month. Her eyes crinkled at the idea.

Flipping open the hatchback, she pulled out her basket of Fair Trade chocolate and coffee, plopped her library book on top, and, arms filled, made her way to the grand entrance to this month's host's home.

"Lilly!" Marva opened the oversized mahogany door, its weight lightened by inset laminated glass. Very modern. She was the one who'd invited Lillian to join the club over a year ago. "You'll enjoy these women," she'd said that day after a Bigger World presentation at her temple. "And they will learn so much from you."

Now they were friends. "Let me help you with some of that!" Marva took the book from the top of the basket and then extricated the basket itself from Lillian's arms, placing it on the walnut credenza that rested against a wall of glossy slate. "May I take your coat?" Marva asked. "I love the length." It was a trim, fitted design for a down coat, all white, extending below Lillian's knees.

"It was my daughter's," Lillian said as she slipped out of the coat. "I'd never have a white coat otherwise. The zipper broke." She shook her head. "Nina doesn't sew, and she couldn't find anyone to replace it, so she offered it to me. I got out my sewing machine and put in a new zipper! Voila!"

"Well, it's a lovely gift from your daughter, and I love that it keeps your tusche warm!"

"Nina is taller than I am—she got her height from Cal—so it covers more of me."

With the coat hung, Lillian picked up her basket before Marva led her across the lustrous landing and further into the living room, where the others were already gathered. A fire glowed from a sleek fireplace, a contrast from the overcast sky outside the floor-to-ceiling windows. The glass framed a heritage oak in the expansive backyard, its twining muscular limbs exuding strength, endurance, and wealth, Lillian thought to herself. Marva had once toured Lillian through the home, describing the contractor's challenge to build around the monumental oaks that graced the property. It took means to reside in the architecture set into this landscape.

"Lilly," several of her book friends warmly murmured her name as she made her way into the circle, still clutching her basket. Philomena patted the open space beside her.

"Happy Rosh Hashana!" Joan said with enthusiasm from the opposite couch.

Lillian smiled. "Thank you." She made a note to look up what Rosh Hashana meant when she got home. She was a lousy Jew.

"Lilly, that turquoise cowl so suits you. The way it sets off your stunning white hair!" She took a long look. "It looks so… *familiar.*"

"Phil, you have one like it!" Shira said. "I complimented you on it—you must remember. A while back."

Philomena looked thoughtful. "You're right! I did have that sweater!" She remembered aloud how she'd found it in Carmel one year, and when it got a little threadbare, she gave it up. "You know," she said, "I donated it to the Echo Shop."

Settling into one of the velvet wheat couches, Lillian giggled inwardly. It was highly probable that she was wearing Philomena's sweater. And she knew it cost her under five dollars. She nodded to the offer of mulled wine while she reached into her basket to display the chocolates and packaged coffee on the sleek cocktail table.

"This is the sweetest, creamiest dark chocolate," she smiled at her ten-years-younger friends, "seventy percent cacao, and Fair Trade, of course."

"What's this?" Lillian heard Shira whisper to Joan.

"Lillian brings chocolate and coffee every time," Lillian heard Joan whisper back. "You don't remember?"

"Five dollars a bar—how many would you like?" Lillian ignored the whispers, her eyebrows raised with friendly persuasion. This book club did actually feel like hard work at times. Keeping up the cheery countenance, the appearance of confidence around these poised women. She reminded herself if she succeeded in recruiting even one of these friends to experience a reality tour with Bigger World, it would justify her efforts. And, after all, one recruit usually leads to others. Chocolate sweetened the chances!

Most of the women unclasped their logo-clad handbags to retrieve their wallets while Marva refilled everyone's mugs. Lillian's own woven bag sagged a little against the box of coffee in the Kenyan basket.

It was after this that the book discussion began. This month the club read *Unsheltered* by Barbara Kingsolver.

"Lilly," Marva said, "thank you for this suggestion. I found the book intriguing and prescient, truly, for our times."

"Isn't it?" Lillian agreed. "Actually, Nina is who recommended it to me, and she said the same thing… that it was so relevant to our awareness of climate change but also to the… how did she say it… the threshold between an old way of thinking, and a new one…"

"And that the chapters alternate between the centuries—so we see that same 'threshold' dividing old and new thinking, over and over," Philomena offered.

Shira chimed in. "And the love story was charming."

"Love story? What love story?" Lillian couldn't remember a love story.

Shira again. "Between the two botanists. You know, in the utopian community."

Joan agreed but added, "It was really a love story about Darwin, I thought."

"Or evolution itself," Marva said.

"Well." Lillian was caught up. "It was the *ideas* in the contemporary chapters that engaged me the most. All that reference to Cuban ingenuity, in the face of U.S. sanctions."

Marva deftly segued by acknowledging how Lillian and Cal's Bigger World trips to Cuba contextualized Lillian's remark, "which helped them all," before moving to how the financial struggles of the modern-day characters exposed the fragility of capitalism.

"The crumbling house in the modern-day story is such an apt metaphor for that, don't you think?" Philomena asked.

Some nodded and the rest of the conversation flowed smoothly. After an hour, Lillian brought it to a close, leaning in with an addendum: a set of printed flyers in her hand.

"Next month—the last week of January—our Guatemala tour is on." Her adrenaline surged whenever she pitched a trip. "We're limiting it to ten, and we've got two more spots!"

She noticed a subtle movement as the women shifted a bit against the damask pillows plumped on the couches. She took it as a cue to go deeper.

"Lake Atitlan is the most beautiful spot—a mile high, temperatures in the seventies, no mosquitoes, a magnificent volcanic lake, marvelous people…" Lillian pushed the flyers toward each woman as she continued. "And we'll be learning about the fascist dictatorship and brutal legacy of the conquistadores, along with the ingenuity and spirit of the Mayan people." Lillian pulled her bag to her shoulder and stood. "Join us!" Eyes bright, full smile. "It will be amazing!"

Shira and Joan folded the fliers into their handbags, smiling politely while rising. Philomena stayed seated, opening her glasses case (Lillian noted the word "Fendi" on the leather and wondered if it was a family name) for her readers so she could scan the details. Lillian felt optimistic and then heard Shira reminding everyone that the book for the January meeting was Joan Didion's *Year of Magical Thinking*. "We'll miss you, Lilly. Maybe you want to bring it with you to read in Guatemala?"

"Unfortunately—or fortunately," Lillian shrugged, "too much to do. But enjoy it without me!"

"Not sure if 'enjoy' is the best adjective for *A Year of Magical Thinking*?" Shira said. "It's about the first year after her husband's death."

Lillian shuddered at a chill, but her unease changed quickly to relief that she'd miss the next meeting.

"Thanks, everyone," Marva said as goodbyes were exchanged. She helped Lillian get into her coat. "You really are a marvel."

"A marvel?" Lillian raised an eyebrow, trying to appear modestly dubious.

"Your eyes are open. You come into our discussions with a perspective we wouldn't have otherwise."

"That's exactly why Cal and I founded Bigger World. To open people's eyes." After a beat, she added, "I learn from all of you, too." Her eyes got round. "Oh—I forgot to ask if anyone wanted to buy the coffee!"

"Next time, Lillian, there's always next time."

When Lillian hurried through the cold to her Prius, the other cars were gone. She considered Marva's parting words, which filled her heart with warmth along with buoyancy. *It's true what she said,* she thought. *Their wealthy world doesn't include the perspective I bring. Even though it's uncomfortable for me, it's good for me to be with these people. It's good for them. It's a way to bring them a bigger world.*

She started the car and realized Marva was standing outside her oversized front door, wrapped tightly in a cashmere shawl, gazing in her direction. Lillian reversed, pulled closer to the entrance, and opened her window.

"You look so cold! Everything okay?" Lillian asked.

"I was just reading your bumper stickers," Marva said. "I can understand why you're keeping the Bernie Sanders ones."

Lillian nodded. It was still too soon to take them off. Maybe she never would. She was still grieving the election. "There's so much work to do."

"One more thing, Lilly."

Lillian waited.

"You mention your daughter. Nina, right?"

"Yes."

"Are you close?"

"Oh, she's marvelous!" Lillian said it declaratively, with gusto, not really answering the question. It was her go-to answer. She felt something twitch. She really didn't know how Nina was. *Were* they close? She quickly absolved herself. There was always so much to keep up with in her own life; she didn't keep up with Nina's.

"Does she visit often? Call?"

"She lives in Sacramento. It's a long way from the Bay Area. And the phone, no. I'm not good on the phone. I'm not a… chatter. Even with my eldest daughter…"

"Another daughter? Oh, I didn't realize you had two children!"

"Yes, Jenny lives in Chicago. Married, with two adult sons and a grandson. Very full life!" With that, she waved goodbye, hearing the gravel crunch as she pulled out of the curving drive to rejoin her bigger world.

So much to do.

Chapter Twenty-Three

Nina

As the wheels of Nina's suitcase crossed the cracks in the walkway from the platform, the percussive repetition echoed the cadence of the train as it had slowed to a stop in Sacramento. The tunnel leading to the terminal amplified the sound, especially as it crowded with other passengers arriving at their destination.

As he had texted, Myles was double-parked outside the main entrance. After heaving her case into the trunk, Nina climbed into the passenger seat.

"Husband!" She leaned into his sideways hug. "I am so glad to see you. So glad."

"Wife!" He kissed her. "Tell me everything. Did it meet your expectations?" Myles navigated around another double-parker and headed out the exit.

"It's what I needed."

"Inspiration?"

"Inspiration. See those colors?" Nina pointed at the gingkos in the median, brilliant yellow flitting in the breeze as they approached. "I found inks at the festival in that very shade, something I never bothered with before because anything I lettered in yellow would just fade into the paper—or get sucked into it, really. But I brought home a bottle of the most luscious, deeply pigmented yellow that I can use on black paper. It stays on the surface, doesn't get absorbed."

"Quite a find." Myles signaled to turn on 24th Street, heading to Curtis Park, while Nina quietly drank in the complexions of the trees they passed: plum, variegated lime green, deep umber, blazing pumpkin. After the lettering festival, everything she saw equated to colors of ink. Fall in Berkeley was less vibrant than the theatrics of her own city's lush canopy.

After emptying her suitcase of her new collection of ink bottles and a line of nibs, she showered and then joined Myles on the back deck where he waited with cups of steeped honey-ginger tea. Before pulling out a chair, she placed a pad of fine-grained paper onto the table and flipped open the cover.

Myles put his mug down. "Wow! What are we looking at?"

Nina grinned. "Pretty fun, right?"

"It looks like a sampler… is this from one of the classes?"

"It's a compilation of scripting I learned over the whole weekend." She pointed to the top line of letters. "Monoline script is sort of the most basic." Her finger moved down. "This loopy one is Florist script. It's got so many embellishments and flourishes that it's best for stand-alone words. You know, you wouldn't use it for a whole page of text. Too distracting."

Myles nodded. "I get that."

"This," Nina continued, "is called 'chunky faux calligraphy.' Not exactly sure why it's considered 'faux,' but whatever. You can use a thin tip or a thick one. I have the pens already for it. And here's 'Elegant,' which is a little bouncy, right? Floaty?"

"Floaty," Myles agreed. "Such evocative descriptors, darlink."

Nina leaned down to give him a kiss. "You are most generous."

She pulled out her chair to sit and nearly squashed Mingus, who had gotten comfortable under the table.

"Oh, buddy, I'm sorry!" The dog momentarily forgot his stoic bent, forgivingly licking her hand before curling up again in exactly the same spot. "And honey," Nina resumed, "look—I promise I'll stop after this. It's called 'Brush Pen Faux Calligraphy.' Again, not sure why 'faux,' but see the double stripe? It looks kind of like a shadow?"

"It does."

Nina turned another page. A menu appeared, lettered exclusively with Brush Pen Faux Calligraphy.

"Zen Breakfast? Eggs Lola? Soy Chorizo? What's this?"

"A job!"

At the end of the sampler class, her instructor pulled her aside to introduce her to the owner of a restaurant in Benicia.

"This woman came down to the festival to find someone to create the menu for her chalkboard."

"Looking for artists on the cheap?" Myles took a sip.

Nina ignored him. "She'd been looking over my shoulder and at some of the other calligraphers' work, and I guess she liked my style. I'm surprised, you know—it's not as if I've been practicing these fonts for years and years."

"My point rests. And a question: how sustainable is a chalkboard menu?"

"Liquid chalk lasts forever. She's been waiting to finalize her menu before making something that only changes once a year." Nina paused. "It gives me a legitimate way to start a portfolio."

Myles asked if there was more.

"Sure." Nina flipped past the menu to a page with one line of Florist script in vivid turquoise.

"'Happy Birthday, Lilly?' You getting ready already?"

"It's not too soon. I told you, right? It's going to be at the Institute for Nonviolence. There will be lots of signage. Banners. Cards."

"The big nine-*oh*."

"I wish you didn't have that recital."

"Me, too. When I call her that day, I'll have a plan for a belated birthday visit. And let her know about Stubby Clapp."

"What?"

"Who. He played briefly for the St. Louis Cardinals."

Nina laughed. They lifted their mugs, toasting the success of the weekend.

It felt good to be home.

CHAPTER TWENTY-FOUR

NINA

The Institute for Nonviolence barely contained itself in the 1910 two-storied house. It leaned left in its old age, never settling in complete comfort as it occupied prime downtown Los Gatos real estate. Surrounded by Victorian houses and newer upscale retail properties with residences above, it stood out with its "Schools, Not Bombs" placards in the unwashed windows. It was home for peace and justice activists to organize and educate. And today, to celebrate Lillian's ninetieth birthday.

As she turned into the driveway, Nina overlooked the rainbow banner and the myriad peace signs hanging from the dormers upstairs. They'd long grown so familiar they'd faded from her attention, and it was only after she climbed out of the driver's seat of her mother's car that she noticed the cheerful sign hanging over the backdoor: "Saludades, Lilly!"

When Riva opened the door, its creaking squeak caused Lillian, clad in her usual ruana, to turn, which signaled Riva to start singing "Happy Birthday." She was soon joined by basses, baritones, altos, and sopranos, all enthusiastic and mostly off key.

Lillian smiled indulgently, waiting for the song to end, and then:

"Can someone help me bring in the Fair Trade chocolate?" Her arms were already committed to a large basket filled with Central American textiles and South African musical instruments. Nina waited behind her with a box of burlap-bagged coffee beans. She was accustomed to this. Lillian carried her inventory to most meetings she attended, including Nina and Myles's wedding rehearsal dinner. Her mother stormed into just about any circumstance as an opportunity to raise funds for the next Bigger World scholarships.

Worming their way through the dimly lit back hall, the house smelled its age. Nina took care not to topple the folded chairs resting uneasily to her right, familiar with employing the same kind of caution she used when navigating Lillian's crowded home. The institute's hall led to an impossibly small kitchen, its counters stacked with mismatched coffee mugs and soup bowls. The dish drain held sponges incubating new forms of life, so as much as she wished she could pull on some latex gloves to start clearing and scrubbing, Nina did what she learned to do: restrain her impulse to scour and instead ignore the disorder and remember the big picture. This place represented her parents' lifework.

The year Nina was born was the same year Lillian co-founded the Institute for Nonviolence. In the chase for cheaper rent the first thirty years, it occupied a number of locations. Finally, Cal and Lillian and their cohorts made a concerted effort to raise money to buy a property so the Institute could continue in perpetuity. A famed folk singer even agreed to hold a concert to help their dream become reality.

"Over here!" Nina heard someone say. She twisted in the direction of the voice.

It was Nola, the office manager. She wheeled closer, pointing to a table that had been recently decluttered to make space for

Lillian's goods. Books and yellowing literature weighted the bookshelves, bowing on both sides. Bold titles popped out: *The People's History of the United States, Beyond Apartheid in Palestine, Imperialism, The Highest Stage of Capitalism,* Nelson Mandela's autobiography. The U.S. Constitution. Nina smelled mold and rot, but the intellectual resources here were relevant and values-based in the present. *Big picture,* she reminded herself.

Nina had been around the Institute's community for decades, but only as a tertiary presence, helping her parents get organized for events. Still, no one here knew her name; certainly, most didn't know who she was. She didn't think Lillian and Cal had ever explicitly introduced her. There was always just so much to do, of course, that there really wasn't time to talk about family.

She addressed the office manager. "Thank you. Nola... I'm Nina. We spoke this morning on the phone. And we've met a few times."

Nola smiled warmly while glancing past her. "Thanks for helping Lillian on her birthday."

Nina nodded as her fists tightened and she stepped away from herself. As much as she wished it, what difference would it really make if folks here recognized her as Lillian's daughter?

Meanwhile, more Lillian fans squeezed through the front entrance, greeting each other, peeling off fleece-lined gloves, hanging up jackets and coats, making room for Sam as he swung his crutches through the hall and into the main meeting room. It was a mix of ages and races, but most folks were white and over sixty. Regulars of the Institute for Nonviolence came wearing their better sweats or jeans, with winter thermals poking under T-shirts. Nina observed a range of silk-screened statements on several: "Feel the Bern," "We the People," "RBG," and one that was bulleted in such a small font that she couldn't help studying the wearer's chest for an inappropri-ate amount of time: PRO Black Lives, Queer, Trans, Woman, Weed, Science, Sex, Choice. Others showed up dressed for busi-ness: two men in suits and ties, one carrying a toddler, and a woman, also wearing a suit. Nola served as host, directing people to the back through the tight hall to keep the traffic pattern con-sistently headed in one direction. Few paid attention as they clam-ored toward Lillian from the front, behind, and every side.

"Lilly! Happy birthday, happy birthday!" The salutation echoed through the house while Lillian used the attention to sell raffle tickets:

"Ten for five dollars! The winner gets to choose between this Cuban rum," she pointed to it on her display table, "and this re-markable painted parchment from Ethiopia."

Nina looked closely at the bottle of rum. Two conspicuous inches were empty from the neck. Did her mother not realize it had been opened? Would it matter? These were the moments she wished Myles was with her so they could elbow each other.

A bell interrupted the commerce. Folks got quiet to hear Nola's directives.

"If each of you could please bring a chair from the hall to the main meeting room." She caught Nina's eye: "Make sure Lilly has a seat in the center of the front row."

Let the games begin, Nina thought.

And the games began, starting with Nina seated by Lillian on one side, Nola's chair wheeled next to her mother on the other. Nola angled herself so she faced the sea of fifty or so faces, waiting for quiet.

"We're here today to honor Lillian on her birthday, and to in-form some of you who are new to the Institute for Nonviolence—

that Lillian cofounded it over sixty years ago." Nola continued to read Lillian's accomplishments from a list Nina had emailed to her the week before.

After that, the Institute's tech expert Paulo projected a video compilation of Lillian and Cal over the years at various demonstrations and peace marches. The last shot lingered, showing them holding a sign together in front of their bodies: "NO JUSTICE, NO PEACE."

Nina looked over at her mother, seated by her side. To her surprise, Lillian's eyes were filled with tears. It was the first time she'd witnessed her mother cry since Cal died. *Finally*, she thought. *Finally, Lillian shows she's human. Allows it.* She reached into her cross bag for a pack of tissues. Lillian beat her to it, now dabbing her eyes with wadded Kleenex she'd pulled from her sleeve.

Next came the suits, who, it turned out, were Santa Clara County Supervisors who brought with them speeches and signed commendations. Each time Lillian was handed one of the framed certificates, she turned to Nina, rolling her eyes. After the third one, she said so only Nina could hear, "What am I going to do with all of these?"

"Raffle them off at your memorial," Nina whispered back.

Lillian laughed.

The speeches gave way to South African drums and plunking mbira. A flash of color swept into the room as a turbaned woman, arms open and unabashedly exuberant, danced directly in front of the guest of honor. Lillian's smile went wide. The rhythm accelerated, driving the dancer's moves until she was frenzied and breathing hard, then gradually slowed, and, as the music stopped, so did she.

"Dear Lilly," the dancer reached out to hold Lillian's hands, "I am a dancer for Peace, and I wish you *min'emnandi yokuzalwa!*"

Flushing, Lillian returned the sweaty-handed squeeze. Nola wheeled in front of the applauding assembly to invite Lillian to say a few words.

"Well," Lillian began after she stood and faced her audience. "It's lovely that you have arranged this birthday party for me, and..." she paused, "I hope to use the time I have left to push for a peaceful world. A peaceful, just world. Ninety years has not been enough time to see this through!"

"AMEN!" boomed a loud voice, which was echoed by the throng.

Nola led another rendition of "Happy Birthday," followed by an invitation to line up for the potluck. As most of the group headed to the growing line, a few hung back to connect with Lillian.

"Mom, relax, stay where you are," Nina said. "I'll get you a plate."

Already deep in conversation with one of her devotees about the next reality tour to Cuba, Lillian nodded absently.

Nina thought of the similarity of these events over the years. The parties her parents hosted as she grew up blended into one general memory with few distinctions. Folk dancing was a staple. For a moment, the Institute for Nonviolence faded into the background while she recalled a typical gathering from her childhood:

"Over here, kids!" She remembered how the folk-dance teacher herded the half-dozen children in attendance to the side of the Nearing's front yard. She'd set up a portable phonograph on the lawn, connected by a long, frayed extension cord through an open window of her parents' study. "In a circle, hands by your side, facing me," she said with gentle authority. Her skirt was tiered with color, and Nina noted the bric-a-brac design circling the hem. Silver hoop earrings flashed against her dark skin and close-cropped hair.

The children followed the dance instructions shyly; they didn't know each other apart from these particular occasions, occasions orchestrated for the adults in their lives. Jenny hid during these events except to come out to fill a plate from the potluck, so Nina often felt particularly awkward by herself. She forced herself to take part so the dance teacher wouldn't feel abandoned. And, she had to admit, she did experience a rush when the dances got to parts where boys faced girls and brushed each other's hands.

The dance teacher warmed up with the children and then ordered them to disperse and bring their parents outside for the adults' turn.

While Jenny sequestered in her bedroom, Nina wandered through the rooms of the house, each one filled with adults she recognized, holding drinks, resting paper plates on the fireplace hearth next to the bronze Paul Robeson bust her grandmother sculpted and cast decades before, shaking their heads, talking between bites of macaroni salad.

"Vietnam…"

"Daniel Ellsberg…"

"Cambodia…"

"What a dick…"

"Last night on KPFA…"

Two young men shook hands. Lillian had guided them to their selective service status as Conscientious Objectors. They were meeting for the first time.

"Lillian is righteous," Nina heard one of them say.

"She saved my life," said the other.

Just as the dance music came to an end, little Nina stepped out the front door. The folk-dancing adults streamed back inside to fill plates with tamales, Frito casserole, lasagna, crusty whole wheat bread, and Lillian's favorite, pickled herring. They ladled punch from the repurposed nose cap of a small airplane ("My mother made it—I inherited her resourcefulness," Lillian explained) or, more conventionally, poured Chablis into clear plastic cups from a gallon jug. Cups that always got washed to use at the next party.

A memory bubbled up for Nina of Lillian and Cal sitting together on the window seat, holding court. Behind them was a view of the Jacaranda. In front of them, across the table, other adults listened intently as Lillian spoke. The table she'd polished the day before to help them get ready. She could still smell the teak oil.

As inconspicuously as possible, she would interrupt. "Hungry? I'll bring you something to eat." She didn't want to disturb the discussion about blocking napalm shipments. Her parents were always thinking about very important things, and she didn't want to get in their way. Her father found her eyes and smiled as he mouthed his thanks; her mother kept her audience rapt as she dove deep into napalm production as further evidence that people's deaths fueled and profited the military-industrial complex.

As she filled two paper plates with cold pasta, Jello, three-layer salad, Nina sensed the weight in Cal and Lillian's lives. The gravity of their work. How much did she register on their scale? Did she count?

Now, forty-five years later, at Lillian's honorarium of a life's work, she loaded her mother's dish again and still wondered.

CHAPTER TWENTY-FIVE

LILLIAN

Canceled book club, canceled vigil, canceled travel.

At first, living in lockdown wasn't that different from life as usual. Lillian was still catching up from the Guatemalan trip—so much to do organizing the pottery and weavings she'd brought back so she could price them for the sale at the Peace Fair. Following up on the contribution commitments Bigger World made to various organizations, then coordinating a trip for Bay Area middle schoolers to build a school in Nicaragua and lining up a Venezuelan speaker for the Institute for Nonviolence—so much to address that she hardly missed the canceled book club meetings, or the paused peace vigil in front of the Los Gatos Community Library. But the gym's closing because of COVID? That changed everything.

"No meditation in motion," she complained to Siti on the phone. "Swimming is what gets me going every day!"

"Lilly, we must have patience," she said. "It will not last like this forever."

"I don't know… how *can* we know how long this will last?"

"Remember, I left Thailand in 2003 and went first to Singapore. Same time as SARS, Lilly. We couldn't leave, not for three months! *No* one could leave the country."

"Really?"

"Oh, see, you don't even remember! But it worked. Very strict, but it worked. So I learned to have patience, and you must, too."

Lillian shook her head. "But you said... *three* months?" It had already been a month since the Y emailed the news of its closure. A month that felt like a year. How was she going to live without going to the Y?

Lillian was famously a late sleeper, but now she slept in even longer. Still in her nightgown and robe she sat down at the dining table with half a banana, almond milk, and a cup of coffee to the side. She picked a letter from the top of one of several piles. Papers were mushrooming.

I have more time to do everything, but I'm getting less done.

The letter was from Partners in Health.

Such good work. She and Cal had been supporting them for years. Nina explained how Partners in Health was now on auto bill pay, so why do they keep sending requests for more money? Wasting the earth's resources. She tossed it into the Namibian basket she used for recycling paper. The next item she pulled was so heavy it threatened to throw the stack off balance. The manila envelope was packed tight with, oh yes... after Cal's death, she'd stuffed all the condolence cards into this envelope until it nearly exploded. When she first opened them, she'd only just scanned the handwritten messages. Lillian again set the envelope aside to look at later.

Time to move her bones. The nearby park offered a circular walking track; she decided to ask Freda if she'd join her. After she zipped the velour running suit she'd nabbed years ago at a consignment shop, she knocked on Freda's door. Freda was wearing a surgical mask.

"Lilly, where's your mask?"

"I'm going for a walk. Want to join me?" Lillian smiled.

Freda had already schooled her on wearing a mask. Sometimes, she remembered; sometimes, she didn't. Nina had ordered special turquoise surgical masks to entice her use. But it was still always with reluctance.

Lillian laughed. "Oh, I didn't really think about it."

Freda backed into her entryway several feet. "We need to protect ourselves and *each other*. And I can't walk with you, I'm sorry. But if you're going anyway? Put a mask on."

All of this about the masks, Lillian thought. It's a little excessive. She'd always believed exposure to germs *contributed* to her good health.

"Cal and I have traveled all over the world and eaten in places without refrigeration and excessive sanitation, and we're healthier for it!" This was her go-to line whenever Nina pressed Lillian about keeping the house clean to her daughter's standard. Nina hadn't been to her house in quite a while, nor had she been to Nina and Myles's. However, her past visits to see them in Sacramento left her self-conscious whenever they came to see her. Well, not Myles, but Nina. Obsessed with cleanliness. Within the first moments of their visits to her house, Nina barged in to move things from counters and desktops and the dining room table, cleaning the surfaces before replacing items in neat geometric order. She threw out expired food in the fridge, which Lillian later retrieved and put back. Lillian wondered if this compulsive cleaning was hazardous to her daughter's health. Maybe the cleaning products she used contributed to her migraines? It made Lillian feel like Nina thought she was messy, dirty, unclean. Very... judged. Judged for a trait so insignificant when contrasted with what was most important. Why wasn't her daughter as obsessed with cleansing the planet as she was with keeping an immaculate bathroom?

Two can judge.

The stack of mail beckoned. She first needed to sort through the mélange of time-sensitive coupons and newsletters overflowing in the vertical file she kept on the kitchen island. As she pulled out a flyer discounting new tires, the corner of a deckle-edged Mother's Day card caught her eye. It must have been from the year before. It pained her to throw away Nina's cards. They were always heartfelt, filled with Lillian's favorite color, and meaningful each time she came across one.

Turquoise calligraphed lettering said, "Mom, you've always been an inspiration for all your good works. It is because of you that I know my legislator's email addresses by heart. How many daughters can attribute this to the way their mother raised them? Love and kisses, Nina."

Lillian felt her heart fill but then abruptly drop. How *was* Nina? When had they last talked? She noticed the lightness in her grasp as she picked up her phone, along with a slight numbness in her fingers. It seemed to correspond with her shoulder pain, which she knew was arthritis. She hit speed dial.

"Nina?"

But it was only Nina's recording. She needed to hear her daughter's voice. Live.

CHAPTER TWENTY-SIX

NINA

I t was Nina's turn to facilitate the writers' group, so she'd set aside the morning to prepare. She'd located a poem to share at the opening and closing the following morning and was working on the prompts for the twenty-minute writes when she got a call from Cori.

"Nina, I have to tell you, I'm… not comfortable meeting in person."

Nina felt a tremble, the kind that made her wonder if she was feeling a small earthquake.

"It's not only about me," Cori continued. "Remember how hard it was to find someone to take care of Lulu?"

"Gosh, yes." When Lulu began to have accidents, Cori realized she couldn't keep up with her mother's needs and her therapy practice without finding help. Incontinence was the turning point, and it took her weeks to find a recommended caregiver with an open schedule.

"Well, I've required Lulu's caregiver to wear a mask in the house. And I've asked her to commit to caring exclusively for Lulu. I mean," she paused, "Moli's here five days a week, but she often works for others on weekends. I know that's a hardship for her to cancel her weekend clients, so I'm paying her more."

Nina pushed away from her desk to focus on the conversation. "That's good of you. Caregivers often have a hard time making ends meet."

"Well, it's pretty self-serving generosity."

"Still."

"And tell me about it. It's costing an arm and a leg for this care, but I know it's exploitative. Twenty-five dollars an hour for this care? How do these caregivers survive? I mean, I interviewed one woman who lives out of her car. It's awful."

Nina shook her head. The values in this economic system, she thought. Again, mostly impacting women: sisters, daughters, nieces, granddaughters who scramble to find caregivers to lighten the weight.

"But back to my thread." Cori's words were more pointed than usual. "I need to be as careful as I'm asking Moli to be. I can't afford exposure to anyone who, you know, may have COVID."

By the end of the conversation, Nina expressed clear agreement about the inherent risks of meeting in person. She hadn't really thought deeply about it, but already, two writers had missed the previous week because of concerns about the virus. It was a hard call to cancel a session, but it served everyone's interests to avoid gathering until things cleared. The governor had, after all, strongly suggested a lockdown. And it wouldn't be long, Cori said assuredly, before the lockdown would serve to slow the virus, and then they could resume their sessions.

Nina's efforts wouldn't be wasted. She emailed all of the writers about the canceled sessions and then called The Friends Meeting

House to put their rented sessions on pause until the lockdown lifted. Her poem and prompts would be used soon enough.

"We understand," said the office manager on the phone. "We're all on hold. We'll credit your missed meetings—just let us know when the River Rock Writers are ready to return."

Nina ended the call, grateful for the Friends' generous response. She sat outside on the deck of her house with her phone, her calligraphy pens, and her art pad. The cancellation of so many activities opened up time to spend practicing her lettering—a strangely wonderful gift. Before she opened the laptop, she took in the signs of spring all around her: the nascent leafing of the jacaranda she and Myles planted to honor Cal. The azaleas, deep pink. The impossibly tender green everywhere. How could it be so gorgeous outside? How could the sky be so clear, inhalations so sweet, the horizon so filled with blossoming redbuds, ornamental pears, plums, almonds—all while the planet's humans were recoiling and afraid to touch one another?

She spun the patio chair so she faced the table, still benefitting from the umbrella's shade. After she hit "favorites" on her phone, she heard the ringtone fade into the voicemail recording. "Mom," Nina said, "give me a call when you have a chance."

The screened metal backdoor clanged open as Myles came to join her on the deck. After the CDC recommended two weeks of isolation to "flatten the curve," he'd been inside canceling his lessons.

"How are your students taking it?" Nina asked him.

"They've all accepted it. I mean," he shrugged, "what else can they do?"

"Kind of a forced vacation for you, right?" Nina said.

"Guess so."

Neither of them were overly concerned. This was not going to last.

Nina nodded over her laptop. "I'm researching books on fonts... between distractions, anyway."

"Are you going to call your mom?"

"I just did, that is," she qualified, "I left a voicemail. You know, as per usual. See if she even listens to it."

Myles pulled a chair out and sat next to her so they both faced the young jacaranda. Mingus had followed him from the house and was now prone on the deck, twitching his nose in the air.

"You realize how lucky it is that she got back from Guatemala when she did?"

Nina pointed to her phone. "I've been reading about the canceled flights and closed borders."

"We are getting a forced break, aren't we? We're the lucky ones. Oh my god," Nina said, "I can't imagine teaching during this nightmare." She felt for her friends still in the classroom. Or not in—really, teaching virtually was the current reality. How school districts were having to rethink their annual schedules. So much uncertainty. Teaching was hard enough when things were *normal*. *At least*, Nina thought again, *this wouldn't last forever*.

Myles was thinking differently. "I've gotta figure something out... in case this lockdown does last longer." He hoisted Mingus off his lap and walked back inside.

As Myles shut the screen door behind him, Lillian's ringtone sounded. Marimbas. But at that moment Nina resolved to work on a sample of geometric contemporary capitals she'd originally planned to submit during the next Berkeley calligraphy conference. Even though the gathering had been cancelled, she wanted to maintain momentum. She set her timer and lost herself in repetitive curve strokes.

After the timer pinged, Nina gathered her oversized drawing pad to return to her office. A tug pulled from inside as she noted her worktable covered with an abandoned design project, protected with an overlay of vellum. The poster was intended for a one hundredth birthday celebration, a live event long canceled. Yet another cancellation due to COVID.

"We can't risk gathering so many elders together," the granddaughter's voice rose and fell on Nina's voice mail. "I hope you didn't work too long on the piece."

Nina returned the call to offer the piece as a commemoration. "It's just about finished. I even used gilt foil for your grandmother's monogram. Maybe she'd enjoy having it?"

The granddaughter coughed back a sob. "Nina… Nana didn't make it."

"Oh, no. I'm…so sorry." Very hard to find words. *Was it COVID?* She didn't ask.

Setting everything onto her desk, Nina opened the blinds to the afternoon's lovely spring light. The sun hit the framed picture she kept there of her dad, which reminded her of her mother's phone call. She clicked on the voicemail from Lillian and hit speaker. What she heard was historic. She played it again.

Nina shot off her desk chair to race, phone in hand, to find Myles. He was in the garage on his poor man's stationary bike, headphones on, eyes focused on the illuminated iPad on the music stand.

"You. Will. Not… *believe this!*" Nina's voice was loud but not loud enough to break through her husband's concentration. She circled to the front of him, hands waving for him to stop.

He pulled off his headphones. "What's wrong?"

"Listen to this," she said, hitting the speaker on her phone. She played the voice mail.

"Nina, please call me. I love you so much. It had been so long since you've been here. And now I don't know if... will I ever... will I ever see you again?"

Myles turned to Nina. "That's *Lilly*?"

Nina, eyes wide, nodded.

"You're going to call her." It was a statement.

"Yes, of course. I just had to have you hear this first. As a witness."

Nina could not remember another time in her life when her mother cared one way or another about seeing her. She didn't call Nina, remember her birthday, or acknowledge Nina's losses or achievements over the years. When Myles's mother died. When she'd been awarded Teacher of the Year in her district. When the restaurant mural she painted was featured in a regional magazine.

"Will I ever see you again?" The words echoed in Nina's mind; she felt an unexpected tenderness. Her mother wanted her. Needed her. *Loved her.*

Nina came inside and settled into the library's leather club chair. She hit favorites on her phone for the second time the same day, feeling for once that her mother belonged on that list. "Mom," she said when Lillian answered.

"Darling," Lillian said, "oh, it's so good to hear your voice. When will you be coming down? I miss you!"

"Mom, I want to visit; it's just tricky right now. I'm trying to figure out a way to see you, mitigating the risks."

"Dear, you're my *daughter*, I need to see you."

Nina gulped back a sob. "And I need to see *you*."

She could not have imagined this exchange.

"Mom, I know you're following the news. You know how some families are unable to be together in person. It's true for everyone!"

"Oh, yes, it's just terrible. New York City and all the make-shift morgues. And right here. Lien can't leave her assisted living facility, and her son can only visit from outside the window of the main hall."

They shared anecdotes of others, including Jenny's family in Chicago, unable to get together. Sylvana stranded in a European airport. Someone else they knew who couldn't leave Beijing.

"I'll figure something out, Mom."

"Thank you, dear. I can't wait to see you."

After the call ended, Nina stayed frozen in place. The warmth she felt toward her mother was unfamiliar. She texted Jenny to share the eventful exchange with Lillian, and as she waited for a response, she called Cori.

"Oh, Nina, that's amazing," Cori said with joy. "Something good coming out of this virus. Who knew?"

They talked some more. After consciously distancing herself from Lillian for so many years—decades—Nina found this turnabout too abrupt to fully accept. "Is it that she has no distractions that she is turning to me? Remembering me?"

"You mean, needing you? Does it matter why?"

"I suppose not, but…" Nina was talking rapidly. "…I'm not sure I trust this. I mean, the proof will be when the lockdown is over. Once everything is back to normal. When her meetings and protests and vigils and Bigger World tours are back. Will I still factor in her life then?"

Cori's voice was calmly reassuring. "Enjoy the moment, Ninacompoop. This is a surprise gift. Treat it as the *current* normal and try to relax into it for however long it lasts!"

Which is what she finally decided to do.

NINA

"**M**om." Nina made the call in the middle of April.

Lillian rushed her words. "Are you coming?"

"I'm coming, but we need to go over some precautions."

"Sure."

"We both need to be masked."

"Really?"

Was Mom watching the news? Nina's stomach lurched. Her mother's customary obsession with current events was not evident.

"Yes. We can meet outside."

"You'll spend the night, right? How long can you stay?"

"Mom, I'm coming for the day. And we'll spend it outside."

"You aren't spending the night?"

"It's not safe for you, or for me, to be inside together."

"But you'll be… sleeping!"

"We'll both be breathing, Mom. COVID transmits through the air."

Nina heard Lillian sigh.

It had been four months since she'd last driven from the Central Valley to the Bay Area. Now on the freeway, Nina marveled at the spaciousness. So few cars. The foothills on both sides of the freeway were covered in green, tight to the surface, like moss. The old oaks rooted there cast the look of wizened age. Of endurance. Untouched by the human virus. The coastal mountains to the west silhouetted sharply against the brilliant blue sky. There was still beauty on the earth even while humanity was being ravaged. A digitized highway sign interrupted her with a jolt: "COVID-19. LESS IS MORE. AVOID GATHERINGS."

Nina began wondering if there was a gift in this big pause. She immediately stifled the thought. Too many people were dying and lonely to allow for such an indulgent idea. As she continued across the Benicia Bridge, the San Francisco Bay stretched to her west, a plane of steel blue. Absent of recreational sailboats and cargo-carrying freighters, it was hard to sequester the idea that a gift came with the halting of human activity. A gift, maybe, to the earth.

Pulling into her mother's driveway, Nina saw the plum was in bloom; walking past it, she took in the scent of her childhood. Warm tortillas. Her dad had smiled at that description of the tree's fragrance but after he buried his nose in the blossoms, he agreed. "Corn," he'd noted. "Not flour." She rang the hanging jumble of Tibetan bells to the left of the turquoise door.

"Nina!" Lillian was masked, as they'd discussed. Her white hair, usually pixie-short and cropped close to her head, now waved down her neck. Almost to her shoulders.

"Mom!" Nina stood a concerted six feet away, miming a hug.

Lillian mimed it back. "Do you need to use the bathroom?"

Nina reminded her that she wouldn't be coming inside. "You have plenty of ivy on the side of the house."

Lillian's eyes questioned her while she shook her head, giggling. "This is all so strange." Lillian motioned to the back gate so they could eat lunch in the backyard.

While Lillian organized her own lunch to bring out, Nina brushed dry scrub oak and acacia leaves from the camping chairs already open in a circle near Lillian's clothesline. She placed two chairs six feet apart.

Lillian took care picking her way over uneven stepping stones while balancing her tray. The path led her past the jacaranda to the acacia tree where Nina had set up the patio table. It had once been a part of a handsome set but was now peeling and covered with a separate larger round top, a little precarious if leaned on the wrong way. Ivy tangled into the slats of the neighboring fence, choking the row of olive trees Cal planted fifty years ago.

"Mom, sit." Nina pointed to the furthest chair. "I can't get over your hair."

"I have no choice—" Lillian was scrutinizing her daughter. "Gina isn't cutting anyone's hair right now. I don't know how her business will survive. Why isn't *your* hair long?"

Nina laughed. "Remember how Myles always grooms Mingus? He's good at it. So he offered to give me a haircut. Do I look a little like a Scottie?"

Lillian giggled, then tugged on an ear. "How do we eat with these things?"

Nina did a double take, observing now that her mother's mask gaped open on both sides.

"Mom, you're not wearing the masks I sent you."

"I had this one already."

"That's an eye mask. For sleeping."

"Dear, it works."

Nina pulled a zip lock bag from the exterior pocket of her insulated lunch bag. It had several surgical masks in it. She handed the N95 to Lillian.

"Please wear this instead. Just take a bite and put it back on while you're chewing."

Lillian sighed, exasperated, but pulled off the sleep mask and replaced it with one of Nina's masks.

They ate in silence. When Nina finished with her shawarma wrap, Lillian fished for another piece of pickled herring. Still her mainstay, Nina noted, along with the carrots and hummus.

"I've never seen herring come like this in jars," Lillian noted.

"What are you talking about?"

Lillian pointed to the jar, one of hundreds she'd probably consumed over the decades. "This."

"Mom?' Nina felt her stomach give way. "You don't recognize this jar?"

Lillian shook her head, unconcerned. "It's delicious!"

Nina didn't know what to do with this memory lapse of her mother's. Events, yes, those might be forgotten; she could understand that. Or at least accept it. Dates, yes. The third step of any instruction, yes. But Lillian and pickled herring? This shook her, but all she could do at that moment was store it. Her attention returned to their extraordinary first lunch since the lockdown.

They shared their experiences. How all of their shopping and socializing habits had been reworked. How Lillian was most aggrieved about missing her swimming and the Friday peace vigil. How Myles had to cancel lessons. How Nina's writing group was on hiatus. How her calligraphy commissions for wedding invitations and addressing had all been either postponed or canceled altogether.

"People's lives are on hold. All of us. Everywhere." Nina widened her eyes to show her wonder above her mask.

"Well, not everyone," Lillian reminded her. "Healthcare workers, EMTs, grocery store workers, delivery people. They're busier than ever. Overwhelmed."

They talked about the news. The whiplash madness of the White House.

"And something good, Mom, for me."

"Oh?" Lillian had her fork in the jar of herring.

"I was asked by a publisher to calligraph the cover for a book."

"A book?"

"A memoir… by a South African who writes about his post-apartheid life."

"Does it remind you of the time we visited you in South Africa?"

"Of course…" Nina paused. "And more than that. It reminds me of when you and Dad were election monitors when Mandela ran for president." She paused. "I'm heading the chapters, too. The publisher is paying handsomely for it."

Lillian smiled. "That's marvelous, dear." She speared another piece of fish. "Have you heard from Jenny? I wonder how Theo is doing since daycare is closed."

Theo was Jenny's grandson, Lillian's great-grandchild. Any big news of Nina's would be eclipsed by something else. She felt a familiar tightness in her gut. This was status quo. Even with Lillian's dismissive response, however, there was at least a new lightness that came with figuring out a way they could finally visit, if only for a day at a time. How they'd do it every week. As Nina talked her through it, Lillian's eyes were wet.

Dusk approached. After Nina used the ivy and Lillian went back to the house to get a heavy sweater and an afghan, Nina pulled out her iPhone. "What music would you like to hear before I go?" She felt a surprising tenderness about leaving.

"Pete Seeger."

As Pete struck his banjo to the pull of "Waist Deep in the Big Muddy," mother and daughter exchanged appreciative looks across the rusted metal patio table. His music had filled the Nearing house during Nina's growing-up years, and his concerts had been special events for the whole family. His storytelling, forever compelling, always standing up to power. Lillian sang every word with conviction. Some things never change.

But some things do. After she and her mother choreographed air hugs, both wiped their eyes.

Chapter Twenty-Eight

Lillian

When California's governor lifted the lockdown mandate in May, Lillian could swim again. What a giddy relief. It wasn't as easy as before since now she had to drive ten miles to another Y with an open-air pool, and online reservations were required. Only four lanes were available for single swimmers, so the competition to reserve online was daunting. Her first attempts failed. She couldn't manage to hit the right key the very moment the digital clock struck the hour. She felt panicked, and the unsettling numbness in her fingers was back. Her swim routine was *essential* to her well-being; she would go berserk without it.

In tears, she called Nina. "I need help!"

After she explained the situation and Nina assured her she'd find a way to reserve her slots, Lillian breathed more easily. Her fingers returned to normal. She decided the pile of mail could wait until after a nap. She made her way to the padded window seat and repositioned the pillows she'd covered years before with Panamanian molas. Climbing onto the soft mattress, she curled onto her side and closed her eyes. At that moment, her phone buzzed. Her eyes fluttered open, and she reached for her phone on the mosaic table by her side.

"Jenny?"

"Mom, Nina called about the swim reservations. I will do that online here from Chicago three days a week. And Lauren offered to make reservations two other days of the week."

Lauren had married the son of dear friends and was an honorary member of the Nearing family.

"Oh, Jenny, that's marvelous!" Lillian felt relief fill her being.

Jenny explained she had to reserve a week ahead for the day and timeslot to secure a lane for her. "So, unfortunately, you'll have to wait a week before you're back in the pool, Mom."

"Oh, so what! Just knowing I'll be able to swim is enough. I can wait a week." She ended the call, shut it to off, and returned to her nap. She could finally relax.

A week later, she entered the YMCA, breathing in the sharp fragrance of chlorine she'd missed so much. One of the staff approached her and handed her a mask.

"Oh, thank you. I forgot!" Her hands full with her swim kit and ID, Lillian shook her head in apology.

"No problem, Mrs. Nearing. Just want you to be safe."

"Lillian," she cheerfully corrected him. "Call me Lillian!"

She leaned into the swinging door that opened into the pool area. After hanging up her clothes in the family changing room, she was met by Siti's unmasked, beautific smile.

"So good to see you, Lilly!"

They sat on separate molded plastic benches by the pool's edge. Lillian kept her eyes on her friend as she leaned over to pull on her flippers.

"Isn't it wonderful?" Siti, dripping from her pre-swim shower, mirrored Lillian's excitement. Now that lane reservations were so limited, neither of them expected to see each other. The locker rooms were closed, and the staff was skeletal.

An hour later, Siti and Lillian sat distanced from each other outside the main entrance. It was early spring and not warm yet.

"So glorious!" Lillian exhaled contentedly. "Have you seen anyone else?"

Siti shook her head. "You're the first I've seen." She caught herself. "No, the second. I saw Lien once. How are you, Lilly?" She pointedly tightened her mask to the bridge of her nose.

"Oh, you know. Just waiting for all of this to be over." She sighed as she fished for her mask; after it was on, she had an inspired thought: "We should do Thai again together. Let Lien and Rita know!" Lillian was excited to finally be talking in person with a friend who wasn't in her immediate circle. Someone who wasn't Nina, Myles, or Freda.

The smile in Siti's voice faded. "Lillian, you must not know about Rita."

Lillian shook her head, wary.

"She passed."

Lillian pulled off her mask, showing her shock. "What!?"

"Yes, she passed. Last month."

"Was it COVID?" Lillian asked.

"I don't know. I don't know how she died. But Lien is forwarding the link to Rita's Zoom mass. I'll email it to you." Siti gestured for Lillian to pull her mask up.

Lillian shook her head, not to the gesture or the Zoom link, but to the news. So many losses. And probably more, she realized, she didn't even know about. "I still think we should meet for lunch at our Thai place."

"Oh, Lilly. Restaurants aren't serving inside yet. But we can maybe order takeout and meet outside in the park. What about that?"

Lillian pouted. "We *still* can't eat at a restaurant?" She managed to stand, hoisting her swim kit to her shoulder. "Well, let's go with your idea. I think we should meet at the park sooner than later. Marvelous thought. Can you let me know where and when?"

After their goodbyes, she walked to her car parked in the blue placard zone. Still strange to think that she qualified for a placard simply because she turned ninety. She tossed the swim kit behind the driver's seat and sat with one hand on the steering wheel and the other on the ignition button. As she pushed it and maneuvered into reverse, her thoughts were on Rita. She had been a steady swim friend. It's not that they were particularly close. She didn't even know 'til today she was Catholic. But she was a positive individual and valued swimming. Her musings were interrupted by the crunch of metal. "*Damn* it!" Her quick reverse jammed the rear of her car straight into the post that held up an overhang.

She pulled forward, placed the car in park, and looked behind her with some relief. She hadn't hit a car, just a post. That post was really positioned too close to the parking space. She'd have to talk to the director about that but now was not the time. She was too hungry. As she reversed again, she was peripherally aware of two Y employees running from the entrance toward her; one hit the hood of the Prius with his hand. At the sound, she stopped, shaken, and brought her window down.

"I'm fine," she assured them.

"No, Lillian, you need to park again."

"Really, I'm fine, I need to get home."

They wouldn't take no for an answer. She re-parked, and recognized it was the lifeguard whose hand had pounded her car. He spoke now.

"Lillian, we heard the sound. It's great you're okay, but…"

"I hope you're not concerned about that post. It should never have been placed so close to the parking line. It's just ridiculous."

"Lillian," now it was Grace the director talking. She had quickly rounded the car to survey any damage in the rear. "Do you know about your tire?"

"My tire?"

"The right rear tire."

This was such an inconvenience. No one was hurt; she wanted to get home. She grudgingly followed the director to the back passenger side of the car.

"Oh good god," she said. All that remained of the tire were a few shreds of rubber still clinging to the wheel. It reminded her of a West African ceremonial neckpiece.

The director was clearly agitated. "Lillian, when did this happen?"

"I have no idea," Lillian replied. "Really, none."

"You didn't notice anything while you were driving? Noise? Imbalance?"

Lillian shook her head.

The lifeguard volunteered to change her tire just as a piano riff sounded from the swim kit behind the driver's seat. It was Nina.

"Nina," Lillian answered, "I'm in the parking lot at the Y, and some good Samaritans are changing my tire." She paused to listen and then said, "Not flat, they saw I had… a blow-out." Again, she listened. "I have no idea. But I'm fine, yes. Let's talk later, dear."

After thanking the lifeguard for his labors, she drove the freeway back to Los Gatos. A little unsteady. After twenty minutes in the slow lane, she wondered, *Where am I?* Nothing looked familiar. *What in the world?* Had she taken the wrong freeway entrance?

She took the next exit, looking for a gas station. When she parked by an air and water station, she called Nina.

"Nina, I'm so turned around. I don't know where I am; I was just driving home from the Y, and I must have gone the wrong way on the freeway."

She listened to her daughter.

"I just said I don't know. Let me look around."

More from Nina.

"That's why I stopped at the gas station. I'll find out. What? Yes, I'll keep the phone on."

The door jingled as she pushed open the door to join a line of customers waiting to pay for gas. Al Jazeera blasted the news in Arabic from the TV behind the counter. The attendant motioned to the others to usher her to the front. He gestured toward his own mask and then to her face.

"Oh." She pulled her mask from a pocket and quickly asked how to get back on the freeway to get to Los Gatos.

"Follow me," he said. "Easier to show you outside." He told the others waiting he'd be right back.

"Where am I?"

"Milpitas." He pointed the way to the freeway entrance. He turned toward the Prius, his eyes narrowing. "That is your car?"

"Yes."

He walked around behind it. "You shouldn't be driving on that tire."

"I just had it changed," she said. "That is the replacement."

"That's a donut spare tire," he said. "Not for the freeway. It's just so you can get your car a new tire. A real one."

"I'll be fine now that I know how to get home. Thank you so much."

Lillian smiled behind her mask, hoping he could see the gratitude in her eyes as he hurried back to his customers.

Now that she was heading in the right direction, her shoulders loosened a little. The radio was already dialed to KPFA, but when it was yet another story about COVID, she turned it off. Half an hour later she pulled into her double driveway and hit the remote for the garage. Freda was walking from the mailbox toward the apartment, but when Lillian waved Freda motioned for her to pull on her mask.

For god's sake. She hadn't seen her tenant's face for months. *I'm not about to wear a mask when I'm by myself in my car or standing at my own front door. Some people are taking this caution to the extreme.*

She pulled her swim kit from the back, extricating it out from the "NO JUSTICE, NO PEACE" sign leaning on the floor mat. She was famished. Exhausted, which is when she heard Nina's voice calling to her.

"Mom!"

"Nina! How did… what are you doing here?" All she wanted was to have something to eat and lie down, and here was Nina. In person!

"I'm so relieved you made it home! After you called from the gas station, you left your phone on but never let me know what was going on. All I could hear was a bunch of sounds…"

Lillian shook her head. "Everything is fine. That's behind me. I need some lunch." She looked at Nina. "You haven't told me why you're here?"

Nina looked confused. "Mom, you have this on your calendar. I'm here today and for the rest of the day."

Lillian realized she was eyeing the donut tire.

"What happened?"

"Oh, it's fine, I need to get a new tire. But I didn't know you were coming, dear! Are you hungry? I'm famished."

Lillian dug her thumbnail into her index finger. Numb again. She had no memory of what happened to her tire. She'd gotten lost. And she didn't remember that Nina was coming. Her chest tightened. What was happening?

CHAPTER TWENTY-NINE

NINA

"Mom, please give me a call." It was the fourth voicemail Nina left that day.

She texted Freda. "Can u please ask Mom to call me? Not picking up."

Freda texted back. "She's not home."

Not unusual. Nina wouldn't allow herself to worry. She finished filling Mingus' ever-growing pill dispensers to last for a month. Heart, gall bladder, arthritis. He had more pills to take than she did, and she was ready for a break. She pulled a book from her bed stand and sank into the leather club chair in the library.

Fifteen minutes later, Lillian's marimba ringtone jarred Nina from page 132 of Heather McGee's *The Sum of Us.*

"Nina?"

"Mom, are you okay? I've called a bunch of times."

"Oh, I don't always hear it. Sometimes it's in the other room. Was there something you needed?"

"Mainly to tell you I'll be coming down Tuesday, and I'm bringing fifty Vote Forward letters for us to write. We can do it outside."

"Marvelous," Lillian responded. "Did I tell you about the George Floyd protest at City Hall?"

"You did, Mom." Nina didn't mention that she'd told her twice already that earlier in the week, she'd driven to the Los Gatos City Hall parking lot to kneel with an anguished and seething crowd. There were so many George Floyds, but finally, this one drew attention. Lillian shared how moving it was to kneel together for nine minutes and twenty-nine seconds. No boot on their throats. Just the time that stretched as a single moment of torture. "Just horrific and tragic and unjust and criminal."

Nina remained quiet. She appreciated Lillian's action. She also worried about her COVID exposure in a crowd. As much as she and Myles wanted to take part in the George Floyd marches in downtown Sacramento, their concern about the crowd's proximity had stopped them.

When is it worth the risk? she wondered. *The risk of exposure to COVID?* The question remained lodged and unresolved in her brain. *Is a humanitarian crisis worth the risk? Is quality of life worth the risk? Is a relationship worth the risk?*

The questions haunted her.

"Dear?"

"Mom?"

"Darling, I need your help. I'm trying to get to Kaiser for my hearing aid appointment, but I can't remember how to get there."

Nina's heart dropped. "You're driving?" Lillian didn't have anything set up in her car for hands-free calls. More than that, Lillian was asking for help to get to the Kaiser facility she'd been driving to for decades. "You're talking on the phone and driving?"

No response. Then, "I have you on speaker. I'm at an intersection. It's Kiley and..." The phone went dead.

Nina hit "recents" to immediately call Lillian back. No answer. She rose from the leather chair, pacing across Myles's study and the library while repeatedly hitting redial. The heat of the afternoon sun burned through the open slats of the rooms' plantation shutters. Nina flipped them closed to keep the room as cool as possible. With temperatures forecast to be in the triple digits, days like these made the seduction of air conditioning hard to resist, but she and Myles held off as long as they could. Like most homes in their Curtis Park neighborhood, the Visser's house was constructed in the 1920s, with great insulation—something they never took for granted. "Lathe and plaster," Myles often reminded her. "You can't beat it."

"Nina?" Finally, Lillian answered.

"Mom, if you're driving, pull over where it's safe." She knew her mother was holding the cell phone in one hand and the wheel in the other. She'd witnessed this in the past. Her tirades about its dangers hadn't sunk in.

"Oh, let's see…" Lillian's phone was on speaker. Nina could hear a car horn. She froze. Someone Lillian probably cut off or swerved too close to. "Oh, I found it!" Lillian started again. "Everything is fine, thank you, dear." She ended the call.

Oh my god. If her mother kept answering her cell phone while driving, how could Nina know when it was safe to call? When was Nina going to get notification saying, "Your mom is dead." Or a call from the police that Lillian had hit and killed someone? Nina's right temple throbbed. Now, her mission was to avoid a migraine. Right now. After pulling her meds from the bathroom cabinet, she swallowed one and made her way back across the house to the bedroom. With the ceiling fan going and the blackout shades down, she held off switching on the AC and lay down on the summer coverlet, eyes closed.

Hours later, she awoke, ready to make dinner. Wrapping coconut rice in lettuce, she heard Myles's last student say goodbye over FaceTime. This was the way Myles's lessons were now—all on FaceTime. It was working. Myles walked in.

"*Mmm…* smells good!" He wrapped his arms around her from behind and kissed her neck. Her hands were wet and sticky, but she stopped and softened into him.

"Maybe I'll open a Riesling," he said, to which she shook her head.

"Not for me."

"Best thing of your day?"

"Well…" she said, leaving out her relief that she didn't get a migraine, "Mom's reengaging with the world."

But couldn't the best thing also be the worst?

The freeway choked with traffic. Instead of an hour and forty-five minutes, the drive from Sacramento to Los Gatos took three hours and ten minutes. Good thing she left early; it was getting tight.

When's the last time I had to consider the best time to get on the freeway? Nina caught the context of her reflection: she was used to COVID conditions. What was once normal (bad traffic) gave way to spacious driving (new normal), and today's stop-and-go seemed like old times. Before Times.

Eventually, she pulled alongside Lillian's long curb. Plenty of time, fortunately, to still make Lillian's doctor's appointment.

Ducking to avoid nature's archway of pittosporum, the arc of which never touched her mother's head but met Nina at her collarbone, she jangled the Tibetan bells. No answer. Knocking loudly on the door instead, she waited. Nothing. Her heart beat faster. Mom had this appointment on the calendar. This was the sole purpose of this visit. *We talked last night! Where is she?*

Pulling out the key her mother copied for her, she opened the front door for the first time that year.

"Mom?"

She walked gingerly past the kitchen island, taking in the leaning towers of literature and bills next to the unplugged radio. Everything looked frozen in time but with more political detritus than ever everywhere. Right on top of one stack rested Lillian's car registration notice. She swiftly folded it and stuffed it in her pocket, making a quick mental note to take care of this as soon as she got home. Her mother could reimburse her later.

She tapped on the closed bathroom door. "Mom?"

She stepped outside the back door, noting the empty hummingbird feeder. Something Cal always took care of. Where was Lillian?

She rounded the overgrown backyard. *Lillian always makes a point of saying she likes living in a forest, but this? This is dried brush on steroids!* Seeing nothing, she made her way back to the front to knock on Freda's door. Not home either.

Nina called Lillian. No answer. She left a voice mail: "Mom. I'm at the house. It's Tuesday. Your appointment with Dr. Sharma is at 11:30. We need to drive to Campbell. Please call me."

Max, the neighbor's lab, barked from across the street. Nina, mask on, crossed in time to catch Mr. Van Arsdale in his red and black striped boxers inside his garage just as his finger was poised on the button to activate the door. He'd lived there with his family during her childhood, the non-descript father to two girls younger than herself. Now in his eighties and divorced, he was her mother's younger neighbor.

"Oh, hey," she said, leaning down to scratch Max's ears.

Mr. Van Arsdale tilted his Greek sailor cap. "What can I do you for?" he asked, muffled behind his mask. In the background, she heard his mynah bird squawking for Mr. Van Arsdale to "Call Helen!" It was the first sentence Mr. Van Arsdale taught the bird twenty-five years before, but the only sentence that stuck. Helen was long gone.

"It's my mother," Nina explained. "She has a doctor's appointment, and I don't know where she is. She doesn't answer her phone."

"I haven't seen her," he said. "But give me your number. I can call you if I hear anything."

"I'll check the Y." She crossed back over the street and got in the car.

Nina parked at the Y, rushing through the entrance but then back again to retrieve the N95 hanging from the steering wheel.

When the entrance doors automatically opened, the sharp smell of chlorine accosted her nose. She hurriedly joined the line of members waiting for the receptionist. A crowd of kids clamored around the corner of the main wing, led by a teen counselor. The summer day camps were in full swing. After the elderly couple in front of her scanned their IDs, she stepped to the desk. The lanyard around the staffer's neck spelled out his name.

"Hi, Akio, has Lillian been swimming today?" she asked, trying to slow her delivery to sound calm. "Lillian Nearing?"

"Lillian! She was here earlier," he said. "Let me check the log."

Akio pulled a clipboard from the counter and turned one page back. "She signed out at 10:33…" He paused. "Earlier than usual."

Where was Mom? She found the doctor's assistant, Justine, in her contacts.

"I'm trying to track down my mother," Nina rushed. "We won't make it in time for the appointment."

Justine listened. "Give me a minute," she said. "Dr. Sharma actually had a cancellation later in the day. We can do video or in-person at 2:10."

"Oh, my gosh, that's amazing. Let's try for in-person." God willing.

As soon as Nina returned to the house, Lillian pulled into the driveway. Nina put on her mask, pushed open her door, then counseled herself to calm down. Breathe. Again.

"Nina, dear! I didn't know you were coming today!" Lillian beamed as she walked out from the garage and hit the remote. "Come inside!"

"Still can't come inside, Mom. Do you remember that I came down for your appointment with Dr. Sharma?"

"Oh, is that today?"

"Already came and went."

"Oh dear. Can I get you some lunch?"

"Mom, when I couldn't find you, I talked to Justine. She's got you rescheduled for 2:10."

"Oh, that's good. I'll have time to nap. I'm really bushed."

"Mom, I was worried." Nina stretched her neck to one side, then the other. She could not get a migraine. She'd be no help to anyone if she were felled by that dreaded pain on the right side of her head. "I couldn't find you. I called, you didn't answer. I drove to the Y, and they said you'd left at 10:30 this morning."

"Well, dear, after swimming, I drove to The Dollar Store. I needed sherbet. I've got to get it into the freezer, especially because it took me so long to get home. It's probably melted. I..." Lillian hesitated. "...really must have been distracted because I couldn't remember the best way to get here. Suddenly, I was on my way to downtown San Jose—going north instead of south." She laughed. "I've done it a thousand times; I'd know that drive blindfolded."

Nina winced. Maybe her mother's driving would be more reliable if she *were* blindfolded. "Go eat something and take a nap," Nina told her. "I'll get a walk in and eat my lunch at the park. I'll ring your bells at 1:40 so we have plenty of time to get to the appointment."

She passed homes she knew from childhood. The neighborhood was built in the 1950s for working-class families. Those days were long gone. Sixty-plus years later, each block had replaced some of its single-story slab homes with McMansions, some farmhouse modern, some grandiose Mediterranean, some with soaring contemporary interpretations of mid-century architecture. She sat, taking in the view of the street from her bench. The robin-blue house across the soccer field still looked as it had when the Reeds lived there. Mrs. Reed had been the troop leader for the Brownies, which Nina had longed to join in second grade. Lillian adamantly refused to sign the application. "How do you think the Hitler Youth started?" Case closed.

Sitting by herself on that bench and eating the sandwich she'd packed helped distance Nina from the morning's chaos. She closed her eyes and felt the sun on her face. Los Gatos's weather always remained near perfect, hardly changing from one season to the next. Leaving the high heat of Sacramento's summer for the South Bay's temperate weather was a gift.

Maybe the four seasons are overrated? But Nina quickly remembered that one of the appeals to Sacramento was that very aspect of its climate, the four seasons. Fall looked stunning as the tree-canopied streets filled every sightline with yellows, golds, deep russet reds. Winter's lovely overcast cold, along with the rain—not that it rained much during these drought years—invited cozy days of reading inside the house, curled up under the weight of her grandmother's hand-made afghans. Sacramento's springs brought forth fresh baby greens and lush violets of bougainvillea and lavenders in wisteria and lilacs. The air fragrant with freesia and jasmine. Summer? *Well*, Nina thought—she'd rather be anywhere but Sacramento in July or August.

So here she was, in summer, sitting on this bench in Los Gatos. This bench made up part of her childhood architecture, and she remembered a time (*was I four? Five?*) when her mother made sandwiches (*probably liverwurst on that yellow poppyseed bread*) just for the two of them, and she brought her here to meet a new friend. The new friend turned out to be a cloth doll Lillian had sewn just for her. The body was soft, bronze-colored cotton stuffed with batting, the eyes black buttons, and the hair made of masses of brown yarn. She had expressive embroidered eyelashes, lush enough to comb. Nina loved the doll then and now treasured it as an adult when she brought it out to place under the tree every Christmas. Tears sprung to her eyes. That was love. Willing her mind to clear its crowd of thoughts, she took in the sounds of nearby red-winged blackbirds and the brushing of the gentle breeze through her hair. It felt good.

Back at the turquoise door, Nina rang the Tibetan bells. Her mother answered. "Is it time?"

Nina motioned at her own mask. Lillian turned to pull from the masks stacked on a shelf of the entryway divider she had built in a woodworking class decades earlier.

"Let's have you drive for a change, Mom." The preceding year, Nina had been driving her mother in her own car for errands while in Los Gatos, but these getting-lost episodes of her mother's made her realize that she needed to witness and experience her mother's driving for herself. She needed a "last straw" reality check to support her belief that Lillian would be safer if she weren't driving. As would everyone else.

Lillian smiled broadly. "I'd love to drive!"

Nina waited outside on the driveway as Lillian backed out of the garage.

"What the hell…" Nina opened the passenger door and climbed in. "Mom, you're still driving on the donut tire?"

"I haven't been going far. The Y, the vigil, The Dollar Store."

"Mom, it's been two months! Or three! And *The Dollar Store*? That's probably ten miles! During rush hour!"

Lillian tugged the seatbelt across her muumuu patterned with the peace signs. "I can go on the freeway as long as I stay under fifty miles per hour."

Snapping in her own seatbelt, Nina took a deep breath, incredulous at her mother's calm dismissiveness of… everything. Her right temple pulsed. "Mom. It's illegal to go that slow on the freeway. It's against the law because it's unsafe to go that slow with the faster traffic all around you."

"Relax, Nina, really." Her words came out stiff. "I'm sorry I ever told you about the tire." Lillian reversed the Prius and thumped over the high curb of the driveway.

"Well, seeing it first-hand again speaks volumes. Where's the tire that blew out? And the wheel?"

"In the trunk." Lillian pulled down the shaded visor against the sun. "When we get to the medical offices, I'll pop it to show you."

"Just don't take the freeway to the doctor's office." Nina heard the nag in her voice, but if nagging saved lives, she would nag.

"I never do, Nina. I always take side streets. It's not that far."

As Lillian hurtled toward the first stop sign and turned right without looking left, Nina stifled a shudder and took another deep breath. She yelped as her mother narrowly missed hitting a young woman crossing the street. And then? Lillian got lost. Nina pulled out her phone to plug in Dr. Sharma's address, slightly disconcerted that she herself had grown unfamiliar with the route. Siri guided them the rest of the way. At the blue placard parking spot, Nina reminded her mother to open the trunk. Nina went to the back of the car and found the distorted wheel, a few lonely strips of rubber clinging to its pocked rim. She took a picture on her phone before slamming down the hatchback. *This is bad. She could kill herself. Kill someone else. This is truly bad.*

The designated seating in the waiting room kept them distanced. Nina, without conferring, called the closest Toyota dealership for an appointment for a new tire ASAP. They'd do a full-on maintenance check while they were at it. Nina figured one was long overdue.

Dr. Sharma's assistant came through the swinging glass door to the waiting room.

"Lilly! So glad to see you! Follow me."

Lillian's eyes beamed over her mask. "I'm delighted to see *you*, Justine!"

Dr. Sharma didn't keep them waiting long in the exam room. Even with her mask, Nina could see she was smiling to see her patient of many years. She gracefully reached over to give Lillian a gentle squeeze on her good shoulder.

"I'm so happy to see you, Lilly!"

"How is your family?" Lillian asked.

"Oh, thank you for asking. My daughters are fine but their online classes are…" she raised both hands to fill in the blank. "But we're managing."

After she checked for blood pressure and oxygen levels, the doctor's deep brown eyes softened over her mask, which was color-coordinated with the Michael Kors dress peeking from her unbuttoned white coat.

"Your vitals are good, Lilly. Do you have any concerns today?"

"No, but Dr. Sharma, how is your family?"

Nina had heard over the years that most of Dr. Sharma's family lived in Mumbai. COVID currently swept over that city. Was that why Lillian kept asking?

"Oh, thank you, Lilly, they're fine, very fortunately. It is very difficult for so many. It's hard to isolate, and the hospitals are dealing with an oxygen shortage. But you are here today, for *you*. There isn't anything I can do for you? No questions for me?"

Lillian shook her head, but Nina practically jumped out of her skin. She swallowed and willed herself to stay calm. She desperately wanted to bring up Lillian's driving, and her memory issues, and this was the perfect opportunity. But to voice her worries in front of her mother? She knew Lillian would feel embarrassed and, worse than that, shattered by the lack of confidence others might have about her facility as a driver, as well as about her cognitive abilities. There had to be a better way. She decided to employ the collective "we."

"Dr. Sharma, our biggest concern is that we need to get some… supports in place so we can honor Mom's wish to stay in her home… maybe a transportation plan, and someone to help clean the house and maintain the garden…?"

Lillian snapped. "I don't need a transportation plan! I drive!"

"Lilly, are you experiencing any problems driving?"

"No."

Nina couldn't help herself. "Mom, you've gotten lost at least a couple of times that I know of. What about that?"

Lillian's eyes were hard. "Everyone gets lost. Besides, I only drive to places I know," she insisted.

"What about today? I came to take you to the appointment, and you weren't home. You didn't remember. And then, when you drove here, you needed directions. What about that?"

Dr. Sharma shifted in her seat, making eye contact with Nina before turning to her patient. "Lilly," she began, "when we become less young, our reflexes slow. Let's do a test."

Lillian passed the simple cognitive function test with flying colors. Same with the test for her reflexes. She looked back triumphantly at her doctor. Then, at Nina.

"Let's check in again in a few months," Dr. Sharma said. She looked at her screen. "Lillian, can you access the site online?"

"Can you please just have Justine call me?" Dr. Sharma's assistant was on Lillian's speed dial. "I have so many emails now I might miss seeing the appointment."

The doctor made a note of that, then said, "Nina, you're your mother's primary health agent. You can access her email account to see when I schedule her and then remind her. That sound good, Lilly?"

Lillian nodded.

"It means you need to answer the phone, Mom."

Lillian glared at her. "Yes." It came out in a hiss.

Nina appreciated that Dr. Sharma picked up on her mother's diminishing capabilities but grappled with the creeping awareness that this shift of communication mode marked the start of a new chapter for Lillian and for her. Up until now, her mother had been facile on the computer and with her iPhone. She prided herself on it. That facility was now unreliable, and Nina was starting to conclude that she would need to be directly involved in her mother's care. There was no time to process this new reality, no time to ready herself. Everything had been unraveling slowly, and now it was happening *all at once*.

She had crossed the threshold.

Back in the parking lot, Nina opened the passenger door for her mother.

"Mom, may I drive your car to the dealership?"

"Fine," Lillian said. "Are we going there now? I really feel ready for a nap."

"I have to leave tonight, so let's get it done. You can snooze on the way."

When Nina showed the Toyota mechanic the destroyed wheel in the trunk he gave out a low whistle. He led Nina and Lillian to sit outside on benches for waiting customers. Half an hour passed.

"Here's what we've found," he said after checking out the Prius. In addition to a new wheel and tire, the assessment sheet listed several other to-dos.

When Lillian saw the dollar estimate for all of the work, she turned to Nina, exasperation in her eyes. This particular expression Nina recognized in her mother whenever money was involved.

"That's ridiculous! That much money!?"

"Mom?"

"Dad would have handled this… maybe I should just get rid of it."

"Excuse me. What did you say?"

"Maybe… why don't we call Myles tonight. See if he can sell it?"

Nina couldn't suppress the grin on her face. She tried to hold back. This was more than she could have hoped for. "Okay, we will talk to Myles about that," she said as calmly as she could.

She saw Lillian grimace a little. "I know this makes you happy, Nina."

"Well, yes. It does! But let's have you… sleep on it. How about we leave the car at the dealership overnight, talk to Myles, think about it." Nina's mind raced. She tried slowing her thoughts for some clarity pointing to the next step. The next step of extricating the car from her mother… *with* her mother's blessing? Who could've guessed?

"Sounds reasonable."

"And," Nina said, "let me show you how easy it is to arrange a ride with Lyft. Once you've done it a few times, it's a piece of cake." Then and there she arranged a Lyft to drive them back to Lillian's.

"See how easy?" she said when they were both seat-belted into the back seat of the gray Camry. She showed Lillian her app, which indicated the driver's name was Ammar. Lillian immediately questioned the driver's navigation choices.

"Ammar, you should have turned right on Winchester."

"It's okay, Ammar," Nina interjected quickly, then looked at her mother. "Mom, let's let him do his job."

By the time Nina headed back to Sacramento, it was dusk. Driving east on 680 between Milpitas and Walnut Creek, she'd updated Myles over the phone, after which he called Lillian to explain that he and Nina would come down to get the Prius off the dealer's lot, drive it to Sacramento so he could prepare the car for sale. He could get a good price for it. "For lots of Lyft cash," he'd said to her. Then, reporting back to Nina, "She'd seemed accepting. Thanked me, even."

"Unbelievable."

"Maybe because I had another baseball name for her."

"Nice diversion. Who?"

"Skye Bolt. Oakland A's."

Nina laughed.

"Will you need dinner?" Myles asked.

"No. It'll be so late."

"Even if I braise reindeer heart in a bed of pine needles?"

"Even then."

"What about dessert? Pistachio sorbet in a beeswax bowl?"

"Many thanks, but no thanks," she said. "I just want to crash."

"Just wait 'til you get home, please."

They ended the call. Crossing the Benicia Bridge, she talked into the dusk. "Dad, are you there?" She stayed quiet, waiting to find the place inside herself where he still resided. The place she went when she teetered, trying to find her footing. The place where she felt his assurance. "I think selling the car will keep Mom safer. Protect her. Protect your beloved."

It was deep dark when Nina pulled into her own driveway. As she opened the front door, the Giants game play-by-play buzzed from the living room. She remembered this was what Myles had been looking forward to. It was a relief to know she could simply shower and collapse in bed with one less thing to worry about. One less *immense* worry. Her mother giving up her car, hands down, was the best outcome she could have imagined. The best part of her day.

CHAPTER THIRTY

LILLIAN

Two years without Cal.

Lillian opened her eyes and yawned, turning to face his side of the bed. The bedspread stretched to touch those two stacked, unused pillows. The sun was high, but she stayed in place, taking in the reading lamp that hadn't been switched on since he died, his dust-covered magnifiers beside it.

Being without him seemed to affect her in layers. The first was the most immediate. He wasn't next to her to reach for. To nestle her head into. To warm her hands in his. The next involved the series of daily shocks. She'd be reading an article in *Politico* and have a need to share it with him. She thirsted for the shorthand language they'd created over six decades. How they finished each other's sentences. His terms of endearment. His kiss. They'd been a team, with an easy choreography at home as they lived their day-to-day lives. Of course, their routines had changed even before he died. But something that hadn't been affected, even when Cal lost his mobility, was their teamwork involving their Bigger World work. Now that everything shut down, she had to reach out to folks on the list for the canceled reality tour. Send them refunds. Deal with the airlines. On her own.

Lillian closed her eyes. She missed going with him to the Y. For her, it was swimming and yoga for osteoarthritis. For him, water-walking and the recumbent bicycle. His particular sense of humor made everyone smile. She remembered how she'd said to a friend, "Let's meet at the Y."

Cal, overhearing, said, straight-faced, "That's a profound place to meet, at the Why." Her friend had looked puzzled. Cal made a small smile, then said, "Wouldn't it be easier to meet at the Because?"

She swung her knees to the bed's edge. These sheets had been a wedding gift over sixty years ago, the cotton thinned and softened from decades of laundering. She slipped her feet into the fleece-lined slippers she'd placed in ready-position the night before. Making her way past the dining table, she pulled up the accordion blinds so she could see the scrub of wild lilac climbing the lanai. She made her way to the swim kit in the bathroom, and as she pulled on her suit, the elastic hung loose around her legs. Her fingers were too arthritic to replace the elastic herself, which meant Freda needed to find her another suit when she next volunteered at the Echo Shop. And then Lillian remembered: no car. Who could she call? The Y was only three blocks away but too far these days to walk. *Goddam Nina.* Everything was harder without Cal; Nina taking the car made everything—the few pleasures she still could access—even harder.

"Freda," she said when her tenant picked up the phone. "I don't have a car. Can you drive me to the Y?"

Freda explained she wasn't home, but maybe, she suggested, Mr. Van Arsdale across the street could do it?

"Great idea. I'm… just not used to having to ask anyone for a ride."

She couldn't find his number, so she slipped into her Hawaiian sandals and crossed the street. She noticed the garage door was open and the car was there.

As soon as she knocked, Max began barking.

"Max, it's me."

Mr. Van Arsdale opened the door. "Lillian! Everything okay?"

She heard "Call Helen!" from deep in the house.

"Can you drive me to the Y? I don't have a car."

"Happy to... I'm about to head out, so if it's now, I can do it. But I won't be able to come get you to bring you home. That work?"

That worked. Lillian knew so many Y members that she was confident someone could drive her home. Getting there was the challenge. She thanked him.

Mr. Van Arsdale drove the short distance and double-parked in front of the entrance. As Lillian reached for the latch to climb out, he asked if her car was on the blink. "Getting something fixed?"

Lillian shook her head. "No, not fixed. It's a long story... too long. I'm not happy about it. I am not used to feeling dependent on others just to live my life."

"Well, you just let me know the next time you need a ride, got it?"

She cut short Mr. Van Arsdale's response as she shut the car door.

When she swam, her tears mixed with the warm chlorinated water. By the time she climbed out of the pool, no one could tell she'd been weeping.

CHAPTER THIRTY-ONE

THE BOOK CLUB

Since the shutdown, the book club began meeting over Zoom. Today's conversation was about the book Lillian had recommended, *The Hundred Years' War in Palestine* by Rashid Khalidi.

"We're missing Lilly," Marva said.

"I called her yesterday and offered to set things up for today's Zoom meeting." added Shira, who preferred to stay off video. A picture of a cat filled her Hollywood Square. "Maybe she already forgot?"

Now Joan chimed in, "I talked to her last night! She told me she'd renewed the book so she could lead the discussion and that she had book club on the calendar and looked forward to seeing us today."

"Can you all please put yourselves on mute?" Philomena was on her phone. "I'm calling her right now."

The book club members muted for the most part while Philomena's face filled her square, eyes on her phone. An unframed abstract on canvas hung behind her. Her art studio was set up for Zoom meetings, and since she'd recently undergone a facelift, she'd installed halo lighting. She had decided to make the most of her recent cosmetic surgery, considering the limitations of the COVID environment. Other than over Zoom, she'd counseled herself, what opportunities did she have to present herself? She was determined to benefit from the investment.

She mouthed something before rolling her eyes and unmuting. "I honestly worry about Lillian. She's ninety-one. Ninety-two? She lives alone. Who is looking out for her?"

"Her daughter…? She has a daughter who lives hours away. Does she ever even visit?" Shira asked.

Joan gestured expressively from her square before the rest of the group yelled for her to unmute herself. "Lillian says her daughter is the one who took the car from her!"

Variously delayed echoes of disapproval filled the audio.

"She has another daughter, too, but she lives out of state."

"Chicago," Marva noted.

"Lilly is very angry about the car. And then the DMV letter she got? Saying her license was revoked?"

"No! Is that the daughter's doing?"

"Lilly thought it was a scam letter. She threw it away."

"Recycled it," corrected Shira, raising a knowing eyebrow.

Joan's hands dramatically filled her screen when Philomena shouted, "Joan! Joan! Unmute!"

Joan's eyes flitted to the upper right corner of her screen. Her voice joined her lip movements as she said, "Maybe we should call in a welfare check."

"How does one do that?" It was Shira. "Call APS? Call the police?"

Joan reminded everyone that she was a retired social worker. "It's not a bad idea to call APS. It's for Lillian's safety. They can find out what she needs."

"What if that gets her daughter in trouble?" Marva asked.

"Or if they end up taking her from her home?" Shira's eyes looked worried.

"Adult Protective Services is largely misunderstood," Joan said, as she had many times over the years. "Its goal is to protect the client's self-determination. Lillian would be considered a client, and APS would try to discover her network of support as one way to be sure she's safe, comfortable, and has access to food and health services. APS would not take her away; they'd be there to find out her needs and to assure her that she is free to determine how she wants to live."

Everyone listened intently.

As host, Philomena needed to keep her friends on track. "Well, before going to those lengths, let's see first if we can reach her. After the meeting, I'll try calling again, and if she doesn't answer, I'll drive over to her house. So," she said, shifting gears, "Lilly will be disappointed to miss this today since our book this month was *her* recommendation."

Marva interrupted. "She told me her daughter Nina read it first and gave it to her. They often talk about books, apparently. So—I know we need to get a move on, but I did want to mention that."

"Thank you," Philomena said. "So, ladies, I'm putting everyone on mute while I wing it here... I'm trying to open a link on my phone with discussion questions." Everyone waited. A moment later, Philomena was back but looking down. "Let's get started discussing the Palestine book. Speaking for myself, it was eye-opening."

Chapter Thirty-Two

Nina

Nina did not waste time moving forward with selling her mother's car. Her prayer—that her mother stop driving—had been answered by Lillian herself. Making an extra trip, Nina sandwiched in a visit to the DMV so Lillian could sign off the title. Nina was pretty sure Lillian wasn't clear about why she was signing, and while Nina didn't avoid the truth, she skimmed over a detailed explanation by mentioning a place to stop for frozen yogurt on the way home.

Myles was practiced at selling cars. Nina hadn't cared enough about the cars they'd lived with over the past thirty years to pay attention to the cycles her husband was attuned to: the number of years beyond which a car's depreciation became significant, the importance of repairing the dings without delay, the need to keep the car in such good condition that future buyers would be impressed. Myles and Nina's own history might be detected by a single popcorn kernel tucked behind the rear floor mat from a trip to Tahoe, a speck of red clay from Southern Utah still clinging to an interior passenger door, or a peanut shell from a Giants game in San Francisco, but overall, Myles made sure a used car looked new.

Lillian's Prius was a challenge.

While he spent time when he could on the car, Nina avoided mentioning it to her mother, petrified that Lillian would change her mind and they'd face yet another argument. So many friends had to confront their parents about their dangerous driving. There were a few lucky stories: After too many years careening on freeways and side streets, Cori's aunt, when she turned eighty, sweetly asked Cori to sell her car. When Lauren's great-uncle turned ninety-one, he had handed his keys to his son, saying, "I'm not driving anymore." But those were exceptions. Many adult children felt pressured to take the car keys or the car out of fear for the parent's safety and for the safety of others. And after forcing the issue, some never returned to the good graces of their parents. That rang true for Myles's brother-in-law, whose father, on his deathbed years after his keys were taken, refused to see his son. This was the hardest issue Nina grappled with regarding her mother, and she experienced a fresh appreciation for those who'd gone before her. Duty was the hard sole of love. The underside.

Myles kept Lillian's car in their garage to work on it over the weekends. He found a pre-owned wheel, exchanged the donut for a new tire, and found a replacement for the waning secondary battery. He decided it was worth the money to contract out some body work to mallet out myriad dents and creases from years of ricocheting around the state on road trips the Nearings took to see friends and present programs at Social Studies conferences.

"It was a little sad, actually," he told Nina as he poured a glass of wine, "to soak the bumper stickers off. "Bernie Sanders." "Work for Peace." They sat on the double swing near their front door. Evenings like this acted like a balm for both of them, and Myles loved pouring one of his finds, this time a Cakebread Sauvignon Blanc splurge. "This one is crackly dry," he said. Wine was generally wasted now on Nina; she drank it less and less out of fear that it could trigger a migraine. But a single glass, if she wasn't too tired, was a pleasure—mostly as an opportunity for Myles to share his discoveries.

"Crackly?" she said. "Such erudite vocabulary, darlink."

Myles closed his eyes as he sipped, the same way he closed his eyes to listen to music. Shut away the visual sense to intensify his olfactory and taste senses. "And tender."

So sincere, she thought as she gave him a kiss. "I really appreciate the time you're spending on Mom's car."

The least Nina could do was clean the interior, which proved to be an archeological adventure. Her parents had not cared in the least about the appearance of any of their cars, inside or out. They prided themselves, really, on the lack of attention they paid to their cars' appearances. As long as they could trust a vehicle to get them where they needed to go, in such a way that left a minimal carbon footprint, they were good.

Nina donned her latex gloves.

It had always been this way for her parents, but it had never been that way for Nina. When Nina saved up for her first car, she was embarrassed to share with her parents how much emotion she invested in the hunt. It needed to be a Karmann Ghia—the older, the better, but with a body that didn't reflect its age. When Nina turned sixteen, she found a 1960 hardtop for sale. Despite the kindly but futile advice from her car-savvy uncle ("You do see that the floorboard behind the driver seat has a hole in it, don't you?"), she proudly drove it home. She cared for it with a devotion she kept hidden from her parents, and when she'd saved more, she had it painted cherry red. Shortly after its transformation, she asked her father's help to add a ski rack. As soon as Cal began forcing the clamps of the rack, Nina heard the scrape of metal on metal.

"Dad!" she'd yelped. "I just had the car painted!"

Cal stood with his palms to the sky. "I want to help, sweetheart. But if you care that much, you'd better find someone else."

An acrid smell snapped her back to the Prius. How could her mother ignore this stench? Nina followed her nose to the dried stain emanating from the double cup holder and leading down the console to the floorboard under the mat behind the driver's seat. Coffee? Soured milk from hot chocolate? Worse? Nina poured boiling hot water to scrub over the stiff carpeted surface and was astonished to see, after steady brushing, the dry mottled stain rise and vanish. *Some* things can get ugly and go away.

After discarding years-old crumpled tissues, plastic spoons, clip-on sunglasses, a set of binoculars, and a half-torn twenty-dollar bill (*shouldn't it be worth ten dollars?*), Nina emptied the front door pockets of worn antiquated maps. She pulled out all of the rug mats and then vacuumed and scrubbed the seats and floorboards so everything emerged clean and fresh. As she brushed out the corners of the hatchback, dusk darkened her visibility, so she opened all of the doors for the lights to come on. She was almost finished and really only needed to vacuum once more against the grain of the car's carpeted surfaces, an empty-headed task.

As she clipped on the best attachment for vacuuming tight corners, her mind opened to consider the book cover she'd been tasked to design. Her lettering skills were starting a small income stream. The publisher's list of changes triggered a cascade of potential redesigns, but her best-laid plans kept getting interrupted. Real life—meaning her mother's life—continued to surprise Nina with urgencies she couldn't work around. Fortunately, the publisher's rep had been pretty relaxed about her delays. She was grateful, and as the vacuum traveled its last tracks against the surface of the hatchback's bed, she refocused on the car.

The used-car market favored the timing of the sale. COVID was to thank for that. New cars were in short order due to supply-chain issues, so the demand for used cars climbed higher and higher. As soon as Myles posted the car's picture and description, offers rolled in. He set up an appointment to meet the first prospect, and after a test drive, he'd made a deal. The buyer was a refugee from Afghanistan who would be working as a Lyft driver. He especially appreciated the Car Play navigation feature camera Nina had previously installed after Lillian started getting lost. As Myles warned, his mother-in-law never got the hang of using the touch screen. She'd instead engaged in long corrective conversations with Siri and was disgusted when Siri just didn't get it. Nina had witnessed one of these:

Lillian: "Siri, take me to the CVS near Thomas Expressway."

Siri: "You have some choices. There's a CVS at Thomas Expressway near Hamilton. Would you like that one?"

Lillian: "No, Siri, the one I want is by The Dollar Store. The new one that carries sherbet. That's the one I want. And I want to enter from the back entrance, not the front. It's less congested."

Siri: "I'm sorry, I'm not sure I understand. Can we start over?"

Lillian: "Goddammit, Nina, turn her off."

After Myles passed the title over, the new owner drove him home. He came in with a broad smile on his face. He'd gotten over the asking price.

"I feel good about this. Lillian will be pleased that an Afghan refugee is now driving her Prius."

"Not sure I'll mention it. You know... refugees are here only because of our intervention there. But," Nina agreed, "she would certainly wish this man well."

She steeled herself as she prepared to call her mother about the car sale. She needed to sandwich it between two happy things:

"Hi, Mom."

"Dear."

"Can you check the calendar for me to come down next week?"

"Oh, you're welcome anytime, you know that."

Nina asked her to note her visit in the calendar, then said, in the most casual voice she could contrive, "Myles has a new baseball name for you."

"Oh?" Lillian said. "Can't he tell me himself?"

"Let me see." Nina listened for a moment. "He may be between students." She walked into the living room. Myles sat at the piano, writing in his planner.

"It's Mom." Nina motioned to her phone. "Your latest baseball name?"

Pointing at his watch, he reached for Nina's phone to clearly enunciate, "Lars Nootbar. St. Louis Cardinals," then handed it back.

"Not as good as Cannonball Titcomb," Lillian laughed, "but pretty good."

How did she remember *that*? Nina marveled. "It's me again. Myles sold the Prius for you, Mom." She shared the sale price, considerably higher because of his work reconditioning and detailing the car. "We've sent the check directly to your bank account, and you now have a lifetime balance for using Lyft."

Lillian didn't say anything.

"Mom?"

"I heard you. I'm just... digesting."

"And the other thing," Nina quickly followed, "is that Dessa is leading Qigong classes over Zoom. You interested?"

"Oh, I'd love it!" Lillian's voice was joyous. "My body needs to move!"

It had been the right sandwich. All Nina had to do was guide her mother over the phone to connect to Dessa's Zoom link.

CHAPTER THIRTY-THREE

LILLIAN

At first, the Qigong Zoom sessions seemed worthwhile. The movement felt good. Lillian was intrigued by Dessa's Zoom prowess—her sister was so comfortable with technology that she apparently didn't require assistance the way Lillian did. She was slightly younger, not yet ninety, but still. Every week, half an hour before the sessions started, Dessa would get a call from Nina in Sacramento so she could set Lillian up in Los Gatos for the Zoom presentation Dessa led from her home in Redwood City. That Dessa could host Qigong *and* lead a group of women, all decades younger, was impressive.

But Dessa had always been impressive, Lillian observed. She had an ease with smaller conversation, even as she actively engaged in the civic affairs of her city and was widely admired for her decades-long work fighting for affordable housing. Lillian, on the other hand, was well-versed globally but impatient with personal exchanges unless it was with a Honduran seeking political asylum, or a woman in Myanmar fleeing corrupt military control in her village, or families forced to migrate from Guatemala because of government-sanctioned violence. To chat with someone privileged about... how their day was going… dismissed the seriousness of other lives on the planet.

Lillian and Dessa grew up in the same environment, but over the years, their personalities diverged. In the beginning, when their mother careened into one of her abrupt rages, they were each others' rescuers. Lilly and Dessa would take off running through foggy avenues of San Francisco's Sunset district to the beach. The running itself helped shake the terror of Clara's wrath. The pounding on the walls, the knocked-over furniture, the fury in their mother's voice unleashed when the girls least expected it, so they'd figured out go-to escapes. The times between Clara's thundering accusations and demands never felt relaxed.

It's how I learned the expression "walking on eggshells." That's what it felt like. That's what we both did. Daddy was always working, so we had to find safety ourselves. Inside and out.

Lillian thought of her father. When he came back every night from his job driving an egg delivery truck, he scooped her and Dessa up, one in each arm, tickling them as they squealed. She smiled, remembering how safe she felt. Which was the way she felt with Cal. She knew it was the same for Dessa and her husband.

Thank you, Daddy, for showing us the way to our partners.

These days, when Dessa left messages to check on her sister, Lillian seldom returned the calls. What was there to say? But she noticed a small comfort in keeping the voicemails to listen to later if she needed to.

CHAPTER THIRTY-FOUR

LILLIAN

The Prius was gone. Would she get over the shock of this? It had been months, but whenever she had to rely on someone else to get anywhere, heat traveled up her neck. *Goddammit.* What else would her daughter take from her? There were so many ways Nina controlled her life. Granted, she and Cal had pointedly asked her to take over various aspects of their financial affairs, so she couldn't really object. She had never been interested in managing any of it anyway, but when Cal started to have trouble with numbers, they began relying on Nina to step in. It started with their taxes one year when Nina was visiting and Cal admitted to being confused with the return. This eventually moved to Nina setting up all of their bill payments so she could pay them online, including their charitable contributions. There was no denying that Nina was helpful. But Lillian felt slightly disembodied when they'd go together to their years-long financial management office, and the advisor would look first to Nina for decisions.

"Nina," Melody said, her eyes on her screen, "now that I've shown you a few scenarios, how much risk are you comfortable with for the coming year?"

As Nina responded that she'd like to keep things 60/40—more conservative than risky—Lillian shifted in her seat. Nina turned toward her.

"Mom? That sound right to you? It's how we approached your investments last year."

"That's fine."

Melody hit a few keys and brought up a screen with bar graphs both vertical and horizontal.

"You're in solid shape, Lillian, until you turn a hundred and four."

"Good god," Lillian grimaced. "I am not going to live that long."

"You never know, Mom," Nina elbowed her. "But this is all good. You and Dad were good savers."

"We were always frugal," Lillian replied. "And we were also very fortunate. My father…" She didn't elaborate because Melody knew all about her client's inheritance. Lillian's father had acquired rental properties over the years, starting as an immigrant with nothing. "But don't forget: we want no investments in armaments or fossil fuels."

"That's been a given from the start, remember?" Melody said. "You and Cal were very influential regarding the investment culture of our office. We don't offer investments in fossil fuel or arms to any of our clients. And the truth is that green energy investments are now out-performing fossil fuels."

"Oh, that's marvelous!" *Doing the right thing always had rewards but so often felt subtle and unseen.* "Even self-serving people will invest in ways that help the planet!"

Melody nodded and brought up the next subject: Lillian's long-term health care insurance.

"It's a waste of money," Lillian said. "I want to stop paying for it."

Nina rushed in. "If you don't pay the premiums, Mom, Jenny and I will."

"What? What are you talking about? It's my insurance!" Lillian tightened her grip on the chrome arms of the Scandinavian office chair.

"Cori has been paying for her mother's care out of her pocket," Nina said. "She's had to dig into her own retirement savings. It's unbelievably expensive."

Melody concurred and offered Lillian a few scenarios with the average annual cost of caregiving in Silicon Valley. She turned her huge monitor in their direction to display graphics illustrating this point.

"I won't need that." Lillian shook her head. "I feel fine."

Melody's voice stayed level, as was customary during these meetings. "Lillian, when we play out your future needs, we need to factor in the *what-ifs*. And the good news is that even though your premium seems like a lot of money, your policy started so long ago that you, in fact, have a very low annual payment."

"Myles and I pay six times that amount." Nina's voice shook a little, and Lillian noticed her daughter's face flush. "Your insurance protects me and Jenny, too, Mom."

"What are you talking about?"

"If you can't pay for your health care needs, your expenses will fall on us."

Melody stepped in, looking up from her giant screen. "It's true, Lillian. All of those reasons you've been advocating for universal healthcare are valid. Even people who are well off can be bank-rupted when their healthcare needs escalate."

Lillian sighed. "I'll listen."

Nina squeezed her mother's hand as Melody explained that the policy factored into Lillian's long-range plan, and that current benefits were most generous if she were to go into a nursing home versus having help at home.

Lillian tightened her grip on the arms of her chair. "I…" She fought for the right words.

"Mom," Nina placed a gentle hand on her arm. "We know you want more than anything else to stay in your home."

"Absolutely!"

"And I respect your wishes. If you need help, we'll cross that bridge."

Lillian startled. "What are you talking about? What bridge?"

"I will do everything I can to support you staying in your home. If and when you need help, we'll find good people to come in."

"I don't want people."

"If you need help, we will do all that we can so you can stay at home."

Lillian had been holding her breath. Now she exhaled.

"That may mean we bring in someone to help you," Nina repeated. "Someone you are comfortable with. Do you understand that this is a way for you to stay home?

"Promise me, Nina."

"I promise."

Lillian let Nina hold her hand as they left the office. After Nina reached over to strap her in the passenger seat, Lillian turned to face her daughter. "You promised me something. What was it?"

CHAPTER THIRTY-FIVE

NINA

After Nina inserted the nozzle into the pump at the gas station, her phone dinged. The two-worded text from Cori was heavy in its brevity: "Call me."

With the tank filled, Nina strapped herself in, set her navigation to quickest routes from Sacramento to Los Gatos for her weekly Lillian visit, and pulled out of Al Jazeera's exit. She and Myles identified the gas station this way because that news station always played on the television when she went to pay at the counter. It served as their go-to fueling station because the family of owners was always warm and called them by their names. Plus, their prices were even better than Arco's.

After she cleared the freeway entrance, she punched in Cori's number and steeled herself.

Cori picked up immediately. She'd been crying; Nina could hear it in her voice. She knew what was coming.

"Lulu. My mamma." Cori broke.

"I'm here," Nina said softly.

"She died this morning."

"Oh, Cori."

"I was with her." Her friend's breathing was jagged.

"I'm so glad you were there."

"I knew…" Cori paused. "I knew it was coming, but still."

"Still."

"Remember how last week I told her about my dream, even when I wasn't certain she could even hear me—we always shared our dreams, you know, and this one was where I was reaching for her hand and I couldn't find it? That's when she squeezed my hand with her fingers? It was so light, it was… almost indiscernible. But she definitely was letting me know she heard me."

"I remember." Nina saw in the rearview mirror a train of speeding cars bearing on her. She carefully changed lanes.

"I'm so grateful for that last squeeze."

"I'm grateful, too," Nina said.

Cori related that she had to go—there were so many arrangements to make. Years before, Lulu had planned for a green burial, but a great many things demanded attention.

"Call me whenever you need me. And I'll be back in Sacramento in three days."

"Love your mother, Nina."

Nina was working on it.

CHAPTER THIRTY-SIX

NINA

As she guided the car onto the curve of her mother's street, Cori's loss stayed in her awareness, but Nina shifted her focus to some good news. Today was a big day. The previous week she'd taken Lillian to get her first COVID shot, and they were both feeling celebratory. The thrill tempered a bit for Nina since she was lower on the priority list for the vaccine. She could come inside, they agreed, if they were both careful. Still masked, still distanced. Still air-hugging according to their established choreography, mask-covered cheek to mask-covered cheek. It had been almost a year since Nina had been inside her mother's house, except for the time she'd come in to look for her missing mother before that doctor's appointment.

Just as she pulled up to park a safe distance from the mailbox, her phone rang. Her mother's ringtone.

"Mom, I just pulled up."

"Where is my car?" Lillian's voice sounded cold.

"Mom," Nina said, pushing off the ignition. "We've gone over this." A pang of pain started to erupt on the right side of her head. *Breathe in. Breathe out.*

"Where is my car?" Lillian repeated. "Where is it? I need it."

Nina pulled her car to her usual spot, leaving space to access the peace-sign-covered mailbox. Skirting a puddle in a sunken part of the driveway, she got to the front door and jingled the bells.

When Lillian opened the door, KPFA news blasted noisily into the air.

Nina mimed a hug; Lillian mimed back.

"Can you turn that down?"

"What?"

Nina walked over to the kitchen island and turned the radio off. "Can we visit without the radio?"

"Sure," Lillian said. "Are you spending the night?"

Nina noted that the car appeared to be forgotten. "Not yet, Mom. After you get your second shot and I get my first, we'll revisit that."

Lillian gestured to the stacks of papers on the island. "I have so much paperwork! And there's more on the dining room table."

As Nina came around the corner to the dining room, her sweater caught the rim of a Namibian basket, emptying its collection of political pins. Scooping down to pick up the basket, her elbow nabbed the corner of the Laotian weaving draped over a CD tower. The tower flipped forward, CDs avalanching across the oak laminate. *Fuck*, she thought, reviving her pet peeve about the house. *Every time I turn around, something falls or breaks or scatters. She doesn't even listen to these CDs. They just impede the passage between rooms. Crazy making.*

"Oh dear," Lillian said. "Let me help."

"Mom, I've got it, it's fine."

Lillian paid no attention, stooping low and grasping a single CD with her arthritic fingers.

"Mom!" Nina gently reached to hold Lillian's shoulders with both hands. "This is not worth a fall."

"Oh, brother."

As Nina swept carefully through the political buttons, she found one from the days of Richard Nixon and the Vietnam War. "Look at this," she showed Lillian. "You used to have this as a bumper sticker on our car. The mean-looking black Valiant."

Lillian leaned over to read it. "PULL OUT DICK." She giggled. "Did I really?"

Nina laughed, too, again relieved they'd moved on from any discussion of the Prius. "I was mortified. I was nine? Ten? I hated when you parked outside on the driveway. I didn't want anyone who knew me to see that bumper sticker."

Under her mother's supervision, she replaced the silk runner and the basket exactly as they had been, poised and ready to fall again. The surface of the dining table was obscured by stacks of papers. Nina walked past it through the open partition to Lillian's office. More of the same.

"I've set aside some things for you by the front door. And there's more stuff by the window seat in the living room."

"Okay," Nina said. "Would you like me to help you sort these things? What to keep, what to recycle, what to shred?"

Lillian emitted a loud sigh.

"Let's set a timer. See how much we can accomplish in an hour."

Lillian winced. "Are you really of my loins?"

"I have a birth certificate to prove it. You signed it."

By the end of the hour, a third of the papers were sorted. A great many redundant pleas for money were dropped into the re-cycling bin. Many were from organizations Lillian and Cal had listed for Nina to pay for online. Coupons for pizza, which Lillian didn't eat, competed with pages ripped from catalogs advertising anti-aging skin plumpers, turmeric supplements, and discounted tires. Then there were the periodicals. More than a year's worth. Lillian decided to put *The Nation* in chronological order for Nina to drop off at the Institute for Nonviolence. Do the same for the *YES* magazines.

"Is anyone even at the Institute during COVID?"

"I don't know." Lillian called and left a message with Nola. "I just told her you'd leave the magazines outside the back door on your way back to Sacramento."

"Oh my god," Nina started on another end of the dining table. "This is your property tax notice. I've already paid this. Did you, too?"

"I don't know."

"Where's your checkbook so I can see."

Lillian shuffled some of the organized papers. "It's usually right here."

Nina located the checkbook lodged between some overripe bananas on the kitchen counter, a cloud of tiny gnats hovering above. She checked the register. Nothing about property taxes. To be sure, she opened Lillian's laptop to access her banking information and brought up her checking statement.

"Found it!" she said, victorious. "It's been double-paid. I'll make a call."

While on the banking site, she checked Lillian's credit card statement too. Not something she'd been doing. While she managed all of the bills, her mother still had control over her check writing and credit cards. Nina hadn't really been concerned enough to routinely check balances. Irresponsible, perhaps, but her hands were full. With the credit card statement opened, Nina felt the pang again. Pages and pages of Act Blue charges met her eyes. Most were for three or five dollars. Harmless. No doubt made Lillian feel she was contributing something of value. But some outliers caught Nina's attention. Three hundred dollars. Five hundred dollars.

"Mom?"

Lillian came over, eating dark chocolate. Fair Trade dark chocolate.

"Just checking. Did you mean to contribute this much?" She showed Lillian half a dozen donations of several hundred dollars each.

"What!? No!! I only push the button for three or five dollars."

"This is not good," Nina whispered to herself. She steeled herself from spiraling into overwhelm but couldn't stop her mind from asking what else might be happening. Her mother had misplaced decimal points. What other charges had been overlooked?

"We'll take care of this," Nina said. She located the Act Blue phone number, walked out of her mother's hearing, and, within a surprisingly short time, spoke with an understanding representative. Not only were the outliers credited to her mother's credit card, but Act Blue willingly agreed to unsubscribe Lillian and block future clicks if she should somehow log in again.

Next, however, Nina found something even more disturbing.

"Let's sit," she said to Lillian after she'd been outside.

She explained what she'd done over the phone with Act Blue and why. Lillian was quiet but then said, "This is one of the few ways I can still make a difference."

"There are other ways, Mom. It's too easy to accidentally hit the wrong key online." She set the copy of her mother's credit card statement so the highlighted entry showed up. "A lot of these emails kind of trick you into making bigger donations than you mean to. Look," she pointed at an entry on the statement. "This is a contribution you made to…"

Lillian's face paled. "That can't be right! I *never* would have made a contribution to him! That's… that's FRAUD." She turned to face Nina. Her voice was quiet. "How much?"

Nina pointed to the total.

"Five hundred dollars!? That's impossible, Nina!" Lillian's voice shook.

"Keyboard mistakes are easy to make, Mom. I've unsubscribed you from that one. How you got on that list, we'll never know." Nina hoped her voice sounded calm. "I'll try to get the money back."

Lillian was still trembling. "But how else can I make a difference if I can't make contributions…" she interrupted herself, "…to the RIGHT organizations. You know what I mean."

"Mom, stop. You're already making big contributions all year long. They're all on your autopay, every single month. Remember?"

Lillian nodded, but her eyes were shiny.

"You can still attend the vigil."

"Except I don't have a car." Lillian's tone darkened. "Nina, where is my car?"

Nina gathered herself and aimed for calm. "You asked Myles to sell the car for you. He did, and the funds were deposited into your checking account. I showed you, Mom. Do you want to see it again?"

Lillian's eyes looked hard, and her lips stiffened into a straight line.

"Mom, walk with me." She led the way to Lillian's computer and pointed to the paper taped on the wall above it. "See this list?"

"I know."

"Good, you know. When you want to go to the vigil, call one of these drivers. You have so many choices. And it can be spontaneous, you don't have to plan ahead. I've already programmed your frequent destinations."

"I'm not comfortable in a stranger's car."

"These driver services are all vetted. This is how Myles and I get around now that we have only one car. So much easier—I don't have to deal with parking…"

"…you just get dropped off, I know, I know."

"Would you prefer for *me* to arrange transportation for you?"

"We'll see," said Lillian. "It doesn't change how I feel."

"I know," Nina said. "It's hard." She brought her mother into her arms. Lillian allowed herself to be held.

Driving home to Sacramento that night, the timing was good. Fresh Air had just started on NPR. Nina needed to make room for other voices, and Terry Gross offered a soothing distraction. It almost didn't matter who she interviewed. Nina knew soon enough she'd be preoccupied with further Lillian entanglements. *It's just problem solving*, she thought to herself. *Try to hold it lightly*. However, the unknowns in her mother's cognitive state made a slippery baseline for troubleshooting. She stopped, mid-thought. Terry Gross was interviewing Dr. Fauci about President Biden's COVID plan now that vaccinations were rolling out. *Wait*. Did she really want to hear more of this? She reminded herself that maybe it was worth a listen. Who knows, maybe her qualifying date for the vaccine had moved up. She and Myles had laughed about their sudden wish to be older so they could be vaccinated sooner. After that she'd be able to stay the night in Los Gatos, and…

An incoming call interrupted the radio program. Lillian.

"Mom?"

"Nina," Lillian's voice was cold. "What happened to my car?"

CHAPTER THIRTY-SEVEN

NINA

The calls came in steadily that month, always about the car. Where was it, what happened to it, why was it taken away, what right did Nina have to usurp Lillian's independence? It didn't help that Lillian either wasn't wearing her hearing aids when she called or that she neglected to use the speaker function on her phone.

"Nina?" she'd say, mid-tirade. "Are you there?"

"I'm here, Mom."

"Nina?"

"I'M HERE, MOM!"

"Nina, I can hear you, but I can't understand you."

This pattern became a new norm.

In a brisk walking conversation with Cori, her "second sister," the first since they were both vaccinated, Nina felt spacey. She didn't notice the greening of the roses pruned to their thorns, the unfurling of leaves in the London Planes, or the young T-shirted parents strolling past with babies swaddled to their fronts. Several Swiss Bernese doodles and various other doodles were walking their people. This particular day McKinley Park just functioned as a setting with a flat walking surface, a safe place for her to inhabit and air her circular obsessions. All at once, like she'd punched the ignition, her emotions were on "go."

"She *still* keeps calling about the car, and she's furious." A sob stabbed her rushing words. "The hardest thing is she doesn't remember that we've had this conversation already, time after time. It's as fresh for her each time she brings it up as it was the first time. And her anguish is deep. I feel it every time, too, and... it's like whiplash. Just as we have gotten close, she slams me about the car again and again like it's just happened."

Cori listened. Offered her silence. With one hand, she led Nina to a bench inscribed with a loved one's name. They huddled close to each other. Close, like in the Before Days.

"You feel the pain like she does, right? It's as acute for you each time as if it's the first time she's lashed out at you, right?" Cori had been through this with her mother as she'd slowly descended. She understood the shade of Nina's future. "I have something hopeful to offer. Would you like to hear it?"

Nina jerked her head toward Cori. "Yes."

"You remember my mother raged at me too. It killed me. That was completely counter to everything we used to have. I worried that after she accused me of something, she might die before I could offer any reassurances. I worried our relationship would be inexorably damaged."

"I *so* remember."

"But what I discovered," Cori continued, "that as she entered new stages of dementia, her anger didn't last. At first, she'd be upset with me for a couple of weeks, but then her rage would... vanish. Altogether. She would be... light with me again. Loving. Tell me I was her wonderful daughter. We'd still have fights, but they would be over new issues. She could hold onto her accusations for only a week, and eventually, over the course of her last year, a day after she was upset with me about something, she'd have forgotten all about it."

Nina breathed out. "I'm glad you told me this. It's exactly what I needed to hear."

"I've heard similar stories from others, so it's anecdotal, but I'm convinced it's common," Cori said. "It helps to know she won't hold anything against you forever."

Nina paused. "I can *hope* it develops this way, especially since there is more and more for her to accuse me of."

"What else?"

"Oh my god, I've had to cancel her credit card three times this year because of scams she's fallen for. She's mad at me about that."

"I remember the iTunes gift card scam, and I know you've canceled Act Blue—or gotten them to block her contributions."

Nina nodded. "I know I keep repeating myself. It's not just the gift card scam. She ordered anti-aging skin cream online, and now she's getting charged a hundred-thirty dollars each month from her checking account. A recurring charge." She shook her head. "I should have caught it, but I didn't. So, guess what? Because Mom has so many automatic payments in the pipeline, I had to cover almost three thousand dollars in overdraft fees. Oh, and they haven't sent her any product."

Cori sighed. "Oh, no. You're reimbursing yourself, of course."

"I have to. I can't afford to rescue her this way. I don't know what else she's spending on her credit card or writing checks for."

"Have you told her financial advisor any of this?"

"I called Melody right after the skincare event. I already needed to tell her that Mom has forgotten all about our conversation about long-term health insurance. She refused to pay for it, so I had to pay the annual premium. Melody and I keep missing each other, but she left a message for me."

"And?"

Nina nodded. "She wants to talk with Mom about making me Power of Attorney. But Mom's forgotten how to retrieve voicemail, so she's never returned those calls. When I bring any of this up, it's as uncomfortable for me as it is for Mom. Mom doesn't see this as protecting her. She sees it as interfering."

"Well," Cori said, squeezing Nina's arm, "keep in mind… *If* she's like Lulu, she may not remember any of it for long. You must keep monitoring her finances anyway. Maybe you can revisit the Power of Attorney with Melody and your mother at the same time."

Nina nodded, taking it in. She needed to do this soon.

"Another positive," Cori noted, "you said Lillian isn't spending as much time on her computer, which is good."

"Thank god for that," Nina agreed and added, "and it will be easier now that I'm paying attention to her statements." One more thing to do. Nina realized that a lot of things needed to be shifted from her mother's control to her own. For her mother's sake. For her own sanity. When she voiced this out loud Cori reminded her she'd already traveled that road.

"I had to do it, too. It felt so wrong, but I had to face the very real possibility that if Lulu could still use a credit card, her financial future was in jeopardy." Cori gave Nina another squeeze. "When I finally took over all of the money stuff, I didn't tell her, and she never asked. With her dementia, it never even came up."

"Weird to be grateful for Mom's cognitive decline. It feels wrong to be *glad* about that."

"If it unfolds the way it did for my mother, accept it as an unexpected gift," Cori said.

Nina wrapped her arm around her best friend and squeezed. "Thank you, my dearest of dearests. You are my personal pioneer, paving the way before me."

"It brings up my dear Lulu, which I can do all day. Even," she sniffed, "the hard stuff. I still feel her with me. And the hard stuff is all long gone."

They sat in silence, the shadows behind them now. Canada geese stepped purposefully in the direction of the park's pond, actively depositing as they moved. The sound of a bouncing basketball echoed from a distant court. Children's high voices swarmed toward them along with a breath of scent from the muddy earth at their feet.

"It's freezing, and I'm hungry," Nina said. They unwrapped their bag lunches.

Cori offered Nina toasted almonds she'd brought to share. "I miss our writing together."

Nina nodded her agreement.

"What about your book cover, though? You hear back after the last revisions?"

"Yes," Nina sighed. "They've got more they want me to do. It's involved because it's something they want me to change stylistically to fit the illustration. And they want a new subheading."

"You're good with this?"

"I'm fine with all of it—this is what I expected, but even though the calligraphy itself doesn't take me long, the back-and-forth revision and approval process does. I'm finding it hard to find the time for all of it, and I've already asked for one extension. They want me to work with their finish date in mind, but I'm nervous about meeting the deadline."

They sat quietly, eating.

"Look," Nina said, glancing up as she reached for a napkin.

The clouds had split apart, exposing a blue sky.

Cori followed her friend's gaze. "Nothing stays the same for long, does it?"

They finished their lunches in silence, the sun's warmth finally seeping in after a long stretch of cold.

CHAPTER THIRTY-EIGHT

NINA

Lillian's angry calls came less often, but Nina still tensed when she heard her mother's ringtone.

While Nina's neighbors pulled tired American flags from the perimeters of their front yards, she drove west, relieved to leave the simmering heat. The past year of weekly driving, five to six hours round-trip, was slowly becoming more manageable. And thanks to vaccinations, she could stay overnight now. And? She could hug her mother. Even though they were now double-vaccinated, they'd kept the habit of choreographing a safe hug. When had she ever been excited to hug Lillian? This thought caught her. She realized it was because the hugs meant something. She was receiving something she hadn't before, something sincere. As Cori had urged, she started resisting less and softening, finding more to love in her mother.

When she arrived in front of Lillian's house, she noted the garbage and recycling bins still placed at the curb. Freda usually took care of them, a kind gesture. Once out of the car, Nina stretched, then opened the hatch to pull out her tote bag with the "Vote Forward" letters. Heaving its bulk to the front door, she enjoyed the rush of knowing they'd be helping to get out the vote, something they both believed in. Something in common. She yanked the Tibetan bells and waited. A minute passed. She tried the doorknob, unlocked of course. This is how Cal and Lillian had always lived.

Nina shifted the weight of her tote to open the door. She stepped onto the Mexican tile her mother laid herself fifty years before and was surprised to see Lillian lying on the window seat, her head propped up on pillows while she read from a book. The Bernie Sanders sign still held its prominent spot facing the street, even though tall hedges of oleander concealed it from passersby. Some things were hard to let go.

Nina tried to make herself visible without startling her mother. She was used to doing this at home with Mingus, who was deaf to all sounds except clapping.

"Nina! What are you doing here?" Lillian looked up abruptly from *How to Be An Anti-Racist*.

"You knew I was coming. I'm here!" Nina said, stepping around a pile of *Nation* magazines.

"What?"

Nina looked pointedly at her mother's ears. No hearing aids. She motioned to her own ears.

"Oh," Lillian waved a hand. "I guess I forgot to put them in." She brought her legs over to get up and slowly rose.

Nina followed Lillian's trudge (*when did she start shuffling?*) to the kitchen island where the hearing aid charger was plugged in. It was hard to see it behind the basket burgeoning with papers and mail, opened and unopened. The sink overflowed with dishes.

Lillian inserted her hearing aid and turned around to face Nina. She opened her arms wide.

"Wait! Mom, let's practice first," Nina mimed a hug, deliberately placing her face to look away so they'd have no contact. Lillian giggled, and they sunk into the hug together.

"I didn't know you were coming, but I am so, so glad to see you!"

"Mom, we spoke this morning!"

"Oh, well, you're here now. Do you need something to eat? Something to drink?"

Lillian opened the refrigerator while Nina looked over her shoulder at the crowded contents. The smell told her what she needed to know.

"Mom," Nina tapped Lillian on the shoulder. "It's a beautiful day. Let me treat you to lunch in town. We can eat outside… how about the Mexican place on Santa Cruz Avenue, you know, where we'd go together with Dad?" She thought for a moment. "Manuel's."

"The place with the courtyard? The one filled with jasmine?" Lillian looked wistful. "I haven't been there without Dad." Her eyes shone.

Nina saw it as an opening. "It will be a sweet thing, Mom. We can remember him there. Bring a wrap in case it starts cooling down. We still need to have masks and vaccination cards. Can you believe it? We're going to a restaurant."

With Lillian's blue placard, she parked where they could enter the restaurant from the back. She opened Lillian's side and helped her slide her tiny frame so her feet touched the ground. They wound around an Escalade, both noting its "Make America Great Again" bumper sticker.

Lillian made a face. "I hope we don't get seated by them."

The tiled steps, deep blue, offered a handrail for Lillian's grip while Nina held her other hand. A tiered landing greeted them, filled with wrought iron tables and the sound of the patio fountain's rushing water, and smells of chiles, steamed tamales, and freshly prepared corn tortillas.

A smiling host guided them to the table they requested. It sat in front of the fountain the Nearings had loved for its familiar mosaics and soothing splash. Nina framed a family photo from this very scene. Jenny had brought her boys from Chicago, and Nina and Myles had joined them. That was back when Alessandro and Matteo were still in high school. It was reassuring to find the background unchanged.

When the server appeared for their orders, Lillian asked about the star jasmine.

"Oh," the server said, pointing to the trellis on both sides of the fountain, "it stopped blooming about a month ago. Can I get you started with margaritas?"

Nina caught Lillian's yes eyes. "Really?"

"Let's have a little fun," Lillian grinned.

This is not my mother, Nina thought. *Margaritas? But yes, let's have a little fun.*

They each ordered without salt, and when generous glasses arrived, they toasted each other.

"To my darling daughter. I can't tell you how much it means for you to come down to spend time with me."

"And to my darling mother, for her inspired choice for a cocktail. It's almost as big as you."

They giggled and took off their masks.

"Something else to celebrate," Nina said. "I almost forgot to tell you about the book cover's progress."

"What book, dear?"

"The South African memoir. The cover I've designed."

"Oh?" Lillian made out like this was the first she'd heard of it.

Nina took a sip, again noting the ample glasses. A lot of tequila for her mother's tiny body. Reminding herself too much sugar in the mix could trigger a migraine, she paced herself. She'd have to pace herself anyway since she'd be driving them home.

"Yes, Mom, I'm working with a publisher and just sent back the revisions they had me working on." She reached for her phone to bring up a picture. "This is the latest. The changes they're asking are so small that this is pretty much it."

Lillian leaned closer to see. "Oh, it's lovely. Did you write it?"

"I designed the cover. I didn't write it."

Lillian used both hands to cup her goblet and hoist it in Nina's direction. "Congratulations, dear! I'm impressed!"

A couple Nina guessed to be in their seventies sat at a table six feet from theirs. They lifted their own glasses in the direction of the two women with shaggy manes, one all white, the other a burnt brown. "Nice to be out, isn't it?" the man smiled.

"Oh, isn't it marvelous?" Lillian agreed. "I haven't been here since my husband died. He loved it here." She took a sip of the tart lime and tequila.

The couple murmured some kind sympathies, which Lillian took to heart.

"He was a wonderful, wonderful man," she said, eyes wet. "We were so fortunate to have sixty-two years of marriage. I was... so lucky..." her voice trailed off.

"To Dad," Nina interrupted with a raised glass.

"To Dad," Lillian said as she met Nina's eyes over the rim of her drink.

"To Dad," the couple said in unison as they raised their goblets of sangria.

While waiting for their flautas and chile rellenos, Lillian engaged with the strangers, explaining the life work she and Cal did for forty years.

"And now I am continuing what we started," she said. "As soon as the pandemic is over, I'm leading a tour to Cuba." She stopped to dig into her Guatemalan bag. "Here," she said, handing them a wrinkled flyer with a color photo of decaying Havana elegance. "I carry this with me, even though the dates are wrong. I can't commit to any yet…"

"Who can even *plan* to travel?" asked the woman.

"Cuba?" said the man.

"…but this will be the ninth trip I'll have led there. I'd love it if you could join me!"

Everyone laughed. Nina marveled at her mother's loose exuberance but also felt a familiar tightening in her jaw. Lillian was masterful when it came to exchanges with strangers. She was warm and captivating and open—all the qualities she usually kept to herself when she was with Nina. But now, here they were, sitting across from each other, and Lillian was now all about this couple. A couple of strangers.

Their entrées arrived. Lillian offered to share her flauta, and Nina gave her a third of her relleno in exchange. That's what they always did. Nina was surprised that her mother even ordered a full entrée. Usually, she ordered a diminutive appetizer and then ate bits and pieces of others' dinners. Nina was relieved they were six feet away from the other table; otherwise Lillian would be offering some of her meal to the couple and hoping they would return the favor.

Lillian's margarita glass was now only a quarter filled. "I need to use the restroom," she announced, slurring a little.

Nina insisted they go together so she could offer a stabilizing arm. The novelty of Lillian's tipsiness kept Nina unconcerned and moreover, she took delight in the fun she was having with the mother she normally saw as intense and serious. The words "fun" and "Lillian" did not usually fit together. Just as "cute" didn't fit, either. But today? Today, Lillian was both fun and cute, and their conversation was as fresh as the cilantro in their salads.

By the time they returned to their table, the couple was standing to leave.

"We waited to say goodbye," the woman said, looking at Lillian. "You are such a delight, and we so enjoyed our conversation with you. We just had to let you know. And thank you for the flyer about Cuba."

"Oh, it would be fantastic if you joined us!"

"'Fantastic' is the right word," the husband raised one eyebrow at the dubious glance from his wife.

"Oh," Lillian rushed over to give the strangers hugs. Nina started to stand to hand Lillian her mask, but it all happened too fast. "You are just marvelous people," Lillian gushed. "Don't you just wish more folks reached out to each other like this? We're all in this world together, and this is how we connect and," she reached for the woman's hand to squeeze, "how we appreciate each other." She was sniffing back tears.

The woman squeezed back, then slipped her Chanel bag onto her shoulder. Nina eyed the Escalade fob in the woman's manicured fingers. The couple pushed in their chairs to leave by way of the back steps.

Lillian sat back in her wrought iron chair, which Nina pushed towards the table. The food had cooled but was still appetizing, so they concentrated on savoring tastes they'd missed this last year. It was such a pleasure, they agreed, to enjoy someone else's cooking.

"Darling," Lillian said, eyes still shining. "You know Dad was so appreciative that you retired early to be with him."

"I am so grateful that I could," Nina said.

"And now there's me." Lillian's glass was empty. "You are the most wonderful daughter. What would I do without you?"

"Mom," Nina's eyes filled with moisture, not quite believing her mother's appreciation. "Aren't we so lucky to have both lived long enough to be friends?"

She couldn't wait to tell Myles.

CHAPTER THIRTY-NINE

NINA

For weeks afterward, Nina reminded herself of the "Margarita Effect." That tipsy lunch seemingly opened a door to authentic emotion between her and her mother, and it seemed to hold until the car surfaced in Lillian's shifting memory. Fortunately, that came up less and less.

Maybe it was time for more cocktails. Create another out-of-character evening for some more bonding. Maybe someday they could do it sober, but this would work for now. Ironically, neither of them were real drinkers, but for now, Nina was all about the alcohol.

As she left the Central Valley's haze behind, Nina was hopeful, and as she drove closer to Los Gatos, something clicked. She was looking forward to seeing her mother. *This is what I wanted. This! I want to see Mom. There's no more need for the want-to-want mantra that keeps me up at night. I... get... to love her.*

Instead of tuning into NPR as she headed south on 680, she listened to her playlist. Set to shuffle, it offered an entirely random mood and tone. She wanted to keep things buoyant, so she fast-forwarded through artists to stay in a Stevie Wonder vibe. Someday, she should figure out how to access albums on her car's system, but this worked for now.

The East Bay hills looked hungover and in need of a shave, brown and black nubs where there had once been century-old oaks. California's previous summer was devastated by fires; these were the scars. She thought back to how she and Myles had exhausted their escape destinations from smoke-shrouded Sacramento. The air quality of the Sierra Nevada foothills had been no better than the AQI at home; even the high Sierra wasn't immune. Fire and smoke knew no boundaries, everything at the mercy of the wind. Fire season was at its peak. It was hot and smoke-choked now, even in the South Bay, so it was unlikely she and Lillian would be eating outside anywhere during this visit.

Pulling up to Lillian's, Nina spotted the jacaranda rising above the roof from the backyard in full bloom. She pushed the ignition off and got out to grab her luggage. Her vaccinations now allowed her to stay for a few days at a time. She brought her own pillow along with a couple of bags of groceries. It was evident Lillian was not paying attention to expiration dates, nor did she believe in them. She didn't seem to consistently remember how to use the microwave. Food was either undercooked or rubber-hard. So, Nina prepared simple meals while visiting; it satisfied them both.

On the second evening, Nina stuck a cauliflower crust pizza into the hot oven while she tossed fresh arugula with spring greens. The 1940s Maytag stove was a hand-me-down from Lillian's parents in 1959. It was her pride. It boasted a soup well and a griddle on the stovetop, and its pilot light burned warm even when the oven wasn't in use. When the pizza was ten minutes in, the kitchen suddenly filled with smoke and the smell of tar. The piercing smoke alarm accosted their ears as Nina rushed to turn off the oven and pull out the pizza. A black ooze coated the back of the top rack before dripping onto the oven floor.

Freda came rushing through the front door. "What's going on?"

Nina and Freda raced around Lillian, who rose halfway from her barstool at the island.

"Mom, stay where you are!" Nina shouted to be heard.

Eventually the right alarm was located and its battery removed.

Wondering what else Freda had witnessed over the years, Nina pulled out the tar-dripping rack from the smoking oven and deposited it outside the back door. She would deal with it later.

While they ate a hastily assembled salad, Nina was careful not to sound accusatory when she asked about the melting black goo on the oven rack. "Do you know what that was?"

Lillian responded with confidence. "The pilot light keeps everything so warm that I keep containers of water in it. That way I don't waste hot water."

"But the containers were plastic?"

"Well, I never use the oven, so what difference does it make?" She looked at Nina. "You should have looked inside before you turned it on."

After dinner, Lillian parked in front of the TV to watch Steven Colbert, taped from the previous night. Nina committed to scraping the tarry plastic from the rack before it completely cooled and hardened. Once that was over, she decided she would clean the oven and thoroughly scrub the entire stove, including the shelves on either side of the oven door that stored long-untouched pots and pans. *How many decades since these shelves had been cleaned?* she wondered. She was glad for the latex gloves she'd brought during her last visit. As she got to the back of one shelf, her hand closed around what felt like scads of toothpicks. Sure enough, she pulled out the first of several handfuls to meet the light of the kitchen. Lillian had gotten up for a chocolate biscotti break.

"Look," Nina showed her the mound of sticky toothpicks. "Wonder how long they've been lodged back there?"

Lillian laughed. "Here, just hand them to me. There's more."

Nina indicated the garbage bin. "Just bring that over so I can toss them in."

"No, give them to me. I'll wash them."

Nina shuddered. Her mother was an extreme re-user. Good values she'd absorbed during the Depression. But toothpicks!

By the time she had wiped the last shelf clean and polished the outside of the Maytag, her mother had finished washing and drying the toothpicks. Now she was sorting them.

"Some of the toothpicks have nice ridges, and some are plain. I'm separating them to use the nicer ones for appetizers."

Nina swallowed. "Okay."

Just then, Lillian's phone rang. By the time Nina located it between the pillows on the window seat, the ringing had stopped. She brought it to Lillian. "Who called?" she asked her mother.

"How would I know?" Lillian sounded irritated.

"Check the voicemail, right, Mom?" Nina was alarmed. Lillian had been adept at both retrieving voicemails and checking recent calls. Had she forgotten how? After she reviewed the procedure with her, they saw together it had been Siti. Lillian called her back on speakerphone.

"Oh, Lilly!" Siti said.

"How'd you know it was me?"

"You know how that works. Listen, I called to say I cannot take you swimming tomorrow. I truly don't know how you live without a car. I couldn't do it! I am so spontaneous about everything; I need to be able to jump into my car whenever I feel like it."

Lillian listened. Nina waited for her to say something. Siti was a talker. It was unusual to see someone other than her mother dominate a conversation.

"Lilly," Siti continued, "you asked me to help you find another car. I am not the right one to do that. Do you know someone else? Your daughter, did she even warn you she'd take your car? Does she even come to see you?"

Nina tried catching her mother's attention with her hands making a "time out" symbol, but Lillian was not as well trained as Nina's second graders. Her jaw hardened during the car part of the conversation. The conversation that never went away.

"I've asked Nat. My friend from the vigil. He said he would help me. I said I want a Prius." She still didn't mention Nina. No wonder Siti knew nothing. When Nina waved her hands, Lillian looked up but kept talking, finished the conversation, and thanked Siti for calling.

Lillian started walking away from the island. Nina stopped her.

"Mom!? Siti doesn't know I visit you?"

"I'm sure I mention it."

Nina shook her head. This was too much. The familiar sense of being invisible rose in her throat like bile. "Do your friends know that I drive to see you EVERY WEEK? Do they realize how much time I devote to your life even when I'm not here?" She felt blood rise from her chest, up her neck, into her face. She spent many days every week in Sacramento managing Lillian's financial affairs. Her health. Her hearing aids. Freda's apartment repairs. Mold abatement. Pest control. Replacing sixty-year-old plumbing and adding a sewer intake to the system. Getting someone to repair her mother's irrigation hoses. Filing an insurance claim after the flooding of one of the bathrooms. Having to replace the floor and install a new vanity. Her head hurt. "Do *you* know how much I'm doing?"

"Dear, of course I appreciate all that you do. And darling, I hate being a burden."

"Mom!" Nina's voice came straight from her diaphragm, loud. "You say the words but…" she spluttered. "If you were feeling it, why wouldn't you tell your friends that your daughter is doing what she can to help you? That she visits you? And, Mom, you're not a *burden*. I'm here because *I love you*!" She shot from her chair. "I'm taking a walk."

Nina slammed the front door behind her. The Tibetan bells clanged. It didn't matter that it was dark out. No sidewalks, just long shadows between streetlights. She was almost running. Three blocks out, her eyes adjusted; it was now easy to see as she reached one corner, then another. The houses she passed held warm light as young families gathered visibly around dinner tables. Venetian blinds of the neighborhood's original residents were pulled shut, scant light spilling out. Nina looked up. More stars in the sky here than in Sacramento.

She needed to talk to Myles.

"Honey?"

As soon as he answered, her breath slowed. She filled him in.

"You've felt overlooked since childhood. Why are you surprised?"

Nina's feet hit gravel as she rounded a corner. "I know. It shouldn't surprise me."

"You can let her friends know what you're doing."

"Maybe." As she approached her mother's street, the house's illuminated windows came into view. Her jaw softened.

Before she opened the front door she brushed the Tibetan bells so they chimed. Lillian was perched in the window seat under a bright reading lamp. She looked up when Nina stopped by her side, finger in place on the page she was reading.

"Dear. Are you staying here tonight?"

Nina moved closer to her mother. "Yes, Mom."

"Oh, what a nice surprise!"

"I love you, Mom," she said, bending down. Lillian turned, and they held each other. Close.

"And I love you."

At least there was this.

L I L L I A N

What day was it?

Lillian opened the freezer just as the chimes rattled. With a sigh, she let go of her view of the double chocolate fudge frozen yogurt and headed to the entry. The chimes sounded again, and now someone was knocking.

"For god's sake."

Freda stood outside. "Lilly, you okay? I wanted to see if you were up for a swim. I can drive you."

"Oh, dear. You know…" Lillian looked down at the robe she was wearing. "What time is it?"

"It's 11:30. The lap swim schedule says you've got 'til 2:30, so you'll have plenty of time if we leave at noon."

Lillian sighed again. "All right. I just needed something to eat, but I can do that and be ready at noon."

"See you then, hon."

Hon? Lillian, disgusted by the term of endearment (*I'm not a child*), returned to the freezer and pulled out the half-eaten carton of frozen yogurt. She stuck it in the microwave for ten seconds. From her position on one of the barstools, she studied the self-portrait Cal had photographed for a project. It showed a pair of his shoes, a suede style popular in the '70s, resting on one of their Indian rugs. She wished he was wearing those shoes, sitting next to her, sharing the carton with his own teaspoon. Her eyes glazed over as she scraped the last of the creamy sweetness.

The swim kit was always at the ready. It was just before noon when she stiffly made her way out the front door, through the arch of the pittosporum, and onto her tenant's apartment doorstep. Freda dropped her off at the Y, yelling through her open window, "See you at 2:00!" Lillian would be able to get in a leisurely shower afterward, including a chance to wash her hair, which had not been this long in years, really. With all the COVID restrictions, she found it troublesome trying to get a haircut. Others she encountered at the Y had overgrown grayed hair. Even the men had pulled-back ponytails, some sporting new beards.

Making her way to the pool, she grasped the guide bar on her right to get steady before she sat on the edge of the pool. Legs dangling, she pulled on flippers, wincing at the pain in her right shoulder. With the mask secured for good suction and the snorkel positioned just so, she slid into the water. The temperature shocked her… but only for a moment. It thrilled her each time and awakened her senses. Stretching her arms to hug the Styrofoam paddle board, she launched into the empty lane.

All of her body tingled. She was home.

CHAPTER FORTY-ONE

NINA

At University Art's entrance, a polite poster asked patrons to "Kindly Mask." Once the door closed, the whoosh of cool air smelled faintly like turpentine. How long had it been since Nina had been seduced by these racks of Italian marbleized papers? The displays of pigmented inks, the aisles of charcoal, pastels, watercolors, sponges, and brushes practically singing their siren song? At least a couple of years. After another canceled calligraphy conference, she decided to upgrade her lettering skills on her own, and University Art was one of the few Sacramento purveyors stocking artisan fountain pen materials.

Which nib did she need? The mid-century font she was learning needed a kind of flex. She surveyed the honeycomb boxes, sampling various tips. What was the difference between a "pro flex" and a "semi-flex" nib?

"Ms. Visser!"

Nina jerked in the direction of the voice. Towering over her was a young man in his twenties, perhaps.

"Even with your mask! I can't believe it's you!"

She placed a nib back into its receptacle. "Please forgive me… how do we know each other?"

He lifted his mask. "It's me! Sergio! Sergio Santos! Second grade! El Centro School!" He covered his face again.

Nina had taught in a school twenty miles away, so running into former students was unusual. "Sergio!" She still had no idea who he was.

"Not surprised to find you in an art store, Ms. Visser."

"Oh, gosh," she stalled. "How old are you now?"

"Twenty-two. Remember how you took the class on a field trip to City College? I just graduated from there."

"Congratulations, that's wonderful!" Nina clawed in her brain for some reminder of Sergio. What year would that have been? She did some math in her head. 2007? 2008? "Are you in touch with anyone else from second grade?"

"Sure! Mostly on social, but I see Jenae. She had a baby a few months back."

Nina's eyes widened. *A baby?*

"And Meghna is in med school." Sergio cocked his head. "Hernan got a full ride at Chico. Oh, you know about Jackson?"

Nina shook her head.

"Yeah, I don't want to throw shade, but not good. He's in prison."

It was involuntary, but Nina gasped. She remembered Jackson. His notebook, every page filled with beautifully rendered guns, pistols, rifles, AK-47s. She'd arranged a conference with the principal and Jackson's parents. "We hunt," they said. "Not a big deal."

Sergio interrupted her thoughts. "He was caught dealing."

The six-plus-foot stature had thrown her off, but then her memory clicked. She pictured Sergio's seven-year-old self and the Picasso-like portrait he had made of her from pastels. Framed, it currently resided in her basement. It was one of the few classroom remnants she'd kept. Leaving out the basement part, she shared that with him.

"You kept it?" His eyes brightened.

"I love it! Are you still doing art? Is that why you're here?"

Sergio pointed to a full paper bag he'd leaned against a display case. "I just picked up decorations for my sister's quinceañera. She didn't want me to just go to the party store for something cheap."

"Your sister… Dulce?" It was flooding back. Dulce was a baby when Sergio was in second grade.

He laughed. "Dulce, yeah. Fifteen already."

"So many years have passed." She collected herself. "What's the best thing happening in your life these days?"

"That's sick. You used to ask us that all the time. Amazing what I remember. Like what we had to recite every morning after the flag salute. I still say it to myself!" His eyes warmed as he straightened his posture.

This day has been given to me fresh and clear.
I can either use it or throw it away.
I promise myself I shall use this day to its fullest,
realizing it will never come this way again.
I realize this is my life to use or throw away.
I am the only person who has the power to decide who I will be.
I make myself who I am.

"Unbelievable!" Nina laughed. "That pledge still holds, doesn't it? An educator named…" she thought for a moment, "Marva Collins wrote that, you know, not me. But you didn't answer my question."

"I'd say the best thing right now is that I'm transferring to Sacramento State to complete the RN program."

"Oh, that's great, Sergio. I'm glad you're excited about your future."

"Listen, I'm on Insta with lots of friends from El Centro. We should have a reunion!"

"If you want to organize something, go for it."

"Are you on Insta? Facebook?"

"No social media." Nina saw his eyes widen. "I can give you my email." She fished for her phone and tapped in his number. Before shooting off her contact card, she asked a favor. "Can you please not share it? But I'd love to hear from you if something gets organized."

Sergio swept her into a hug, then swung out the exit, calling back to her, "I'll make this happen!"

Nina palmed a handful of nibs and laid them on the counter. What a treat it would be to see her students as adults. They'd all need name tags, for sure.

"Other way," the cashier motioned for her to flip her credit card so the chip faced the right direction.

"Sorry," Nina said. Seeing Sergio was certainly the best thing that had happened to her that day.

CHAPTER FORTY-TWO

THE FRIDAY PEACE VIGILERS

The group stood in the usual place for the vigil, just in front of the steps leading to the public library's main entrance. Since the pandemic, the intersection saw less traffic, but enough drivers passed by that they could influence when they came to a stop.

Riva hoisted her sign a little higher: "HONK FOR PEACE!"

"Shira texted that she was attending a conference this week, but where is Lilly?" Nat asked. Half-circles of sweat dampened the armpits of his Che T-shirt.

"You know, she doesn't have a car. She just called me to ask for help finding another Prius for her." Elaine said from her end of the "VOTE PEACE NOT BOMBS" banner.

"She asked me, too," Nat said. "It's a tough used car market right now."

Shira gripped the banner's other end. "She seems to be getting the hang of using Lyft. But I don't blame her, I'd want the freedom to drive, too."

"She says her daughter took away the car," John said, "and it's her daughter who arranges her Lyft rides."

"That's cold," Nat shook his head. "That car was her independence." His mouth set in a straight line. "Ageism."

"I wonder if her daughter sold it for her," Shira thought aloud.

"She's never said a word about that." Nat tugged the neck of his T-shirt up to his face, wiping sweat. "Do you think her daughter is on the up-and-up?"

"I've never met her," Riva said. "Lilly never mentions her."

"Maybe we should ask Lilly directly," Elaine considered. "You know, 'Did your car get sold, and can you use the proceeds for a new one?' A new used one, that is."

John weighed in. "Well, let's all keep our eyes and ears open for a Prius. She's only interested in Priuses; she figures it'll be a less demanding learning curve."

"It's possible the daughter took the car so Lilly wouldn't drive anymore. Did you think about that? I had to go through that with my dad. Not an easy thing," Shira remembered.

Lifting his mask, Nat spat onto the sidewalk. "She'd have told us. All she has said is that she wants another car."

"Sure hope she's not being fleeced. It's family members who most often exploit their elders." That was Riva.

As the sun dropped, they kept Lillian's spirited presence in mind. It wasn't the same without her. Her energetic five feet and her snow-covered head drew a lot of welcome attention, regardless of which sign she held up.

A car honked for peace. Nat registered another tally.

Chapter Forty-Three

The Swim Group

That fall afternoon, sitting on concrete picnic benches at Vasona Park meant for cold tushes, but it was the agreed meeting place for a safe picnic among swim friends.

"Where's Lilly?" Lien asked.

"She still doesn't have a car, you know," Shirley said. "It is so limiting. She wants to find another one."

"Why can't her family help? She has that daughter. What is her name?"

The swim friends paused. No one could remember Lilly's daughter's name.

Lien sprayed bleach over the concrete table while the rest of the women hung back. Siti showed up with a box filled with individual lunch orders from Thai Spice. While pulling tom kha gai from the thin take-out bag, she announced she had something important to say.

"Last time I was at Lillian's, I had to wait for her to get ready so I sat at her kitchen counter, and her checkbook register was open, right in front of me."

A murmur came from one side of the table.

"It's not my business, but it was staring up at me. I saw the most recent check she wrote was for twelve-hundred dollars." She looked around the table. "It was made out to Nina."

"Nina?" Shirley asked.

"Nina is Lilly's daughter," Siti sounded surprised to have to explain this. "That's my point."

"So? A check made out to her daughter," Lien said.

Siti raised an eyebrow. "Just to explore a bit further, I opened the register to the page before. There were two other entries made out to Nina. One for five hundred dollars, and one for four thousand-something!"

Shirley and Lien looked at each other. "It could mean nothing," Shirley said.

"But maybe we should be paying closer attention," Lien suggested. "Was there anything written on the memo line?"

"Maybe," Siti said, "I was too nervous to look closely." She held up her phone. "That's why I took pictures of the checks!"

Another glance passed between Shirley and Lien, and as they peered at Siti's phone, the lines on their foreheads deepened. The images were too blurry to make out the writing on the memo lines.

"Okay, change of subject!" Siti dipped her spoon into the steaming soup. "Too bad she's missing this. Our favorite Thai lunch!"

"It's cold out here, though," Lien said as she snapped her down jacket closed. "Don't think she would mind missing these temperatures."

"Let's put our heads together." Shirley wasn't ready to change the subject. "Until Lilly gets another car, we can drive her to our outdoor lunches so she's not missing out."

Siti took a sip of the tom kha gai soup she knew Lilly loved. Just the warmth of it was a balm Lilly could use.

Yes, extra effort among friends was necessary. They resolved to be more involved. Especially if Lilly's daughter was up to something.

CHAPTER FORTY-FOUR

LILLIAN

As much as Lillian detested Zoom, she asked Nina to help her set up for the book club meeting.

"My computer is on," she said on her phone.

Nina responded, "Oh, good morning, and how are you, Mom?"

"I'm just needing to get into this Zoom meeting. It starts in fifteen minutes. You told me to call you."

Nina forwarded the email link, Lillian located it, and clicked it open. "I can't hear anything."

"Just wait," Nina said. "You're probably the first one to show up. Just unmute yourself and click on the video icon."

Shira's face popped up, along with several other friends in their respective squares. She was facilitating. "Long time, Lillian!" The two of them were accustomed to seeing each other more often—the book club as well as the peace vigils on Fridays. Lillian had missed the vigil the last few weeks.

"I don't have a car," Lillian said as an explanation for her absence.

"I'm happy to drive you," Shira said. "It's just been so cold I thought you'd rather wait 'til it warms up."

"True, but still. I really miss my car."

Silence from the squares.

"Well," Shira said. "We've got the updates out of the way. Let's start discussing *All We Can Save*."

"Wait, I need to ask Lillian something," Philomena interrupted. "How are you getting around?"

"That's just it. I'm not getting around."

"How do you get groceries?" Riva asked.

"Freda always lets me know when she's going to Trader Joe's. And my neighbor across the street, too." Lillian paused. "But I miss shopping for myself."

"What about your daughter?"

"Nina is the one who took my car."

"And she isn't around to drive?"

Lillian shook her head. "She tells me to use Lyft. 'It's so easy,' she says. But I don't feel comfortable in a stranger's car."

"Nina lives in Sacramento," Marva interjected.

"That isn't helpful," someone said from the top left corner.

"No," Lillian said, "and even from a distance she manages to control my life."

"How do you mean, 'control your life'?" Joan asked.

"She monitors my credit card and my checkbook. She cut me off from making donations. She decides how to spend my money."

Others murmured from their boxes.

"Lilly, do you need an advocate?" Joan spoke up again.

A bitter taste formed in Lillian's mouth. Her life no longer felt like her own. "Maybe I do."

⌒

239

A few days after the book club, Lillian's morning started slowly. She heard her slippers drag as she left the bedroom/study. She'd hoisted the Murphy bed back against the wall that morning and now wished it was already down. Wanting a cup of rooibos tea, she headed to the kitchen. *Was it always so loud when she walked? Was she… shuffling?*

The kitchen. Why was she in here? She glimpsed an empty ceramic cup on the island counter. *Some tea would be nice*, she thought. Ever since she burned her hand on the kettle, she'd stopped using the stove for boiling water, relying instead on the microwave to heat up one cup at a time. While the water heated, she unexpectedly found a clear plastic container filled with her favorite chocolate biscotti. *Why is it in the cupboard with the empty tuppers?* She pulled one out and took a satisfying bite just as the microwave beeped. She pulled out the cup of hot water and placed it on the island, then remembered she needed to fish out a reused teabag from the collection she kept in a well-repurposed Ziplock bag. That bag resided on top of the stove inside a lacquered container she and Cal acquired from that cooperative years before. *Ten years?* Time was growing increasingly relative. As she made her way through the kitchen, she counted back from this year. Wait, what was *this* year? 2020? Or 2021?

Once at the stove, she couldn't remember why she was there. She walked back to the island, hoisted herself onto a barstool, and sipped from the steaming cup. She sighed. No teabag.

Lillian's attention shifted to the piles of unopened mail taking up more and more real estate on the counter. She began to open one envelope after another, always pleas for donations, every one of them sincerely in need. Many were so familiar she thought she already contributed, but then why would they be mailing her another request? What was it Nina said? She thought Lillian was probably already contributing, so just set these requests aside in a separate place so Nina could confirm during her next visit. NAACP. SCLC. NDLF. ACLU. Planned Parenthood. Friends of the Library. A business card with "APS" printed on it. What was APS? The card was paperclipped to a note, which included a hand-scrawled note: "Sorry we missed you. We'll be by again soon. Call us if you need help." She looked more closely at the business card and read "Adult Protective Services" spelled out under the logo. Protection services? Was this a scam?

Nina always cautioned her about scammers, so Lillian dismissed the letter and added it to the stack she'd show her daughter the next time she visited. Her calendar was open next to the stack, and Lillian saw Dessa's Qigong class written down for Wednesday. What was today? The Y pool kept opening and closing, and without a steady swim schedule, it was hard to keep track.

She cupped the hand-thrown teacup and took a sip. The hot water warmed her chest. So what if it contained no tea? It was a comfort, nonetheless, and she smiled as she remembered how, as teenagers, she and Dessa preferred to drink hot water to tea. Before she'd gotten distracted by the mail, she'd meant to sit for a while to consider the recent book club meeting. She'd read *Lillian Boxfish Takes a Walk* so long ago that she remembered almost nothing about it. Still, she conceded these meetings were stimulating even if she drew a blank about the book. Her friends were bright and interesting and offered a range of perspectives on whatever they were reading. And this time, they'd shown an interest in her. Interest about... she sighed. She couldn't remember. She really missed their in-person gatherings. The delicious charcuterie and the excuse to wear one of her favorite turquoise second-hand finds along with her peace earrings. The novelty of Zoom was well over. Once logged in, she either unintentionally muted or unmuted herself. The little "muted" symbol never meant what she thought it meant. She'd been vocal about her distaste for the whole Zoom experience.

"It's so impersonal!" she'd exclaimed after she finally managed to properly unmute.

The other women agreed but considered it better than the alternative, which was no alternative. Meeting in person was flatly discouraged again, and no one in this group of women was willing to risk exposure to COVID.

"We're in a vulnerable age group," Philomena said gently.

"I suppose you're right," Lillian said, resignation thickening her voice.

She was sick of it. She was sick of the malaise. No tours to lead, no trips to take, no demonstrations to attend, no plays, no Smuin dance performances, no potlucks at her home, no Pete Seeger sing-alongs, no opportunities for gathering signatures on various petitions she had clip-boarded on the entry's gateleg table. Irregular swimming. No family gatherings. No... a sob caught in her throat and shocked her back to the moment. *No Cal. No Cal. No Cal. All of this would have been so much better if Cal were here.*

Cal wasn't here. She rarely allowed herself to think of Cal for very long. What benefit would that offer her? None. While she told people on the phone that the house was filled with reminders of him every moment of every day—and this was true—she didn't let on she avoided nostalgia. The truth was, there *was* comfort in taking in these reminders: the Makondi sculpture Tanzanian friends gave them; the framed newspaper article featuring the two of them as co-directors of Bigger World, Cal in his daishiki and Lillian wearing woven textiles from the Mayan highlands of Guatemala; the Navajo rug given as a wedding gift. The reminders were fleeting. Once she passed a memory, she didn't dwell. She was afraid to dwell.

When Jenny called, she'd sometimes tell stories about Cal. And Nina's visits were often filled with shared sweet memories of him. Lillian liked that. It didn't feel as lonely. Nina would talk about things that were so unique that they were knowable only by their tight remaining family of three, like Cal's inside jokes about the nose he'd passed along to Nina. Lillian got distracted again. Nina didn't seem to care anymore about the nose she'd inherited from her father. That was a relief. *I suppose by the time a person turns sixty, that sort of vanity diminishes*, Lillian thought. How could it be that Nina was… sixty? At least sixty? Which swiftly returned Lillian to her original disbelief: Cal was gone.

The next sip of tea was cold. She felt for Cal's ring. The chain around her neck was missing. The ring must be somewhere. Where could it be?

Lillian climbed stiffly from the stool and was on her way to check for the ring by her bed when she decided to put on a heavier sweater. She pulled a cable knit over her head and wondered what she'd been on her way to do. She looked for a warmer place to settle for the afternoon. The sweater wasn't enough.

The warmth she craved was the warmth that was no longer there.

CHAPTER FORTY-FIVE

NINA

Nina's AWA writer's group was meeting again on Tuesdays, but now over Zoom. After writing ended, she stayed at her desk to work on calligraphy.

Taking a break in the late morning, Nina called her mother just to check in on her. No answer. Nina got up, did a few yoga stretches, and made her way through the living room to the kitchen. She pulled out the Kewpie and arugula for her favorite BLTs and tried Lillian's number again. No answer. *Hmm. Maybe she went to a swim lunch?* Myles walked in as she sliced tomatoes, still a bit green but easily yielding to the knife, just the way she enjoyed them most.

"Good writing this morning?"

"Seems so long ago. I've been working on lettering. How's your day?"

"Piccolo," Myles said as he dislodged his earplugs. "I'm sure you heard."

"Since when are you teaching woodwinds?"

"Sidney asked." Sidney had started viola with Myles ten years ago. "She played piccolo when she was in high school and wanted to revisit it. I said sure."

Nina gave him a hug. "You're a sport."

With the sandwiches assembled, they headed to their little studio in the back. His studio, really. A keyboard resided there for piano practice, along with a music stand for his cello, but Myles built a banquette and table for them to lunch together when they needed a change of scenery. Despite being spring, it was already too warm to eat on the deck; the studio, however, was insulated with a window air conditioning unit and perfect for days like this. After counting their blessings, they exchanged the best aspect so far of their respective days.

Myles: "The baseball strike is over! The Giants start April eighth!"

Nina: "My second graders have scheduled a Zoom reunion!"

"Your babies are all grown up. That'll be fun."

"In-person would be a lot more engaging, but this is smarter."

Even with vaccinations and boosters, COVID still factored in when it came to crowds.

Nina closed her eyes as she slowly savored the tang of the bacon against the sweet tomatoes (then again, maybe *this* was the best part of her day). Mingus nosed his way through the doggy door, exhibiting Scottish Terrier indifference to the enthusiastic welcome. He curled into a ball directly in front of the floor fan. Between sandwich halves, Nina called her mother again. Still no answer.

After lunch, Nina called every thirty minutes, and when she saw it was 3:00, she called Freda.

"Don't know where she is. Maybe her phone's not charged," Freda suggested, "but I'll check the house and call you back." Three minutes later, Freda had nothing to report. No Lillian.

Next, Nina phoned the Y. "Did Lillian swim today?" she asked the front desk.

"Oh, this is Nina, right?" It was the Y director. "As a matter of fact, Lillian was swimming today, and one of our trainers saw her hitchhiking on the road a block from here."

Nina felt the blood drain from her face. "Hitchhiking!? What time?"

"Around noon," the director told her, adding, "and Lillian's phone was found in the locker room. It's here at the registration desk. You're welcome to pick it up."

"I'm in Sacramento," Nina said, "but I'd better head down."

Her to-go bag always remained packed for the unexpected. She raced to the laundry room and made sure Mingus' medications were organized for Myles.

"What's going on?" Myles poked out of the studio for five minutes between students.

Nina rushed through a recap.

"Hitchhiking?" He opened his arms.

Once on the road, Nina scrolled through the contacts on her dash screen, thankful she'd had the foresight to add some of her mother's friends. Most of these people she hadn't met, so she wondered if they'd even answer her unfamiliar number. She left a message for Siti, Shira, and Nat. When she called Lillian's neighbor across the street, he answered on the first ring.

"Mr. Van Arsdale, Nina here. Lillian's daughter?"

"Yes, of course."

Nina heard muffled sounds on the other end, then a three-syllable sneeze she could spell ("her-esh-shoo"), followed by a, "Where's Helen?"

"Bless you," she offered, hoping her impatience didn't make her sound insincere, then explained the situation.

"Your mother hitchhiking? That's a pickle." He said he'd keep an eye on the house and call Nina if he saw any sign of Lillian.

By the time the calls were over, Nina had already reached Sunol, forty-five minutes from Los Gatos. The greening landscape blurred past as she drove, too fast, from Sacramento. Having exhausted the friends call list, she pushed the dash's microphone. "Siri, call the Los Gatos police."

After a dispatcher answered, Nina felt as if she were disembodied, watching herself as she said the words, "I have a missing person to report."

The dispatcher transferred her to the San Jose precinct. The new dispatcher listened patiently to Nina's narrative and, after thoroughly identifying who Nina was, took down pertinent details:

"Time she was seen hitchhiking?"

"Just after noon today, from the YMCA on Miren Road, heading north."

"Full name and birthdate?"

"Lillian Nearing, December twenty-fourth, 1929."

She gave him Lillian's address.

"Physical appearance?"

"Five feet tall, no, she's not anymore. She's more like four foot ten. White hair to her shoulders. Green eyes. Olive skin."

"Cognitive state?"

"She's in cognitive decline. Some days, she's sharp; other days, she calls me, not remembering that we spoke five minutes earlier."

The dispatcher said a report would be filed and a bulletin posted in three counties. "Call us if you locate her."

"Of course, I will, I will."

After Nina thanked the dispatcher, she wiped her eyes to see the road. How could the "missing person" be her mother? Who could have picked her up? She reminded herself of Myles's counsel not to speculate.

"Don't borrow worry. It eats at your reserves and doesn't serve you."

It was hard.

Los Gatos was now about fifteen miles away. The Y would come up first, and it was important to retrieve Lillian's phone. When the YMCA director saw her enter the sensor-opening glass doors, she reached below her desk for the phone and came out to meet Nina with it in her hand.

"I'm sorry, but we haven't heard anything."

Nina didn't know what to say.

"Would you please let us know that she's okay?"

"I will. Thanks for this," she waved Lillian's phone in her hand. Back in the car, Nina checked her own phone first. Three text message alerts.

From Freda: "Your mom's home."

Nina exhaled.

From Mr. Van Arsdale: "Nina, your mother is back. Looks like someone is with her." Nina inhaled sharply.

From Myles: "Things okay? Call me."

She'd call later.

Five minutes later, she pulled up to her mother's house. An unfamiliar car occupied her usual parking spot. She lurched into a U-turn and parked in front of Mr. Van Arsdale's house. Jumping from her car, she raced across the street, quickly taking pictures of the silver Hyundai and its license plate.

Without ringing the bells, Nina twisted the doorknob and stormed into the foyer, her phone at the ready.

"Mom?" Nina's voice was a barely controlled yell.

"Dear? What a surprise. I'm just making us tea."

As Nina turned toward the kitchen entry, her peripheral vision detected someone sitting on the couch facing the front door. A man. She pivoted, eyeing the stranger warily. "I just texted a picture of your license plate to my husband. Who are you?" The man started to rise just as Lillian came around the corner, balancing a tray with two hand-thrown ceramic cups, her tea pot, and a plate of cookies.

"I'll be back with another cup," Lillian smiled, and, after setting the tray onto the coffee table, returned to the kitchen.

The stranger wore sunglasses even in the dim of Lillian's living room. Standing now, he doffed his Oakland A's baseball cap, revealing a shaved head. He introduced himself. "I'm Ken. Ken Rollins." He explained that as he was leaving The Dollar Store in Campbell, this diminutive white-haired lady (he motioned with his chin) stopped him and asked for a ride home.

"The Dollar Store?" Nina tried to stay calm.

"Yes," he said, "The Dollar Store. I had the time to drive her but I asked her to first call a family member so they would know what was going on."

"I didn't get a call."

"Your mom searched her bag," Ken continued, "and couldn't find her phone, so I just brought her home. That was half an hour ago. She insisted that I have a cup of tea… which," he smiled, "is taking a while. I can see you're upset, and," he looked at Nina with furrows in his forehead, "I am not surprised."

Lillian was back with another cup for Nina. "Ken, this is my daughter. Nina, why are you here?"

Nina held out Lillian's phone.

"Oh, you found it! Where was it?"

"Mom! I couldn't reach you. I tried for… three hours! You didn't answer. I called Freda, I called Siti, Nat, Shira—I called the Y, and they told me your phone was there and that someone saw you HITCHHIKING!"

"Nina, calm down. This is my life."

"Mom! HITCHHIKING? You're ninety-two! You had no phone!"

"I needed to go to The Dollar Store. I don't have a car!"

"Mom! Hitchhiking? You could have called a Lyft!"

"Nina!" Lillian's mouth was now a thin line.

"No one knew where you were! I…" the next words ruptured into a screech "…called the *police!*"

Lillian's new friend rose. He tipped his cap to Lillian and reached into his pocket for a billfold, from which he excised a business card. He handed this to Nina. "I was just trying to help, but I think it's best I leave."

"Oh, but you haven't had your tea!" Lillian implored him.

"Thank you, Lillian, this is best. And thank you for the flyer about Cuba." He patted his back pocket and saw himself to the door.

"Please join us!" Lillian called after him.

Lillian turned to face Nina, her rage barely contained. "Unlike you, I live in a world of *trust*. *You* live in a world of fear. You've taken my car, you tell me who I may or may not donate to, you control my finances, and now you're telling me I can't choose how to get around? I can't choose my friends? You've left me with no choice. You've stolen the little bit of independence I still have. Calling *the police?*" She was trembling, her hands in tight fists. "You are not welcome here."

"Mom!" Nina was in tears.

"Go. Stay out of my life."

Nina began backing away. "Mom, I love you."

"You need to leave," Lillian's voice shook into a scream, "or I'll call my lawyer!"

CHAPTER FORTY-SIX

NINA

"Allow yourself to relax into your breath," Cori intoned. She was facilitating the writing group today. "Follow your inhale as it starts from your pelvis, moves to your belly, your lower ribcage. When it reaches your upper ribcage, pause, then slowly exhale, following it back to its starting point."

Nina could neither slow her breath nor shake her impatience. She willed time to speed to the next step. Finally, Cori delivered five single-word prompts:

scratch
salve
shoulder
valley
slam

Nina scribbled associations after each word, priming for the first twenty-minute write. Her mother's last words were hard to shake; they were bleeding over everything. She had no idea how she'd string together her own until all of it avalanched into a poem.

I Slept Like a Baby

That night I slept like a baby;
I shouldn't have slept so well.
I should have been wide awake, reworking the argument,
the soft fingers of it, the howling grief of it.
It was all too raw to be vanquished by sleep,
by an involuntary surrender to the sinking pillow,
a vacant valley I pounded into the feathers.
That night I slept like a baby,
slammed straight to a dream,
someone else's dream,
I think,
while I'm dreaming.
There's no familiar here,
I think,
while I'm dreaming.
No breeze to cleanse this groundswell of
unfinished feeling,
just a hard scratch, digging deep, to reach the
animal in need of
a rest.
A resolution.
I've never had a facility for shouldering
the strength of an argument.
Exhausted, I slept like a baby,
the night peeling me away from battle, readying
me for a new morning.
A new day, but the scars remain, tender,
in need of a salve,
another night's dream,
not mine.

Nina's shock from the hitchhiking episode reverberated for days.

It stung in a way that punctured deep. It was so misplaced that Nina's mind scrambled for some sort of foothold. *How is it,* she asked herself over and over, *how is it that I can be feeling this pain when I am doing everything possible to make sure Mom is safe and taken care of?*

She returned to her ongoing conversation with her dead father. "How is it that Mom sees me as the enemy? It's upside down: if I were to leave her to her impulses, I'd be remiss, but as I try to control her environment and her actions..." Control. There was that word again. And with Lillian's dementia, what place could control even occupy?

Everything was compounded by Lillian's inability to remember things and Nina's determination to keep the signs of dementia a secret from her. Still another way she was trying to protect her mother. And that is where Nina caught herself. Heard herself.

All while sitting in the parking lot at Target.

Control. She didn't characterize herself as controlling, but Myles often brought it to her attention, primarily in terms of planning ahead. "You're doing it," he'd say.

He'd say it when she'd start brainstorming plans before friends came to visit. "Maybe we can borrow a couple of bikes from the neighbors?"

He'd say it when she'd start reserving lodging as soon as they'd picked dates for a trip "When we wait, we get the dregs."

He'd say it when she started multi-stepping on the way to and from destinations. "We'll be by that rug place after the hike, and after that, we can pick up dog food."

It was true, she acknowledged. She did feel more relaxed when she prepared a few steps ahead. It served to ease the stress of having to manage the unexpected.

"Worry isn't helpful," was Myles's mantra. "We'll figure it out."

But guess what, husband. This is how the sausage gets made. And with Mom? Now that she has cognitive issues and is seriously fragile, I no longer have the luxury of "waiting to figure it out." Nina had enough immediate crisis stuff to deal with, so whenever she could plan for ahead of time, she would.

Speaking of crises, she was scrambling to avoid one of her own. After she emailed her second request to extend the deadline to accommodate the editor's latest changes for a book's chapter headings, the publisher no longer offered flexibility. They stood firm on the date they'd issued. When she read their declaration, her stomach dropped. The publisher lost patience; they must see her as a loser. And the panic in her gut crept down her arms to her fingers, a panic that was all about losing control. She had so many Lillian commitments on the calendar and had to spend time in Los Gatos that she was filled with uncertainty. How would she finish?

She might not.

This jolted her back to her surroundings. As she sat paralyzed in the Target parking lot, tears tracked down her cheeks. This book's title and chapter headings, uniquely hers, might not happen. Her mother filled every inch of Nina's calligraphy time. Completing the book project was looking impossible.

Nina reached for a tissue from the console and blew her nose. Why was she at Target? She had to remind herself. She scanned the list she pulled from her jean's pocket:

Canned dog food (no poultry)
Band aids
Air filters
Bananas

Butter pecan slow churned
Mom: biscotti, compression sox, TP

She refolded the list and stuffed it back in her pocket with the N95 mask. Despite two COVID-19 booster shots, she still carried a mask. You never knew.

A rush of retail air and sound met her as the glass doors slid open. She grabbed a cart, deliberately avoiding the sani-wipes the store provided. "What a waste," she heard Lillian's voice say before abruptly realizing now it was not Lillian's voice but her own.

"Nina! Nina Simone!" Cori's voice eclipsed the Todd Lundgren music filtering the aisles.

Nina turned as Cori's cart nearly collided with her own. They never ran into each other doing mundane errands; their meetings during COVID were always planned and outside. This contrast made them both laugh. The surprise meeting pulled them into an exclusively shared space. They were blind to the blur of shoppers passing around them.

"This feels NORMAL!" Cori grinned.

"Right?" Nina smiled back, not ready to talk about the disappointment of her book cover or her mother. She'd do better hearing about her friend's life. "What's the latest, Coriander?"

"Oh, everything is taking longer than we thought. Every remodel is like that, right, but supply chain stuff is really prolonging things… and it's costing more, too. Remember that Hemingway quote about how a person goes bankrupt?"

Nina furrowed her eyebrows. "Two ways? 'Gradually, then suddenly.' Something like that. Oh, boy."

Cori was renovating her mother's home, a bittersweet project. "On the one hand," she'd said in a recent phone call, "it's satisfying to take our family's home down to the studs and start fresh. A way of honoring Lulu's memory while making it my own. On the other hand, it forces me to dwell in my loss in unexpected ways… ways I appreciate as a therapist. There is no avoiding the pain of grief, after all, and working on the house in my few spare moments means I've been mourning almost constantly."

The grief that filled Cori a year after Lulu's death was a grief Nina envied. Would she ever feel that way about her mother?

But they didn't talk about Cori's sadness in Target's stationery aisle. They chatted about the house, about Mingus' regimen, about their next meeting. "We could even go to the movies!" Cori exclaimed just as her phone dinged.

"Yikes, it's the tile guy. He's at the house already. I need to get going!"

By the time Nina wheeled her cart back to the car, she'd resolved to find ways to put some safeguards in place so she could worry less about Lillian's safety and concentrate instead on their relationship. She wasn't sure how to start toward these two very disparate goals, but she did recognize she needed help. As Myles had suggested, it was time to include others in Lillian's care and time to include others to help her find her way back.

Back to her mother and back to herself.

Chapter Forty-Seven

NINA

By the time Nina joined the Zoom reunion, four former second graders' faces already filled the screen. Before hitting the video link, she studied the animated young adults. Maya Winmer! How could someone change so little in fifteen years? But the other three? Not a glimmer. Two more popped up, then three. Catching herself being a voyeur, Nina hastily joined the group.

"Ms. Visser!" All voices buzzed in her earbuds.

"I'm muting everyone!" Sergio broke in. He had organized the gathering and taken on the role of facilitator. "No one can hear anything if you're all talking at once. Ms. Visser, you talk first."

Nina laughed. "Sergio's getting a taste of what it was like to manage a bunch of seven-year-olds."

Sergio took the hint. "Guys, if you have something to say, you know what to do."

Raised-hand emojis popped up on the screen.

"How about we get a one-minute update from everyone?"

Sergio unmuted Joey, a student who had been so enchanted by Nina's classroom piano playing that he'd composed a piece for her to play. She still had it, a page of dots, squiggles, and diagonal lines.

"Hi, Ms. Visser," Joey's voice was deep and resonant. "I'm a music major at American River College."

"So great, Joey! What instrument are you studying?"

"Um, it's Joe. I'm playing guitar, slide guitar, and standup bass, but I'm also doing percussion."

"So wonderful!" Nina said. "You still love history?" In second grade, he was famous for his references to World War II, which mystified both his classmates and Nina. "Do you remember when we had a visiting author who asked for ideas for a story? She said, 'Who has a setting we can use?' and you raised your hand to say, 'The southern part of Poland near the German border.'"

Joey shook his head, but his broad smile matched the faces of his friends.

Adley took her turn next. Pride underlined her words. "Ms. Visser, I'm applying for the teaching credential program at Sonoma State."

Nina applauded her while biting her tongue. She wondered if Adley knew what she signed up for. Whenever anyone shared the idea that they wanted to pursue teaching, Nina struggled with conflicting thoughts. On the one hand, it made sense to support anyone who felt that calling. It was a deeply purposeful, rewarding profession. On the other hand, she always wondered if it would be a gift to provide a reality check. *Well, Adley is an adult. She'll find her way. We all eventually find our way.*

Chanda went next: "I'm working. I help my mother pay the rent," she said. "I got a job at the corner store on the way to El Centro. At the gas station." She smiled shyly. "Raise your hands if you fill up there."

Brandon J. boomed that he was on his college basketball team. Jenae talked about her baby ("Can you hear her?"). Meghna detailed her first year in premed at UC Davis.

"I'm exhausted. And I'm engaged," she said. "We're not in a hurry, though."

"Congratulations," Nina said. "Let me know when you need any invitations addressed."

"Oh, your beautiful calligraphy!" Meghna exclaimed. "I would love that!"

Sergio unmuted Kayla, whose face was replaced by a page filling the screen.

"What?" Sergio asked.

"Oh!" Nina laughed. "The yearbook!"

"You made this monogram next to my picture," Kayla's finger pointed to the Gothic depiction of her initials, outlined in silver. "There was a long line of kids, even from other classes, who wanted you to use your special pens to monogram their names."

Big gestures filled the grid. Sergio turned off the universal mute for several seconds, amplifying a cacophony of exclamation, mostly echoing "I still have mine!" and "I remember that!"

An hour and a half passed, then two hours. Jenae and Chanda had to excuse themselves, but by the time Sergio signaled it was time to tie things up, everyone had had a chance to update Nina.

"How about we end with the 'Pledge to Myself?'" Nina asked.

Sergio unmuted the former students, then led with: "This day has been given to me fresh and clear…"

Fifteen years later, everyone still knew the words.

CHAPTER FORTY-EIGHT

NINA

"Nina, Freda. Call. Urgent."

Nina swallowed her spoonful of butter pecan before hitting the dial button. "Freda?"

"The toilets are all stopped up—your mom's house and in my bathroom."

So much for ice cream.

"I'm on it."

The plumber called Nina two hours later. "Fixed," he said. "For now."

"'For now' doesn't make me feel very secure."

"I'll call back with options."

For the moment, Freda and Lillian could relax.

Nina cleared her desk and opened her laptop to tackle her mother's taxes. Preparing to get to the list of donations, she saw a red alert on the link for bill pay. *What now?*

A long column of "overdraft" notices accosted her, along with a wave of nausea. It made her sick to see the alerts attached to the automatic withdrawals. She immediately called the bank to see if she could pause the onslaught.

"Until I figure out what's happening," she pleaded.

The bank rep stayed with her on the phone as they scrolled down to isolate whatever the mysterious charge may have tipped things over the edge.

"$23,444," the rep pointed out. "Page seven, mid-page."

Nina located it. "American Airlines. Christ."

Next was her call to Lillian.

"Mom."

"I can hear you, but I can't understand you."

"I haven't said anything."

"Dear, I can't understand you."

"Your hearing aids?" Were they lost? In her ears but not charged? Or, still angry about the car, was she pretending not to understand?

"I'll email you."

"What, dear?"

Nina hung up. Who knew when Lillian would open her email? She always waded through mushrooming pleas for money, taking each one seriously and often never making it to the most recent messages. What to do? This was too hard to untangle from a distance.

That evening, Nina pulled up to Lillian's mailbox.

"Dear!" Lillian exclaimed. "What a treat."

And maybe it was, but the delight evaporated quickly once Nina sat her mother down on the couch.

After noting the overdraft entries on the laptop, Lillian turned to her daughter. "I'm sorry, dear. I charged the tickets to my credit card, and then I guess my checking account covered it when the credit card was due."

"But what are these charges? Tickets? For whom and for what?"

"Cuba, dear. It's reopened. I expect to have ten folks joining me in January."

Holy shit. Nina couldn't wrap her head around Cuba. Not yet. "I had to forward a payment, Mom, for the overdrafts. From my own checking account."

"Oh, well then, of course I'll write a check for you."

"You don't have the funds in the checking account, Mom. Melody will have to pull some from your investments to cover this and… have any of these people already paid you for the tickets?"

"Dear, no. I haven't been recruiting. I won't need to. Folks are always interested in Cuba. I just went ahead and reserved for January. I'll collect as people sign up."

It was already dark, but Nina needed to take a walk.

Here we go again. What happens if Lillian starts to collect money and forgets about it? What happens if she has a group of travelers depending on her and she loses her passport? Forgets the itinerary? Loses her way?

It was too late to call Jenny in Chicago, but Nina already knew and dreaded her next steps. She needed to somehow take away her mother's credit card and checkbook, the last vestiges of Lillian's independence. This time, she would do it without asking and hope that being out of sight, it would also be out of mind.

CHAPTER FORTY-NINE

NINA

The time had come, Nina decided, to include Aunt Dessa. Up until now, she had consciously kept details about Lillian's decline from her sister. She'd wanted to preserve Lillian's dignity and didn't want to create anxiety for Dessa about her older sister's well-being. It might be too close to home. Quite possibly, Dessa had started experiencing similar symptoms, herself. Like Lillian, Dessa was recently widowed, and even though the sisters had been very close when they were young, in later adult life, they'd taken separate paths and didn't communicate all that often, even after they'd both lost husbands.

As a confidant, Dessa was much more approachable than Lillian. Even so, it had been a long time since they had really talked.

For her phone conversation with Dessa, she decided to walk a neighborhood route that would take her to the track rounding Curtis Park. The dogwoods were in full bloom, as well as azaleas and rhodys. The orange trees, ubiquitous in backyards, were fragrant with blossoms as she walked from one block to the next. She plugged in her AirPods and punched in the phone number she knew by heart.

Her aunt answered the phone.

"Dessa, Nina here."

"Nina." Dessa's voice was warm as ever. "What's up?"

"Is this a good time?" Nina wasn't quite sure how to start, but once she did, her words cascaded. Lillian's forgetfulness, her drawing inward, her inability to grieve, the issues around driving, the getting lost, the steady increase of unreported car dents, the overdraft charges ("Twenty-three thousand dollars on airline tickets for a nonexistent tour, Dessa!"). Accidental Act Blue contributions, the doctor visits about cognition and driving, her rage about the car being taken away forgetting she, Lillian, was the one who'd suggested it, the letter from the DMV she'd dismissed as a scam…

Dessa interrupted. "She told me about that," she said. "It was especially upsetting because the reason stated for the suspension of her license was dementia!"

"Right," Nina said. "I only knew about the letter after Freda found it in Mom's recycling basket and called me. I assumed her doctor informed the DMV. You know, she's legally bound to report it if she finds a patient doesn't have the reflexes—"

Dessa interrupted again. "But dementia? Lilly has never been diagnosed with dementia, has she?"

"No… Dr. Sharma calls it 'mild cognitive decline' in front of Mom. But in my observations, it's more than 'mild.' So after Freda called me, I emailed Dr. Sharma to ask her about it. She said regrettably the DMV report offered a limited number of reasons to check, and dementia was the most fitting one, if not entirely accurate."

Nina took a breath, noticing suddenly she'd hardly registered her whereabouts during the phone conversation. She'd already circled the park and was now crossing railroad tracks that divided the Curtis Park neighborhood from Land Park. She looked both directions. "So last week, when she didn't answer my repeated calls, I tried to track her down by calling various friends. No one knew where she was, and when I called the Y to see if she'd been swimming that day they told me she'd left her phone behind, but also that someone had reported seeing her hitchhiking."

Dessa was quiet, then said, "Oh, dear."

"Yes, oh, dear." Nina went on to explain the rest of the story, and when she got to Lillian's directive to "stay out of her life and leave," she slowed, unable to finish the memory.

"Oh, dear, Nina, I'm so sorry. That must be terribly painful."

Nina was too overcome to answer. Dessa filled the gap.

"Listen, you know Bubby was so much like that. So much anger without an iota of warning."

Nina listened, nodding. Her grandmother Clara, Dessa and Lillian's mother, was a hot and cold rager. Nina and Jenny had been afraid of her throughout their childhood and until she died, even as adults.

Nina needed to take a breath. "What was it like, growing up with Bubby? You were scared of her, too, right?"

"We came to understand the signals. We knew—most of the time—when she was going to get angry. Things that triggered her were often when the attention drifted from her to us, or really, to anyone else. She was… effervescent, charming, really, when she was the center of attention."

What Dessa was explaining matched up with what she already knew and experienced with her grandmother. "But how did you cope with that?"

"Lilly and I had each other. The Abram Girls. We were a team. And when we saw the storm coming, we would take off down 23rd Avenue to the beach. The ocean soothed us. Rescued us."

Nina crossed another street and approached her favorite block. An old fire station on one corner had been inventively remodeled into a single-family home, residing on a plot among shingled Craftsmen, all shaded by hundred-year-old London Plane trees. Nina asked if her mother and aunt ever confided in their mother or, for that matter, their father.

"Never with Mother. Daddy was much easier and very loving, but he was working so much of the time that we didn't bother him with our concerns. We had each other for that."

Nina listened, thoughtful. Her aunt continued to fill in both familiar and unfamiliar creases of Nina's mother's life. Growing up in their San Francisco home, any expression of sadness was dismissed as a sign of weakness. Same with admitting struggle. Complaints of any kind. Lack of confidence. It was important to always appear to be strong and in control. Dessa speculated that although her parents never discussed their pasts with their daughters, it had doubtless shaped the way they raised them. Some of the family history seeped into the girls' awareness when visiting relatives shared tantalizing bits and pieces: both Mother and Daddy were brought, very young, with their families to the United States from the Ukraine and Bessarabia around 1900. They fled to escape the pogroms against Jews, as well as their sons' fates as involuntary conscripts to the Russian Tsar's army.

Nina thought of the black and white photo on her gallery wall in the back of the house. Twelve children, her grandfather among them, solemnly assembled around their mother and Bubby. No father. The photograph must have been taken in their homeland at the turn of the century; he was ahead of them in the new world, readying their untried life. Her grandmother's story was much the same. How much stoic will and discipline they had to employ, leaving what they knew for the unknown in New York City. And what followed was the high expectation foisted on the young generation to succeed in this adopted country.

"All of that," Dessa repeated, "influenced the way they brought us up. It was understood that they accepted hardship to reach their goals; so did we." She stopped for a moment, then continued. "Complaining wasn't an option."

Nina listened as Dessa talked about her parents' sensitivity to the circumstances of their history, specifically the oppression of Jews by the Tsar, and their subsequent excitement over the Russian Revolution and its potential to flip the social structure in such a way that a more balanced structure of power would ensue. "That planted a seed, for certain, for their respective activism to support the powerless."

"I remember them reminiscing about the Spanish Civil War against Franco," Nina chimed in. "That was all about changing the balance of power. And with the labor movement here. Civil rights. Same principles."

Dessa issued a sound of agreement. "As long as forces of power exploited labor, our folks offered their support to those who struggled. The longshoremen in San Francisco, for sure. Their compassion was rooted in their own history, yes."

Nina had long understood that her own parents channeled their compassion similarly—on a large scale. Toward oppressed people. Masses of people. Refugees. Victims of racism and war. Religious persecutions. That kind of compassion was acceptable. Necessary. And in their view, divorced from compassion toward a daughter, say, who might be embarrassed about her acne, or wishing for a Barbie doll, or shunned by a friend. They made clear that personal problems were trivial problems. Selfish, even. Problems to be dismissed. Now Nina could also see her mother's place in this world, a generation before her own, and how it shaped her as a parent.

"So how is it that I can tell you things I'd never share with Mom?" She looked up, surprised again by her surroundings. When had she started retracing her steps? The Land Park neighborhood was now behind her, and she had started heading toward the hard-packed sand trail around Curtis Park, an expanse of shaggy green with tennis courts in its center and lots of people out walking dogs. Homes surrounding this park were built a hundred years before, more modest than the elegant two-storied homes a few blocks back but charming and architecturally varied. English Tudors sat next to Bungalows, divided by sprawling camphor trees, monumental red-woods, and occasional queen palms and fig trees. A neighbor-hood of privilege, to be sure.

Dessa took a moment; then, "I've thought about it, but I don't know. Lilly has always actively played the older sister. More serious than me, less… yielding. Maybe she's had to hold that sort of pro-tective posture to protect her vulnerabilities."

Nina tried to picture her mother as a little girl. *It must have been hard*, she thought. *Hard to feel unloved by her mother.*

Just as Nina was about to end the call, Dessa's voice lowered in register. "Something you said earlier about Lillian not grieving. I've left messages to talk about Cal, but she doesn't return my calls." She stopped for a moment. "We all mourn differently. She may be going through it privately."

Nina circled the park two more times. She let the conversa-tion steep. By the time she arrived back home, she felt tenderness for Lillian's need to fortify herself against feeling too deeply. Lilli-an didn't have a maternal model for showing love, or receiving it, either. Or trusting it. With Cal, yes. *She let Dad love her,* Nina thought, *and she loved him, that was clear. But who else?* Nina knew it wouldn't be easy, but she was beginning to identify a theme: maybe in her devotions, she was giving her mother what she'd been missing.

"Shower the people you love with love." The lyric from James Taylor's song was one of Cal's favorites, and he lived those words. Could she somehow reframe her dedication to Lillian to fit this way? It made her hopeful to remember that Cori's screaming, knock-down fights with her mother dissolved as soon as Lulu's short-term memory evaporated. Crossing her fingers, she grabbed a glass of water at the kitchen sink, then made her way outside to the swing in front to give her mother a call. A call in the spirit of love.

Which is when Lillian's marimba ringtone clanged. Nina answered, steeling herself.

"Mom?"

"Nina, sweetheart. When are you coming to visit? I miss you so much."

CHAPTER FIFTY

NINA

What did crows do before there were telephone wires? Nina wondered as she looked up to see a murder of them punctuating the sky in a neat row, a line of ellipses, balancing with unthinking agility. Maybe not a murder. Might a dozen crows be a manslaughter?

The sun was as high as it would get, but Nina was weighted down from news she and Myles received about a neighbor who was now in hospice. He was a remarkable human, barely fifty, but he lived better and more exuberantly than both of them combined. His wife's four-year-long caregiving abyss made managing Lillian's life look easy by comparison.

Nina decided to walk.

She and Mingus followed the shade. Block after block, they moved at a senior Scottie's pace from one stand of trees to the next, appreciating a canopy of London planes followed by cool relief offered by deodar cedars. The liquid ambers were still heavy with foliage this time of August, still too early for their spiraling seedpods to rain from overhead.

From a sun-bleached intersection to a sidewalk dappled with welcoming shadows, a yard came into view with an estate sale sign staked near the curb. The space between the house and the sidewalk had been filled with detritus from a lifetime: wire VHS holders, a sagging couch, two maple bedstands dark with age, a console with accordion doors that once held a stereo, a cardboard box overflowing with extension cords and cables, a standing lamp with a yellowed shade. Two walkers.

Nina spotted a simple chair. A steel skeleton held its sturdy seat in place, but the arms drew her to it. She'd been slowly replacing her mother's Danish modern chairs with clunky armed chairs for steadier transitions. A man perched nearby on a worn barstool between two others, sipping from an aluminum can. He watched peripherally as she lifted a coat draped over the back of the chair. She asked to try out the chair with the armrests. "I need to feel how solid it is," she told him.

He nodded, stood, and amenably pulled the chair off the grass to place on the concrete driveway. Nina sat. It didn't matter that it was upholstered in cheap, shiny vinyl. It was perfect.

"It's for my ninety-three-year-old mother," she said. "How much?"

"My father made it to ninety-five," he said. "He passed away a month ago."

"I'm so sorry."

"He lived long."

"I recently heard someone say a long life is a finished life," Nina remembered out loud.

"Well," the man said, "I've been supporting both of my parents for some time. My dad lasted the longest. I say to myself—and I say out loud—that I like to think I helped them to the finish line."

Nina blinked twice. "You were a good son."

"I would like to donate the chair to your mother." He said it formally, then introduced himself. "I'm John. "

Nina rushed Mingus home as much as he could be rushed. At the house, she wrote a quick thank-you note addressed to "John," jumped back in the car, and drove the few blocks to the house where the chair sat waiting. After hurried parking with one wheel over the sidewalk, she saw John at the curb with the chair, ready to load it into her car. As he laid it on its back, she noticed, close up, that the underside of the chair was full of cobwebs. She caught herself. She would clean it at home. She also knew she would paint it turquoise.

With the chair loaded, Nina handed John her thank-you note. He stood in the street, quiet.

"I'm a little lost," he said. "It's a new feeling, having no parents."

She stepped toward him, not asking, and opened her arms. When they let go, they both wiped their eyes.

Chapter Fifty-One

NINA

Lillian opened the door and greeted her daughter at the door with open arms.

"Darling! Can you take me swimming? I already have my suit on." She lifted her muumuu so Nina had full view of her mother's idea of a swimsuit: a top faded from seasons of chlorine and a pair of gym shorts sagging from a loose elastic waistband.

After unloading the car and filling the fridge, Nina helped Lillian out to the car and then dropped her off at the Y. Before she'd driven the distance of a block, Lillian's ringtone marimba'd. Nina pushed the phone button on the car's console.

"Mom?"

"Dear, I left my snorkel at home. Can you bring it?"

"Of course," Nina said. "Where is it?"

"It's in the oven," her mother answered.

Of course it is.

When Nina returned to hand off the snorkel, lukewarm, her mother headed back to the dressing area. This might be a good time, Nina thought, to speak with the director to make sure her contact information was listed for emergencies.

"Yes, we have your contact information," the director said after scrolling down her monitor.

Was it her imagination, or did the director's voice sound cold? Cordial, yes, but cold.

"We were… concerned about your mother driving her car… when that blow-out occurred in the parking lot."

Nina flushed. "That was so awful. She isn't driving now."

"And…" the director seemed about to bring something up just as an employee tapped her on the shoulder.

"Excuse me," the director said, now in a rush, "I'm needed in the weight room. But," she nodded, "Lillian's contact information is up to date." She led the way out of the reception area with the employee following her.

Until now, Nina hadn't really considered how she might appear to staff. They saw her mother several days every week, but for a moment, she wondered. Was it wrong for her to casually drop off a ninety-three-year-old mother? Should she be holding her hand and guiding her to the dressing area? Staying to watch her while she pulled the elastic tighter on her swim shorts? No. She had con-sciously chosen to leave Lillian alone in her swim world. It was one of those few areas of her mother's life where Lillian maintained confidence navigating on her own. Her actions at the pool were embedded in her muscle memory. Nina had become so inserted in Lillian's affairs that this seemed one area to leave alone. But how did it look to others?

Nina headed back to Lillian's house. She wondered if more than anything this hands-off approach was less about Lillian than her own need for an occasional break. A convenience. But put in these terms, her all-consuming involvement in Lillian's life was, after all, a *complete* inconvenience. No. Her mother handling her own swim life was a win-win.

I should relax about this.

When Nina pulled into the driveway, she completed her unloading, including the chair. She'd sprayed the frame with turquoise Rust-Oleum, and as she placed it at the head of the dining room table, she wondered if her mother would even notice it.

A few steps away, she surveyed the kitchen. Where to begin? The decaying fruit in the corner by the window? The gnats hovering over the compost container? The unwashed dishes collecting in the sink? As usual, several stacks of mail, opened and unopened, filled the island counter.

While she had put out feelers to locate a cleaning service, nothing was yet in place, most of all, approaching her mother about it. She knew Lillian would resist anyone coming into the house, but Nina resolved to stop spending her visits cleaning bathrooms and repairing aging window screens. Instead, she would arrange to pay someone, an expense she knew her mother could afford. This way, they could actually enjoy time together. Go on a drive to Mt. Umanum. Visit the coast for a day. *She won't like it, but if Mom wants to stay in her house, this is how we do it.* For now, it was up to her to just clean the damn kitchen. She began with the perishable food long past rescuing. After hoisting the compost container with one hand and balancing the garbage in the other, she headed out to the bins on the side of the driveway.

"Nina!"

"Freda, how are things?"

Freda gestured toward her apartment. "Can you look at my toilet?" she asked. "There's a leak around the base."

"I'll get someone out."

The papers came next. Lillian expected Nina to comb through everything and shred duplicate requests for money, and it relieved Nina to do so. It was a quick matter to separate redundant mailings from organizations her mother didn't recognize. Some months before, Nina sat with Lillian to cull her contributions:

"Narrow it down to two or three to help the environment, two or three for social justice, to support veterans, universal healthcare, Black Lives Matter, etcetera, etcetera."

Nina picked up a note paperclipped with an APS business card. Adult Protective Services. The handwritten note read, "Sorry we missed you. We'll be by again soon. Call us if you need help." *What?*

This appeared to be benign, but how could she be sure? Her experience with Child Protective Services during her decades of teaching signaled otherwise. As a public educator, she was a mandatory reporter, and after any call she'd made to CPS, she'd known that a family would be startled by a surprise visit. Since the closing sentence in this message said an APS worker would be coming by to visit, the letter lessened any surprise. Either way, one thing was clear: her mother would have gotten a notice from APS only if someone reported a concern to the agency.

Nina's heartbeat quickened. She thought again about the YMCA and that vibe from the director. Would *she* have contacted APS? Stepping away from herself again, Nina tried to see her actions as the director might interpret them. The variety of drivers dropping her mother off; Lillian bumming rides from Y members on their way out... and, glaringly, the hitchhiking incident. Didn't look good. Then she paused. What if it *wasn't* the director of the Y? Who else might be seeing Nina through a suspicious lens? Nat from the peace vigil? Someone from the book club? Her swim friend Siti?

It wouldn't be Freda. What about Mr. "what can I do you for?" across the street?

Her thoughts were interrupted by upbeat marimba tones. Time to pick up Lillian.

Nina parked, Lillian's placard dangling from the rear-view mirror. She walked into the lobby, making a show to anyone who might be watching of herself as a good daughter. Lillian looked up from the new swim schedule, smiling.

"Dear!" She said, slowly rising to give Nina a hug.

See that, YMCA staff? Do you see she wants to see me? Nina resisted the temptation to glance toward reception.

After she secured Lillian's seatbelt and lowered the windows, Nina took a breath.

"Mom, did Adult Protective Services visit you?"

Lillian didn't have her hearing aids in.

Nina raised her voice while moving from park to reverse. "DID ADULT PROTECTIVE SERVICES VISIT YOU?"

A woman climbing out of the car next to them looked over.

"Everything okay?" she asked. She was pointedly polite, her eyes on Lillian.

Lillian didn't notice. "I'm sorry, dear," she said to Nina, "I'm not sure what you're asking."

Nina shook her head and motioned to her ears. She also leaned toward her mother's open window to address the concerned woman. "We're okay," she smiled. "Thank you for your concern." She pressed the button for the windows to glide closed.

Lillian reached into the swim kit to pull out the hearing aids and insert them.

"Try now," she smiled.

"Did Adult Protective Services visit you?"

"Adult Protective Services? What is that? Kaiser?"

Nina shook her head again. "Not Kaiser. I'll show you the note I found when we get home."

While Lillian waited for Nina to unlock the front door, she shook her head. "I don't know why you lock it." Lillian hung up her Cuban towel (a great conversation starter in the locker room) over the walk-in tub. Nina washed blueberries and chopped up a large Fuji apple to mix in with plain yogurt sprinkled with flax seed. They sat side-by-side on the newly cleared counter. Nina put her spoon down to reach into the basket where she'd placed the APS business card and note.

"This, Mom."

Lillian took it with her free hand and reached for her reading glasses with the other.

"Oh, I thought it must be a scam. I wanted you to look at it."

"You are very well trained," Nina said. "Someone very skilled must be guiding you."

They both laughed.

"But, still, did APS visit you here?"

Lillian's eyes seemed to glaze. "I don't know, dear. They may have."

Lillian's memory had become so unreliable that Nina expected she'd never know for sure. But one thing was certain. Someone was watching them.

CHAPTER FIFTY-TWO

LILLIAN

Lillian shifted in her chair, stiff from being in the same position for who knew how long? It was a comfortable seat, she conceded, and she appreciated the calligraphy Nina had painted onto the frame. It was her favorite Margaret Mead quote.

The bells jingled. Nina and Myles opened the front door, lugging in suitcases and a cooler filled with groceries. Lillian rose in surprise, leaving open *The Promise*, a post-apartheid novel about a white South African family clinging to their privileged past. Once standing, she surveyed the luggage filling the entry.

"I'm thrilled! Looks like you're staying for a long time!" She held open her arms and allowed herself to be enveloped by Myles, his bearded chin resting on top of her head.

"Son-in-love!" she murmured. "I'm so lucky!"

"I'm the lucky one," he said back to her. "Even luckier than Brooks Pounders, who pitches for the Angels." He let go, and Lillian, giggling, made her way to Nina, who gave her a gentle hug, too.

"I mean it, Nina. You have so much here it looks like you're planning to stay a week!"

Nina asked her if she remembered that their visit was written in her calendar.

"Oh, I don't know. I can check," Lillian said.

Nina told her never mind. They had packed for just one night in Los Gatos and then had reservations for three days at Asilomar on the coast. And they'd swing by Lillian's on their way back to Sacramento.

Lillian fleetingly thought it would have been nice to be included, but at least she had Nina and Myles with her for a little while, before and after. Maybe she missed these details when she looked at the calendar. This happened now and then. Sometimes, she thought, she was even looking at the wrong month! She didn't dwell on this; she didn't want to focus on something that had to do with her memory. It was manageable for her, but Nina doubtless would overreact to it.

"Where's my grand dog?"

Myles had deposited the suitcases in the back room and was back to help Nina unload the groceries. "Mingus sends his deepest regrets," he said. "He's at a conference in Glasgow."

Lillian laughed. Like Cal, Myles always kept a straight face.

"Mingus had a hard time deciding between this conference and the one on Scottish independence. Yeah… registered for a talk on 'Kilts As Regional Symbols.'"

Lillian giggled, stepping back to make room for Myles to enter. Just then, her slipper caught. Twisting, Lillian veered in slow motion and off-kilter onto the low, hard table. Her right arm slammed into the leaf, and she crumpled to the cold tile.

"My arm! My arm!"

Myles perched, not touching her.

"Oh, my arm!" Lillian heard someone's voice scream.

"Mom, we're here," she heard Nina softly say.

Lillian couldn't ascertain what had happened. Only pain. When Nina suggested she go to the Emergency Room, Lillian shook her head. "No." The ER was the last place she wanted to go. But then she moved her right arm.

"Oh!" She went dizzy. Nausea swept through her body. So much pain. "Yes," she said. It came out as a whimper. "Yes, that's a good idea."

The trip to Kaiser was agonizing. The necessity of cradling her pained-to-the-touch arm made everything harder: getting into the car, getting out, moving into the hospital-provided wheelchair, waiting for her name to be called.

Shivering on the exam table, Lillian moaned. "I'm freezing." The ruana Nina wrapped around her was not enough.

Thankfully, her daughter was permitted to come into the exam room. She immediately asked the nurse for a blanket.

Many of the medical staff's questions were answered by Nina, followed by a nod from Lillian. While Lillian's arm was X-rayed, Nina told her she'd text Myles so he could pick up the prescription painkillers. That way, she said, they could get home sooner.

The doctor relayed the X-ray results.

"Your arm is fractured in several places, Mrs. Nearing. It will take time to heal, but we'll know more specifics after you see the orthopedist," he began. "I've written a prescription for pain meds." He offered suggestions on how to cope while she had to wait for the next appointment. "Don't put pressure or weight on your arm," he said. Lillian, given an ice pack and her discharge papers, thanked the ER physician.

"You are so gentle, and you really listened. We need more doctors like you," she said.

He smiled. "That means a lot to me, especially coming from someone who is in pain. You're a trooper, Mrs. Nearing."

"Oh, please call me Lilly," she said. "I want to get this arm taken care of as soon as possible so I can get back to swimming."

The doctor's eyes widened as he seemed to perceive this ninety-two-year-old with more appreciation. "Swimming?"

"I swim five days a week," Lillian said. "It's meditation in motion."

The doctor shook her good hand and assured her that her team supported the same goal. "You are somebody special, Lilly."

She managed to smile as the doctor stood up to leave. "You might want to join me on my tour to Cuba."

The doctor stopped with his hand on the door and turned. "Cuba?" Lillian noticed he looked at Nina, who shrugged.

"Be well, Lilly."

Lillian watched Nina take in all the practical details—noting the administration of the pain meds and the follow-up appointment with the orthopedist, which was when Lillian would either be given a cast or a sling. When Myles returned from the pharmacy, Lillian swallowed the first dose.

"I'm exhausted." Utterly drained, she wanted only to get home.

She slept ten hours straight, apart from waking up once for Nina to give her another pill. When she opened her eyes again, it was the bright light of a new day. Freda was sitting by her.

"Good morning, Sunshine," Freda leaned toward her. "How are you feeling?"

Lillian winced as she leaned on her right arm for an instant. Pain flooded back. "Where's Nina?"

Freda looked back at her. "Myles had to take her to the ER half an hour ago. She had a migraine, and it was so bad she went in to get hydrated."

"Oh!" Lillian's eyes sprung tears. "She's got a migraine. It was because of me."

Freda assured her that none of this was Lillian's fault. Myles had already canceled the reservations on the coast, and as soon as Nina was discharged and she had located someone to look after Lillian, they'd be heading back home.

"Someone to look after me? They're leaving?" She scowled.

"They'll talk to you when they come back to check on you and get their things. But Nina was up early this morning to locate a skilled caregiver for you. Later today you will be meeting someone named Moli who will be with you as you recover from the broken arm."

"Broken? Who is Moli?"

Freda had the background. "Nina's friend Cori worked with Moli when her own mother needed help. She comes highly recommended."

Lillian sighed. This was not good. She did not want a stranger in her house. But something spoke to her. Her arm. What a mess. She was old. She didn't think she needed help, but Nina clearly thought she did. And Nina, well. Nina's health was paying a price now for supporting Lillian's increasing needs. She was going to have to accept this stranger in her house. For Nina's sake, for her own. At least for her arm. She was determined for it to heal. She needed to swim again and to live independently. For the time being, she'd grin and bear it. Maybe not grin. Just bear.

T HE S WIM G ROUP

The white Mercedes approached and came to a stop. The back passenger door opened from the inside, and Lien climbed in.

Ever since the swim friends discovered a shared appreciation for flower arranging and bonsai, they scheduled outings each season. In June, they'd driven to the de Young Museum in San Francisco to attend the Bouquets to Art exhibit. During the drive home they talked about attending the bonsai event held every fall in Redwood City at the Senior Center. Today was its scheduled opening.

From the driver's seat, Siti turned around to greet Lien. "So strange not to be picking up Lilly."

"Yes," Lien agreed, "Lilly loves this. What a disappointment for her to miss it this year."

"She's the one who introduced it to us," Shirley reminded them.

"How is her arm now?" Mary joined in. While Mary had shared lanes at the pool over the years it was only after Rita died that she became part of the group.

"Well," Siti said as she pulled from the curb, "she is not happy with the caregiver her daughter hired."

"I can imagine it might be hard to please her," Lien said.

"Really?" Mary looked surprised. "Lilly always seems so nice."

"She has her moments," Shirley said. "Did I ever tell you how we first encountered each other?"

Siti laughed from the driver's seat. She knew the story.

Wasting no time, Shirley launched into it. "I was swimming in the middle lane—I hadn't been at the Y very long and you know, it takes a minute to adapt to any pool culture. I was sharing a lane with one swimmer, and then a third joined us. It was crowded but everyone was managing fine, all circling the same direction, of course. But then one swimmer passed me. I kicked whoever it was, by accident. I felt badly, but we all just kept going, and honestly, I forgot about it."

"Here it comes," Lien said.

"So afterward," Shirley continued, "I was toweling off in the locker room when Lien introduced me to Lilly."

"And what did Lilly say?"

"She said, 'Oh believe me, we've met.' I was confused. 'Really?' I asked. And that's when Lilly pointed to her black and blue thigh."

"That's funny," Mary giggled. "I've never seen her like that."

"Oh, she can take care of herself, that Lillian."

"But now? Her broken arm? How did she break it?" Mary asked. "Doesn't she have family to help her?"

"No one close by that I know of," Lien said, who shared a look with Shirley. "She has a daughter but she doesn't live around here."

Siti had one hand on the wheel and reached for her sunglasses hooked to the visor. "Her daughter supposedly helps her, but..." she paused. "Sometimes I wonder."

"What do you mean?"

"Sometimes I'm not sure her daughter has Lilly's best interests in mind. You remember about that check? And, you know, she was… *there*… when Lilly broke her arm."

"She was?" Shirley didn't know.

"What are you suggesting?" Lien said.

"Shouldn't she be *safer* when her daughter is visiting?" Siti left it as a rhetorical question. "I need to concentrate; the exit is coming up."

CHAPTER FIFTY-FOUR

NINA

"Your mother doesn't want me here," Moli's voice rushed over the phone, unusual for her relaxed Fijian self. "She has been verbally abusive. Again. I'm sorry, Nina, I cannot continue."

Everything blurred like an over-exposed photograph: too bright. Her ideas bounced wildly as she brainstormed. What options? Her mother could no longer be alone but since her arm healed, she didn't believe it. She certainly was never going to accept paying someone to be in her home all day. How impossible was this?

The phone rang; Lauren's name danced across the screen. Lauren was a family friend she and Myles saw at Thanksgiving and Christmas. An elegant woman who had married Mac, the son of Tanzanian friends of Cal and Lillian's. In addition to their commitment to high-level professions in Silicon Valley, Lauren and Mac were raising two beautiful teenagers.

"How are you, Nina?" Lauren sounded characteristically cheery. Nina burst.

"Nina, oh, Nina, what's wrong?"

She caught her breath and then related Lillian's recent events haltingly, including her cognitive decline and broken arm and the need to always have someone home with her.

"And now Moli is leaving because Mom raged at her." Nina's ears started ringing. *What now?* Who could step in when Mom wanted no one in her house? When she hadn't absorbed that she was a danger to herself?

"I'll take her to lunch every Monday."

"What?"

"Yes, put me in the calendar for 12:30, every Monday. She can get her swim in. I'll be there! I can do it."

Nina felt overcome. She couldn't respond. Lauren hadn't hesitated for a second. She didn't ask for time to think about it or even check her schedule. She just volunteered without a moment of deliberation.

"This is love, Lauren. You don't know how much this means." Marveling, she ended the call and stepped off the walking path to text Jenny.

"Can u talk?"

Jenny immediately called back. "What's going on?"

The words eked out as she explained first the latest development with Moli and then her phone call with Lauren. "I just don't know what to do, long term. I mean, there are other caregivers in Moli's network, but Mom isn't going to treat them any better."

"I feel terrible being this far away," Jenny interrupted. "I can't even fly to California to give you a break. I'm just not comfortable with this latest surge. But you know what? There are things I can do from Chicago. Like anything online."

"Oh..." Jenny *could* help from a distance. It was a breakthrough, like when Nina reached out to Dessa. They went back and forth, then, "Maybe you could order things online. Or set up Lyft rides?"

"I think so," Jenny said. "And maybe the boys will help, too."

Permission to involve her nephews? Lillian's grandsons? Wow.

Jenny asked about Lillian's friends. "Could any of them visit at least some of the time? Like Lauren?" She brought up Freda, Lillian's long-time tenant in the apartment attached to the house. "You think she might be interested in something... daily? She lives right there. She's retired and seems to be home a lot, right? You could actually pay her. You know, without Mom knowing."

After her financial advisor had finally persuaded Lillian to name Nina her Power of Attorney ("She said I should make important decisions like this while I'm of sound mind," Lillian related to Nina after an annual review), everything she now managed for her mother was out in the open. However, Lillian had little sense of the cost of anything, so there were things she dug in her heels about, like the cost of a Lyft to the peace vigil, and the cost of routine yard maintenance. She didn't like spending any money... unless it was to the American Civil Liberties Union or NAACP or Prison Radio or Natural Resources Defense Fund.

But maybe Jenny was onto something. Freda did live right there on the premises. She was a known entity to Lillian. She could probably use the money.

"And if she needs time off, maybe that's when Mom's friends might be able to spell her. Can you talk to any of them?"

"The friends who don't even know who I am? Or you? Like Siti? I've heard her on speaker when she calls. She thinks we are completely selfish and distant—like we don't do anything for Mom and leave her alone in the house."

"Exactly why you need to talk to them. You told me Myles suggested this a while back, and it's truer now than it was then. They need to be included in the loop. They need to understand what is going on, so they can be helpful to you. They're Mom's friends. They'll *want* to help."

"Maybe," Nina wondered, "and after I speak with them, maybe the boys could help with scheduling that sort of thing with her friends—something they could do from a distance."

Still another breakthrough.

At the top of the call list was Freda.

"What's up, Nina? You got the rent check, right?"

"Oh, right on time, as usual. No, I'm calling about something else. I have a proposition." She laid out her plan: if Freda, already a frequent visitor in Lillian's home, could be more intentional about monitoring Lillian's daily life, especially now with Lillian's arm mostly mended, and commit to several points Nina bulleted:

- Drive back and forth to swimming three days a week
- Check Lillian's pill dispenser to insure she takes her blood pressure meds every day
- Ensure her hearing aids and phone are charged every night...

If Freda were open to this ("Take your time to think about it.") Nina proposed an arrangement that would allow Freda to live rent-free.

"I don't need to think about it," Freda said cheerfully. "I'm already over there all of the time. Let's do it."

One down, four to go.

"Siti?" Nina had her mother's swim friend on the phone.

"Yes, who is this?"

"Nina, Lillian's daughter. Is this a good time to talk?"

Siti, who normally cascaded into non-stop chatter, listened as Nina explained that since the pandemic started, she had been driving down every week for the day and that since vaccinations, she spent three or four days every couple of weeks with her mother.

"I didn't know that," Siti said. "She never mentioned you."

Nina shared her observations about Lillian's short-term memory, about her getting lost while driving, about the tire blow-out just outside the Y, and most recently about Lillian's broken arm.

"Really?" Siti sounded surprised. "I knew about her arm, but I didn't know about her blow-out."

Nina paused. She was trying to stay matter of fact. She expressed how anguishing it was to see her mother so diminished, but also how painful it was to open up about it to her friends. "I've wanted to protect her dignity," Nina blew her nose. "I probably should've called you sooner, but it would have made her decline... more real. I just haven't wanted to face it."

Siti's voice cracked. "Nina, I'm glad you called me. Most of the time, you know, Lillian seems so sharp, so when she tells me you took her car..." and here she paused for a moment, waiting, perhaps, for a response from Nina, "...and she never mentions that you visit... I have been feeling protective of her. I worried that she was being neglected. Especially when she said she'd broken her arm at home."

Nina shared the whole drama of the car, and of the fall that led to the broken arm. "Now I'm trying to get some supports in place. It's why I'm calling you."

The phone call ended with Siti offering that once Lillian's arm was completely healed, she could be a backup to take Lillian swimming and let other swim friends know. She would encourage them to be more vigilant. After she gave Nina her house cleaner's phone number she said, "You know I may be able to drive her to other things. Doesn't she go somewhere every Friday? Bingo?"

Nina suppressed a laugh. Siti's friendship with Mom was clearly limited if she thought Lillian played Bingo.

Next on the call list was Nat from the peace vigil. After leaving him a message it took several days for him to return the call. He was not as receptive as Siti had been. "Who reported Lillian to the DMV?" he asked, his tone contentious.

"That was her doctor," Nina replied, struggling to stay calm. "She told Mom that when she judged her reflexive capacity to be compromised, she was legally obligated to report her."

"You know, Lillian thought that was a scam letter," Nat said. "She asked me to find her another Prius to buy. I would never have spent the time tracking down cars that if I knew about a license suspension."

Nina took a breath and exhaled. "This is one reason I am making this agonizing call." Lillian's friends were all younger. They needed to know the truth. Their fellow activist's cognition was unreliable; it colored her requests. And her moments of clarity confused things further. "You spend a couple of hours with her once a week, right?"

Nat grunted.

"In that short amount of time, it's easy to perceive only her characteristically sharp self. You need more time to notice her memory issues."

Silence.

"It took me a very long time to understand what was happening," Nina continued. "Even as I observed her forgetting how to do various things, and, for example, her surprise at my long-planned for visits, I excused it and equated it to my own lapses..."

"I'm going to be direct," Nat said. "Did you sell the car?"

Nina explained how Myles had prepared the car for sale and as a result, gotten an excellent price.

"And the money? Where is it?"

Wow. Nina's face got hot. "We deposited it into her checking account. She knows she has plenty of Lyft money now."

"That's not what she says."

"This is why I am asking for your help, Nat."

Over the line, Nat coughed and spat. "She says she has no checkbook. She says you're trying to control everything in her life."

"Actually," Nina sighed, "I'm trying to support her independence as much as possible," and, hearing silence, "while protecting her. And by the way, all her transactions register on her bank statements."

More silence, then, "Why are you calling me?"

"For your help." Nina worked at keeping her voice level. "I will arrange a driver to take her to the vigil and pick her up, but I wanted to know if you could make sure she gets out of the Lyft safely? And, after the vigil ends, help her into the Lyft?" Nina hesitated for a moment but added another request. "If you notice anything concerning, can you please let me know?" She gave him her text number and email address. "I deeply appreciate this. And please let the other vigilers know about this conversation."

An undecipherable mutter before he hung up left Nina unnerved. She decided to call Lien. She attended the vigil every week but also swam at the Y and was one of Lillian's swim lunch group.

By the time Nina got on the phone with her, Lien had already gotten a call from Siti.

"Oh, I'm on board, Nina. I'm all in. You call me if you need anything for Lillian, understand?"

It was a relief to have covered bases with Freda, the swim group, the vigilers, and now, finally, it was time to contact the book group.

Marva's name seemed to come up most often when Lillian talked about her book discussions, so Nina found her number on the book club's address list.

"Marva, this is Nina, Lillian's daughter."

"Oh, Nina, hello. Is everything all right?"

"Yes, yes, things are okay," Nina tried to keep her voice even, "but since you and the others in the book club see her regularly, I thought it was time for me to introduce myself and to let you know how to get in touch with me… if there is any reason you're alarmed. You know, I live in Sacramento…"

"Excuse me," Marva interrupted, "do you ever visit your mother? I worry about that."

Nina repeated to Marva what she'd explained to Siti, Nat, and Lien. Marva was quiet for a moment before she spoke. "Shira left me a text message to call her about Lillian, but you called before I had a chance to respond. You know, she attends the peace vigil now with Lillian."

"I didn't know," Nina said. Her mother, the influencer.

Marva sounded thoughtful. "I'm glad you called, Nina. I hope we meet. I will relay to the others what you've explained. We honestly have all been concerned. Your mother is very dear to us." She invited Nina to call her in the future "for any reason."

With the calls behind her, Nina's shoulders loosened. While she thought it was disloyal of her to expose Lillian's vulnerabilities to her friends, the relief was overwhelming. *Finally, I have some allies.*

Team Lillian.

CHAPTER FIFTY-FIVE

NINA

Nina's desk was laden with sheaves of rice paper and tule. She was in the middle of assembling wedding invitations for friends who were marrying after thirty years of living together.

"Elegant and simple," they agreed when they consulted with her on her backyard deck about signage and invitations. Mark and Vincente were the Visser's neighbors who lived in a Squeaky Williams Tudor revival three blocks away, a fact they often repeated. Sacramento's park neighborhoods were dotted with fairy-tale homes built by the architect known for the high pitch of his voice and his rooflines. They'd leafed enthusiastically through the portfolio of Nina's calligraphed projects. "Can you make us a logo? Use our initials and intertwine them the way the Tudors did? Almost like code?"

"What a great idea." Nina wondered why she hadn't done this before. Wait, this was essentially how she'd penned her students' yearbooks for years. Two or three initials unified with a flourish. "We can use that as a motif for your signage, your invitations, your envelopes—maybe make a stamp you can use even after the wedding."

She completed the logo and had it approved after Vincente asked to include a circular flourish originating from the right stem of his "V."

Now everything was done except for the final assembly.

As she punched holes through the folds of the linen and rice paper, grosgrain ribbon at the ready, she reflected on the latest Lillian story. Knowing Lillian missed the theater, she arranged for her to attend an August Wilson play with Marva from the book club. A few days before the performance she called Marva to let her know the tickets would be under her name at Will Call.

"Oh, Nina, I was just going to call you. I was exposed to friends who tested positive for COVID this morning. I'm so sorry."

Nina emailed and texted everyone she could think of in Lillian's universe.

A text came in from Lein of the swimming group. "If no one else has volunteered, I would love to take Lillian to the matinee."

Nina called the box office to change the name at Will Call.

The night before the performance, Lien called. "I'm at the ER. I can't believe it... and you won't believe it... but I broke my hip!"

After another last-minute flurry of emails and texts, Nina surrendered and left a message with the box office to cancel the tickets for the following day.

In the morning, her phone rang. It was Freda. She had rearranged her schedule and, if it wasn't too late, could take Lillian to the matinee.

The box office didn't open until noon, and the performance was at 2:00. Nina was breathless when she reached a live ticket agent.

"Forgive me. I hope it's not too late. I called to cancel two tickets for today's matinee but wondered if they might still be available."

"Ah, yes, Nina Visser." The ticket agent knew about Nina from his colleagues, and it was not too late. The tickets had not been resold.

"And please," Nina asked, "can you change the name at Will Call?"

The evening after the performance Freda reported that Lillian had enjoyed the day.

At that moment Nina's phone pinged with a voicemail alert, a text alert, and an alert for an incoming email.

"Nina, call me. Things are changing." Hearing from Freda wasn't unexpected.

Nina punched in the number from her favorites.

"What's wrong?"

"Oh," Freda sighed. "Your mom is okay, but... and I don't want to embarrass her so it's not something I want to bring up in front of her... but..."

"What?"

"Well, first I want to share something that happened this morning. Unrelated. I brought over a newspaper clipping of the August Wilson play. I thought she'd appreciate it."

"Nice."

"Well... she asked me why I thought she'd be interested in the story. I reminded her of the matinee we attended together. You know what she said?"

"What?"

"She said she hadn't seen it, but it sounded worthwhile."

"Oh my god."

"Yes, oh my god. After all of that."

"Too much." Nina was reeling. "What's the other thing you wanted to tell me?"

"Well, I hate to have to bring this up but I don't want to be the one to confront her about her accidents. They're happening frequently now, and I don't know if she just doesn't notice, but she needs protection now and much more cleaning up. She's not swimming as often, so she's not getting that before-and-after shower, and…"

"So she needs more help than you can manage," Nina interrupted. "That it?"

"Nina, I'm sorry."

"Thank you, Freda. I appreciate you letting me know, and you've been great. It's given me and Jenny a lot of peace of mind. This is a new stage. I'm not surprised. I need to get on this as soon as possible." Nina was now understanding that her mother's changes could happen abruptly. There wasn't time to process, only to act.

Freda assured Nina that she'd keep up with the duties until someone else was in place.

Nina acknowledged the generous offer. "You're the best."

Nina glanced at her desk with her creative obligations. She swiveled so her back walled off the pleasure of her revived pastime.

She called Cori.

"The time has come," she said when her friend picked up. "I've misplaced Moli's number. Can you text me her contact info? I need to see if she'd still entertain the idea of working with Mom—after everything."

"Remember, Nina," Cori said after she sent the text, "it's possible your mother has forgotten all about their last confrontation together."

Nina was leaning into that.

Her conversation with Moli did not go as she'd hoped. Moli was already committed to a new client for twenty-four-hour care. But she gave Nina three other names of caregivers in her circle. Nina snapped to it. She learned one had retired, but over the next few days Nina played phone tag with two others. Neither were available.

"Cori," Nina called, not bothering with a nickname nor concealing her frustration. "I've hit a brick wall. None of Moli's leads have come of anything. I really don't want to go through an agency. I want someone personally referred for Mom."

"I understand exactly, believe me." Cori said she'd reach out to friends who'd also had to hire skilled caregivers in recent years. "I need to warn you again, this is not cheap."

"I know, I know. Thank god Mom didn't stop paying for her long-term health care insurance. It's not a great policy but it's definitely better than nothing." Nina ended the call, hopeful that a solution might present itself from Cori's network of friends. She closed her eyes and took some breaths. *Don't dwell in worry*, she told herself, *prepare instead. Who said that?* She wondered, then remembered a quote her father cited from Mark Twain: "I have spent most of my life worrying about things that never happened." Myles reminded her with some frequency that he shared this philosophy; that worry wastes energy. She *was* preparing: *a seed had been planted*, she told herself. But as it took root and began to grow, she needed to relax.

Opening her eyes, she swiveled to face the invitations. The paper seemed duller than a moment ago, the ribbon limp. Before her next launch into Lillian action, she needed to get this done for her friends. She had a deadline to meet for the timeline of their beautiful day.

By the time Nina had gotten to the envelopes, almost three hours had passed. This is what happened when she did lettering. Time filled a space that seemed to grow with every capitalized initial, every sweep of the nib as it completed an embellishment. She had no awareness of the light as it moved into shadow, so when her phone rang, she jolted upright.

"Hello," she said.

"Hello, Nina, it's Moli. Something… not entirely unexpected happened. My client passed. He was one hundred and three, so it is not a surprise. If you are still needing me for your mother, I am available."

"Oh!" Nina felt like she'd awakened from a dream. "Oh, yes!" she exclaimed. "I am so happy to hear this!" She fumbled. "I mean, I'm sorry about your client."

"It's okay, but thank you. It's always difficult."

"Listen," Nina began again, "I know things didn't end well with Mom last time, so I wasn't sure you'd be interested."

"I am open to trying again. Some time has passed, and Lillian's situation has changed. She may not remember the last things she said. I have been working with the elderly for almost thirty years and often have seen how cognitive changes affect behavior. Sometimes people mellow."

Mellow? Mom? Nina didn't say this out loud. "Can you come over soon so I can re-introduce you to Mom? Like we're starting over from scratch?"

"Yes."

That seed Nina had planted? Who knew she'd be harvesting it in a blink of an eye? There must be a phrase in Bartlett's that would capture this. All she could think of was, "Thank you."

CHAPTER FIFTY-SIX

LILLIAN

A melody from "Swan Lake" wafted to Lillian's spot where she read at the dining room table. She was still unaccustomed to the sound of the doorbell Freda insisted on installing.

"Why bother?" Lillian had sulked. "And why doesn't it just *ding-dong?*"

"Why bother!? Lillian," Freda scolded, "you never hear me when I knock on the front door, and you don't hear me when I ring the chimes."

Lillian placed *The Warmth of Other Suns* face-down. Had she read this already? It was a fleeting thought as she pushed back her chair. Such an exceptional book. Walking barefoot past the wall of baskets and through the kitchen, she wondered who had come by. When she opened the door, she was met by a familiar face.

"Lillian! So nice to see you!" the familiar face smiled.

Lillian cocked her head. "I know you, don't I?"

"It's Moli. Is Nina here yet?"

"Nina? I need to check my calendar but please," she gestured with an open hand toward the turquoise couch, "make yourself comfortable."

Lillian wondered about this Moli as she returned to the kitchen to locate the open calendar on the island. Unsure as to what month it was, she brought the Sierra Club planner into the living room and handed it to Moli. "Would you mind locating today's date? See if Nina is coming today."

Moli quickly located the day's date before handing the open calendar back to Lillian. Lillian turned to sit in the armchair so she could access her reading glasses. She glanced down at the date Moli had pointed to and saw at once Nina's note stating she would be driving down to visit today. It also said "Moli" but no reason for her being there.

Just then, the bells chimed, and Lillian beamed. "That must be Nina!" And before she could rise, the door opened. Sure enough, it was her daughter.

"Darling!"

"Mom! Moli! So sorry I didn't get here before you did. Lots of traffic on the Sunol Grade, yada yada," Nina waved her hands.

"It's not a problem," Moli said. "It's good to see you."

Lillian stood to open her arms for her daughter. "I'm so delighted you've come to visit!" She gave an apologetic giggle. "I'm afraid I don't quite remember Moli—well, I know we know each other but for the life of me, I can't place how."

When Nina reminded her that Moli stayed with her after she'd broken her arm, Lillian felt an uneasy flutter. She had broken her arm? She sat back down. These lapses in her memory were not anything she wanted to bring to anyone's attention. "Oh, that's it," she said. "How are you, Moli? And your family?"

While Moli shared a little about FaceTiming her family in Fiji, Nina left to assemble a tray of chocolate dunkers and put water on to boil.

Offering cookies to Moli and Lillian, who took two, Nina asked if she remembered why the three of them were meeting today. Lillian wryly shook her head. "I honestly don't. Enlighten me."

Nina set the tray down and pulled the rocker from its crowded spot between multiple chairs from an earlier era when big groups gathered in this living room. She slid closer to her mother and as she turned to sit back, her ankle clipped the runner. Her face writhed for a split second.

"What is it dear?" Lillian leaned toward her.

Nina let out an exhale, appearing to try to smile. "My ankle caught." She shifted away from Lillian's concern. "Do you remember the promise I made to you that I would do everything to support you staying in your home for the rest of your life?"

"Absolutely. That is absolutely what I want." Lillian's voice was resolute. "You're keeping that promise!"

"Moli is part of the promise, Mom," Nina said. "As you become less young, we…"

"Who do you mean by 'we?'" Lillian interrupted.

"Jenny and me, Mom. That's who 'we' is."

"*Are*," Lillian corrected.

Nina continued, "We need to ensure that you are safe and comfortable in your own home. Moli is here to help us with that. She has agreed to be here five days a week."

"I don't need any more help, dear. I already have Freda."

Moli looked over at Nina. Nina scooted even closer to Lillian. "Mom, this is part of the promise. Moli won't be here all of the time, only half days. When she's not here, Freda is still happily available for anything you may need."

The whistle of the kettle shrieked. Moli rose, "I remember where the tea is, Lillian. Let me."

With Moli in the kitchen, Lillian faced her daughter. "I feel ambushed," she said.

"You don't remember me scheduling this? Our conversation about my promise?"

Lillian shook her head. "I hate this."

"What part of this do you hate, Mom?"

From her seat Lillian scanned the shelves across from her, sagging with books. The Navajo rug covering the adjacent wall. The molas Cal had framed after their trip to Panama. The woven silk pillow covers on the turquoise couch. The woodblock print spelling out "War is unhealthy for children and all living things." Evidence of her full life embraced her in this room and every room in this house, a house she didn't ever want to leave.

"I hate that I must have someone here. That I can't be alone in my own home, that I don't have privacy, but…"

Moli came in with a tray laden with the Vietnamese teapot, three cups, and more cookies. She set everything down on the coffee table, poured the tea, set a cup down next to Lillian and then another cup by Nina.

"Thank you, Moli." Lillian felt a small surrendering inside her small frame. "How is your family in Tonga?"

Lillian thought she saw Moli stiffen. "No, Lilly. I am from Fiji."

"You are such a long way from home, Moli."

Moli nodded. "Most of my family is still there. Remember I told you I FaceTime them every day?"

Tears sprang to Lillian's eyes. "That must be very hard." She reached for Moli's hand. "When will you start coming to be with me?"

CHAPTER FIFTY-SEVEN
NINA

Back in Sacramento, Nina and Myles celebrated the Lillian and Moli reunion by sitting together at the piano to play "What a Difference a Day Makes." Myles took the bass clef and Nina the treble.

After concluding with the sustaining pedal on "and the difference is YOU," he lifted his hands. "Darlink! Time for something special. Let's go to Tower."

They walked the mile to Tower Café, their favorite Sacramento spot.

Even in November, the tree canopy over the outside tables was in full colorful leaf, and in the early dusk, the string lights cast an enchanted light among the queen palms, so tall they obscured the marquee on the theater next door. The bubbling of the fountain washed between conversations and laughter coming from the guests.

"Outside or inside?" the host asked at the podium.

"Outside," they answered in unison, then laughed. It was still kind of amazing they had a choice after the long moratorium on inside dining finally lifted. But even in the Before Times, the choice between sitting inside among the global curiosities (a collection of art from the world over) and outside, with all the gorgeous ferns, palms, and deodar cedars, was definitive for Nina and Myles. Unless it grew too cool in the winter or oppressively hot in the summer, they always opted to eat outside on the multi-level patio.

The host led them to a table squeezed between two others. Just as they were, lots of folks were returning to restaurants, so could they really complain about being too close for comfort? A multiple-generation family sat to one side, a couple in earnest conversation on the other. Once they were seated, Myles pointed to the libations section of the menu. "Should we order Champagne?" He pronounced it "Shampognay."

"Really?" Nina felt hyper-vigilant about the prices of alcohol at restaurants. Instead of ordering it with a meal, they usually enjoyed a glass of wine at home before they splurged on dinner out, but with that evening's walk, they'd hydrated with plenty of water.

"Well, there's a nice Schramsberg. Blanc de Noirs. Not Champagne, but awfully…" Myles glanced up and saw Nina's expectant eyebrow. "Well, you've liked it in the past. It's dry as those sycamore leaves we crunched through on our walk here."

"I'd like to follow your advice, monsieur sommelier. Let's decide what to eat first."

"I protest! You know very well that I first choose the *wine, then* find an entrée to pair with it."

What a goof, Nina thought.

When the server approached, Nina asked for more time to decide. "We're out of practice." Some of their favorites were no longer on the menu, so they had to devote a few minutes to studying the choices. They agreed to split the Santa Fe salmon, which Myles said would pair nicely with the Schramsberg. The sound of live Hot Club jazz filled the air from a trio that included a rhythm guitarist, a violinist, and an accordion player.

As the music swung, Myles reached across the table for Nina's hand. "We're here, aren't we? Hi."

"Hi," Nina's eyes locked with his. Then she looked around at others seated at surrounding tables. Ice tinkled against tall glasses of hibiscus tea, one of Tower's trademarks. The collective sound of excited voices ebbed and flowed across the patio, occasionally punctuated by a spirited laugh. The aroma of grilled shrimp and garlic wafted past, and a couple nearby giggled and stood up to dance to the music. One large party's table was headed by a matriarch in dreads and on the opposite end by a toddler in a highchair. When their server arrived with platters of the restaurant's signature pomme frites, everyone in the party applauded.

Nina, taking it all in, smiled and squeezed Myles's hand. "Yes. We're back."

She closed her eyes to take in the sounds and smells. She'd forgotten about this, about having fun. Things were turning around. Yes, life was opening again, and it was lovely.

CHAPTER FIFTY-EIGHT

NINA

Mingus was expensive.

Nina turned into the animal hospital to park under a shade tree. COVID protocols were still in order, so she stayed in the car with the dog. She called to let the front desk to check in.

"Just pop the back of your car; a tech is on his way."

The appointment was routine at this point: an annual test to see if the dog's heart murmur had changed. Waiting in the shade gave Nina a chance to think.

Moli was expensive, too. There was no question that her service to Lillian was invaluable. And really, for this skilled work, and to have someone trusted spend time with her mother in her home? It was a bargain—she couldn't fairly characterize it as expensive. It's just that it added up fast. Thank god Lillian and Cal had been paying for long-term health care insurance all of these years. And to think that Lillian had almost stopped paying the premium.

"I'm not going to need this, Nina. I am not going to live much longer. I will just stop eating, and that will be it. I don't…"

Nina grabbed the bill out of her mother's grip. "We've been through this. If you don't pay this bill, Jenny and I will have to."

Lillian had shaken her head. "It's a racket. They're mobsters, I'm sure of it. They made everything so hard when I had to file claims for Dad."

Nina clearly remembered her mother's struggles with the paperwork and her raging phone calls with the insurance company. "Yes, it was brutal, but in the end, it significantly helped bring the cost down for Dad's care."

"You deal with the mob, then."

Nina didn't love this kind of thing either. Who does? But now that it was her turn to file a claim, she appreciated the insurance dividend. Thank goodness Lillian hadn't just recycled the bill.

A knock on her hatchback window startled her. The vet tech was waiting.

"All done!" He said from the back, a bit muffled by his mask. "We'll call you soon with any updates."

Later, after Nina pulled into the driveway, she opened the back gate for the dog. The Chinese elm, its elephantine limbs shaggy with yellow leaves, towered over the yard. She took in their urban forest with renewed gratitude.

Since Myles actively taught in the front of the house, she headed directly to her office so she could start her mother's claim. Down the hall, the squeak of a cello informed her that this might be Myles's new student.

"Nice," she heard Myles say. "Let's start again in first position."

Pushing open the office door, she made her way to the desk where she'd stacked the insurance forms.

Maybe my experience with the insurance company will be easy. Maybe Mom's intense dislike of bureaucracy made it even harder than it needed to be. Maybe her deep distrust of insurance companies set her up for frustration.

Maybe it will be different for me if I… approach it with a different expectation. She nodded, optimistic.

Two hours passed while she waited on hold, during which she relocated to the kitchen to unload the dishwasher, then outside to deep water the Modesto ash in the front, and then to soak the Scotch moss at the base of their olive tree. The on-hold music stopped abruptly mid-saxophone.

"We're here to serve. Thank you for your loyalty, and how can we help?" Just as the representative answered, the phone pinged with another call. It was the vet's number. Nina couldn't risk losing the insurance rep, so she scribbled a note to call the vet as soon as she was finished.

The agent coached her on how to access the website and start the claim process.

"Next steps are all listed under the 'Filing a Claim' tab," she said, "but since you asked, I'll tell you over the phone. After the doctor examines your mother and determines her need for home care, he—"

"She," Nina said.

The agent paused. "*She* will need to send a documenting letter directly to us. We will also need a confirming letter from a nurse on your mother's doctor's staff. You'll need to hire a registered nurse to check your mother's vitals once a week. The nurse needs to submit all her credentials and identification and contact information to us, and that goes for any caregivers who will be working on your mother's behalf."

"Got it," Nina said. This didn't sound hard.

"Remember, more details are on the website but don't hesitate to call us if you have questions. We're here to serve."

Nina ended the call and called the vet.

"Sorry," she said when she got the vet's receptionist. "I was on the phone with an insurance agent and…"

"Oh god, say no more. I've emailed over that coupon for the Simparica Trio, and the doc will call you to explain the results in more detail… but he says it looks good."

Nina closed her computer, feeling a sense of relief as well as accomplishment. When she'd called the insurance company to speak with a human, she was not surprised to be put on hold, and in the end, she'd found the agent responsive and friendly. She had easily filed the initial claim on the insurance company's portal. She understood the next steps.

So far, so good.

All seemed right in the world.

CHAPTER FIFTY-NINE

NINA

That sense that all was right in the world—her world, at least—held. With Moli caring for her mother during the week and Freda there on weekends, Nina could finally breathe and carve out time for herself.

This morning, Myles didn't wake her. When she opened her eyes and turned to his side of the bed she saw he was up, and then, as her senses came into the world, the quiet around her reminded her that last night he'd said he'd be going to the gym first thing. She would be alone. What a delicious thought. She peeled away the sheets and coverlet and padded to the bathroom, immediately noting the sticky note Myles left her on the mirror. "Mingus ate. Gone to gym, then Home Depot. Back by 1:00."

The shutters were still closed. She angled some of them to bring in the sight of the Burgundy Belle's deep red leaves and the Japanese maple's delicate gold. Sacramento's falls provided splendid colors.

She sipped hot mint tea while she waited for half a sesame seed bagel to toast and looked through the back window. Mingus lay on the deck, regal as ever. Of course, he hadn't heard her, but she expected his nose would soon inform him she was up. Amazing that his sense of smell was such that he detected food even when walls of lath and plaster stood between him and anything edible. She turned in the direction of the island separating the kitchen from the library. Seeing the leather club chair in its upright position brought a rush of anticipation and pleasure. She could sit back and read her book. No one was expecting her to do anything.

Toasted bagel in one hand, steaming cup of tea in the other, she set both down beside the recliner and walked back to the bedroom to retrieve a Louise Penny book from the top of a leaning stack.

She slid into the chair just as Mingus nosed through the dog door to join her. Nina smiled as she thought of one her father's favorite Groucho Marx quotes: "Outside of a book, a dog is man's best friend. Inside of a dog, it's too dark to read." Once reclined with her feet up, she opened the novel, and before she reached the end of the third page, her eyes closed.

A ramming from the front of the house shocked her awake.

More pounding, combined now with the doorbell and... a bullhorn?

Nina jumped from the chair, knocking over her half-empty cup as she clipped Mingus at her feet. Tracking tea across the hardwood, she tightened the robe around her on her rush through the living room and past the plantation shutters. Shadowy figures showed through the slats.

She swung open the peek-hole to peer through it and the screen of the outer security door.

"Police!"

A uniformed woman stood on the front doorstep. Her name-plate and badge shone visibly in the late afternoon light, but Nina's attention froze in the lenses of the woman's brown eyes.

"Can I help you?"

"Nina Visser?"

"Yes, I'm Nina Visser." *Was it Myles? Her mother?*

The female official motioned to the front door. "We have a warrant for your arrest."

"I'm sorry? What's going on?"

"The Sacramento County Sheriff's Office is engaged in an investigation initiated in Santa Clara County around the welfare of Lillian Nearing."

"My mother!"

"You are under arrest, Ms. Visser."

"Is she okay?"

The officer appeared to incrementally soften. "This is why we're here. We're concerned about her safely and security. The District Attorney's enlisted our unit to investigate an allegation of financial impropriety against Lillian Nearing. There is a charge of elder abuse, Cal Penal Code Section 368."

"What?"

"Who handles your mother's affairs?"

"I do. I've been taking care of things since my father got sick," Nina counted in her head. "Six years, at least."

"Her money?"

"Yes," Nina said, "I have Power of Attorney." She stopped and directed her attention to the officers on the front walk, all of whom had moved closer to the front door. "Wait. You said I'm under arrest? Shouldn't I be contacting a lawyer?" The years of watching *Law and Order* never seemed applicable to real life until today. She pulled her robe closer. This was too bizarre. She had nothing to hide, but this was a dark accusation.

"You have the right to contact a lawyer, yes."

"And aren't I supposed to hear my rights?"

At this moment, Myles pulled up on the driveway, flying from the car without closing the door behind him, rushing to the front walk. Nina eyes stung as he approached the officers and moved toward her. "Is everything alright?" he quietly asked, holding her eyes with his.

"Sir," one of the officers stepped forward. "I need to ask you to stand aside." The police guided him towards the swing.

"There has been a big mistake," Nina said, as slowly and evenly as she could. "It has to do with Mom. I need to get a lawyer."

Myles's face revealed his confusion. "Lillian? Is she okay? And what? *You* need a lawyer?"

"Sir," an officer leaned forward. "I need to ask you to refrain from engaging."

Myles responded sharply, "I'm her husband," then to Nina, "I'll call Alex." Their nephew had recently completed law school. He could get her connected to someone.

By this time, the couple next door had joined a cluster of neighbors across the street. These were Nina and Myles's friends. What could they be thinking, seeing her in her pajamas this late in the day, armed police officers, patrol cars, blue and red lights flashing?

CHAPTER SIXTY

NINA

What stayed with her was the smell. The patrol car ducked into the bowels of the courthouse on I Street, and even with the vehicle's windows locked shut, a rush of stale vomit and sewage filled the air and began sinking into her pajamas. She hadn't been offered the chance to get dressed. The female officer seated next to the driver got out to open the passenger door, guiding her two-handedly as if she were a heavy object, not human. By the impersonal familiarity of the officer's touch, it was obvious she'd done this countless times. Couldn't she see that Nina did not belong here?

Outside the patrol car, her skin cells began to absorb the stench. She closed her lips into a tight line; it was worse to taste the stink than smell it.

The handcuffs chafed, and the restriction of Nina's arms and hands behind her back was unbearable. This was considered humane? Deep breathing was her go-to in stressful situations, but that smell obliterated any hope for relief. This was going to be a PTSD nightmare she'd have to work hard to forget.

Echoes of voices bounced from concrete walls to a high-sheened linoleum floor. The female officer led her to a room—a cage. It was too large to be a cell. Floor-to-ceiling steel and wire made up three of the walls. The fourth was concrete painted yellow with a door leading deeper to the basement level. Nina's neck chilled. Was she going through that door?

She was. The next room was all cinderblocks. A scuffed wood counter dominated the space, behind which another female officer sat looking through plexiglass. Standing in front of it, a security officer nodded to Nina's "guide" as she was passed off into his care. His care? His responsibility. His gun nestled visibly in its holster. Since her arrest on her front doorstep, everyone Nina had encountered was armed, but this gun drew her attention. Did they seriously consider her dangerous?

"Turn around," he said to her. "After I release your wrists, understand that you are to continue holding your hands behind you."

Nina nodded. The officer at the counter then interviewed her, typing Nina's responses. She was instructed to press and roll her right thumb onto an ink pad for prints. Then, a mug shot: Nina looked directly into the camera, then turned for her profile.

Back to the counter, the officer flatly explained the next steps.

"You will be taken into the booking area where you'll remove your jewelry and empty your pockets." *Jewelry? Right, the earrings I have on to match my flannel pajamas.* "You will remove all clothing, including your underpants." *Already halfway there.* "Bra must come off." *What bra?* "After a squat and cough, you will change into a regulation wear jumpsuit. You will remove any makeup, wigs, and eyelashes." *Makeup? Wigs? Eyelashes?* "Your clothing and all of your loose possessions will be placed in a plastic bag and kept secure until your situation is determined and whether or not you'll need to post bail and/or stay the night."

Nina flinched and felt for her wedding ring with her thumb. Would it even come off? Squat and cough? Did they really think she was a flight risk? That she was dangerous? That she belonged here? Where was the dictum "innocent until proven guilty?"

The wood-paneled, soft-carpeted courtroom was straight out of Perry Mason except for the oversized screen suspended above the judge's bench and the slender mics hanging in front of it. The judge's image was projected from his chambers onto the screen, displaying a not-to-scale handsome face and a perfunctory manner. *Like Oz*, Nina thought. She stood in front of a camera suspended from the ceiling of the wood-paneled courtroom. The judge wore expensive looking headphones, looking down, but not at Nina or the confident attorney her nephew Alex had called. Her name was Marla, and she stood at Nina's side.

"To the misdemeanor charges based on Cal Penal Code Section 368," Marla said in her rich, clear voice, "my client pleads not guilty."

The judge didn't respond and appeared to be reading something outside the frame of the screen. He then looked up for the first time.

"You're released, Ms. Visser, no bond is necessary. You must be in court on January tenth at 8:30 AM. It will be courtroom 401 on the fourth floor."

By the time she stepped out of the jail-issued orange jumpsuit and into the lesser embarrassment of her pajamas and robe, that pervasive smell of the place had lodged into the fibers. She'd been allowed a phone call from a bank of payphones. *Perry Mason*, she thought again. *What is this, the 1960s?* When she lifted the receiver, her fingers stuck. Myles picked up immediately.

"Honey?"

Nina sank into the warmth of his voice.

"I'm okay, and we'll talk when we're together. I just want to get out of here. You can pick me up inside the main entrance?" She gave him the address. "You'll go through security, and then to a counter. You'll see it. Let them know you're picking me up, and they'll call for me."

"I'll be right there."

"Oh, and honey, can you please bring me my down jacket?"

"Down jacket, yes."

She scrunched her nose at the stickiness under her palm. "And hand sanitizer?"

While she waited, shifting hard against the back of the plastic bench, she willed herself to review the day so she could immediately start compartmentalizing. This was not a memory she wanted haunting her, and she'd learned this technique worked better than simply suppressing memories that could otherwise show up unexpectedly. She forced herself to visualize the arrest on her front doorstep, stepping from the patrol car into the bowels of the courthouse, and the steps that followed. The peeling away of her identity as her clothes were confiscated, the humiliation of the squat and cough, the ringing panic in her ears, the echo of her footsteps as she followed the officer to the booking counter, the windowless holding cell with women she couldn't look at, the way she was led to the courtroom with her wrists tied behind her, the judge on the screen, her wondering what he must have thought of her and then realizing he didn't think of her at all. In his court, she was no one. She was simply a white female to process for a court date. When Nina's recall arrived at the present, she noted the silent women waiting nearby and willed herself to close a heavy door on the day. To seal it from her consciousness.

The smell that inhabited her nightmare was still with her and got in the way of her forgetting altogether. A retch from her gut propelled spew through her chest and then her throat. Nina locked her lips, searching wildly past the other waiting women to the corners of the cinderblock room. A garbage can? Anything? The bile moved fast and feral, splatting right over herself and onto the floor.

"What the fuck?" the women swore in unison, rushing to the opposite corner.

She didn't care. She'd never see those women again, and she would throw away everything she was wearing. Better, she'd burn it.

Myles finally hastened toward her through the security gate, his eyes finding hers. She reached for him and they held each other for a long moment. She hadn't warned him about the smell. He didn't appear to notice; he only held her tighter.

L I L L I A N

The phone rang into Lillian's hearing aids.

"Moli, the phone!"

Moli came into the kitchen, handing Lillian the phone.

"Help me? I can't open it."

Moli played the message.

"Mom, please call me. We need to talk." It was Nina. She sounded trembly.

Lillian shook her head. She pointed to the yellow sticky her lawyer had taped to the phone case. DON'T TALK TO NINA BEFORE MEDIATION.

"I can't remember all of the reasons for that note."

Moli nodded but said nothing.

"Bring me the calendar, please."

Lillian paged through the month. There it was, in someone else's handwriting: "December 18: Centering Mediation, Santa Clara, at 11:00 AM."

The mystery would be cleared up then. She handed the phone to Moli. "I'm not supposed to talk to her. Hang up."

Was Nina in trouble?

CHAPTER SIXTY-TWO

NINA

Jenny had been calling Nina every day since the arrest.

"Mom won't answer the phone."

"Even for you?"

"Even for me. And when I text Moli, she… wait, I'll forward her response."

It was clear the caregiver was reticent to get involved between the mother and her daughters. Her text read, "Yr mom's lawyer came to the house. Set up a mediation. Contact her."

Nina called the number in her contacts. She'd met with the attorney a few times in the past, most recently to update the Power of Attorney.

Dahlia Crenshaw-Bates answered her phone.

"Dahlia, Nina Visser here. I hope you can help me."

"Your mother is my client. We will be seeing you at mediation on the eighteenth."

"I haven't heard about this."

"You should receive the notice in the next few days."

"You can't fill me in at all? I was arrested, for god's sake!"

"I suggest you contact your own counsel. Have them contact me. I'll brief them, and then they can enlighten you. Bring your attorney to the mediation. It's for your own protection, Nina. See you then."

Nina shuddered. Cold.

NINA

"I feel like our neighborhood is a cemetery," Cori said. They'd lost a Himalayan cedar, which took out the back of their house and destroyed their garage and the roof of a neighbor.

Nina was still so shaken from her own unnatural disaster that it seemed to numb her to the catastrophic effects of the cyclone winds and rain that had torpedoed through Sacramento two days earlier.

This Tuesday morning was the first AWA meeting for Nina since the arrest.

"Well," Eleanor said, facilitating from her Zoom frame, "our two closest freeway entrances are still closed from the storm. At least we don't have to drive anywhere to write together." Even though COVID had essentially lifted, the River Rock Writers continued to meet over Zoom.

After the opening meditation, she shared the screen to read the day's opening poem.

"From one of our own," she said.

"**Winter**," Eleanor began, "by Nina Visser."

Winter knocks on my door.
Not snow, not ice, not the explosive train hauling its
    cyclone bomb,
not bitter wind, not frigid lakes spilling over freeways,
not old oaks with roots reaching for the sky,
not frozen fingers gripping roof gutters, but winter,
winter of my life.

That winter knocks on my door,
a crone there for more than a visit,
more than a borrowed cup of flour,
more than a handshake,
but instead, here to stay, lodge in my bones,
take over my eyesight, my joints, my haste, my worry, even
my ability to warm to each day when I wake to a new dust-
    ing of snow.
Another portent of old age, as winter, like dripping
    icicles, seeps in,
stiffens my body as it takes residence
in woolens and fleece, immovable steel inside soft
    outerwear,
resisting the feeling, not ready for it,
waiting for the warming red of a spring sunrise,
a warmth loosening, unbuttoning, thinning the layers,
shaking the weight for a little while,
before spring opens to summer.
The cycle presses on, but with each season,
even the warm ones,

winter encroaches,
a reminder
in my fingers
that time is passing.

I'm a crone who still has her mother,
older than me by three decades of heroism,
conservation and resistance,
questioning authority,
picketing for fair wages,
her arms sheltering the incarcerated,
the maimed, the refugeed, the undocumented.
Big compassions keep her own winter at bay.

She says she does it so her children
may inhabit a better world—

but her arms don't have room for warming me.

Like winter days, hers shorten, as do mine.
I finger a quilt, add another layer over her as she sleeps,
crawl in beside her,
something soft about it,
two crones touching toes,
a daughter, awake,
a mother asleep.

Hearing another voice read the poem shook her. She scrawled responses to Eleanor's one-minute prompts:

Bitter: acrid, tinge, ache, bitter and sweet, bittersweet, citrus pith, marmalade, dark chocolate—yellow cinderblock, enduring stench, memory—

"Next word: teeter," Eleanor intoned.

Teeter: sway, scramble for balance, panic, moral indecision, unsure, uncertain, tightrope, cliff drop, high altitude—

"Caught."

Caught: net, rescued, captured, fly-ball, between a rock and a hard place, surveilled, unveiled, caught in the act, caught the light, caught the moment, caught my eye, caught me unaware—

"Sentinel."

Sentinel: vigilant, alert to threat, duty, ever-watchful, obliged to protect, protector, on guard, lookout, guardian, sentry—

"Vacant."

Vacant: yawning, empty, bare, hollow—

"It's time for our first twenty-minute write," Eleanor said. She offered four prompts:

1. Write about a time you found out a family secret.
2. Write about "time standing still."
3. Write something about "a skirl of bagpipes."
4. Write about invisible violence.

Nina knew not to think too long about the prompts—best to plunge in before analysis got in the way. "Skirl of bagpipes" brought Mingus to mind, but she was not in the mood to write about him. A family secret? Not today. Time standing still? Invisible violence? Maybe.

She used pen and paper for the one-minute prompts but now pulled the laptop screen toward her and pulled the desk's undershelf out, hovering her fingers over the ergonomic keyboard.

"A false accusation is visceral," she typed, "and evident only to its victim. Even when the layers of contrived proof peel away, like bitter pith, exposing truth, scars remain."

"How do I shake this off? Does Mom even remember her lawyer coming to her house? Have any idea of the case Dahlia was building that her daughter, her guardian, her protector, her keeper" Nina crossed "her keeper" out but made a mental note, shaking her head—she didn't want to be her mother's *keeper.* "has been charged with exploiting her? Abusing her?"

Nina sighed. This was not what she had in mind for writing. She counseled herself to try again.

"How do I stop dreaming of that day in the county jail? That smell?"

Nope. *Inhabit something fresh, bright,* she thought.

"Caught. Captured and… released," she wrote. "Like a trout interrupted on a moon-guided trajectory to its place of origin, its starting point; now its end. A trout toughened and aged from battling miles and miles of counter current, caught by a fly fisher standing solid in waders resisting the rushing water. As the fish is reeled in its scales catch the sun. The fisher's canvas-gloved fingers grasp the wriggling belly, holding the tail by the other hand. Thank you, he says out loud, and as he points the trout's head into the current, his words wash into the roar of the river. He lets his catch go, resuming its journey."

"Three minutes," Eleanor's voice interrupted. "Find a way to come to a close."

Nina shook her head. What did she know about fly fishing? Nothing. Maybe she'd be more successful writing about the skirl of bagpipes. Too much thinking was functioning like a dam… *shit, there I go again*, she thought.

Words were not helping; they were getting in the way. She needed to get to a clearing of sorts to empty her mind of words. Sun lit the spaces between her office's window blinds. It had stopped raining.

"I'm sorry," she said when Eleanor announced from her Zoom frame that time was up. "I can't stay."

Everyone offered quick goodbyes as Nina left the meeting.

Zipping her down coat closed, she made her way through the back of the house. The ragged strains of a viola pierced the living room wall. She lifted the leash from the hook by the back door.

"Let's go, laddie," she said. Mingus didn't hear her, of course, but when she reached down to latch his collar, his ears softened. It was possible his tail moved.

The novelty of a rainy winter in Sacramento begat the novelty of appreciation for clear skies. *Quite the opposite of the customary years of drought,* Nina noted as they crossed the street. She glanced back at the odd sight of their back fence, no longer hidden behind the seventy-foot elm they relied on for shade every summer. Only its root bed and trunk remained, out of sight from the street. She and Myles had already seen the damage done to their closest neighbors, but as she and Mingus ventured further on and into the park, she found herself gasping at the scale of destruction. deodar cedars, magnolias, camphors, Modesto ashes, and other Chinese elms laid out like corpses, all facing south, some root beds as tall as two men.

"Mingus!" A neighbor from another block approached with her Labradoodle.

"Murphy!" Nina called back.

The neighbor crossed the street and shook her head as she pulled out Kleenex. "So many trees." The dogs sniffed each other, and after thirty seconds, Nina pulled on Mingus' collar to keep going. She didn't want to talk (and why didn't she know this woman's name?).

As they passed the park's tennis courts, the wider scope of the damage in Curtis Park became apparent. It was awful. Unquestionably awful. And in that moment, she had a surprising thought: *once these boles are hauled away, saplings will be planted.* And to a newcomer, someone unfamiliar with the density of trees before, there'd be no evidence that there'd been a disastrous loss. An abundance of majestic sycamores and cedars still graced the park. Instead of stately trees in every front yard, it would likcly be every three front yards. *Yes, painful. But,* Nina thought, *Sacramento would still be The City of Trees.*

Nina rounded the park and came to the bench where she and Cori often met up. She sat and lifted Mingus to her lap. He was too big a dog for that and too dignified, but she needed to bury her nose into his sweet-smelling neck.

The mediation was scheduled for December eighteenth.

All will be well.

Why, then, in her mind, did this declaration come with a question mark?

CHAPTER SIXTY-FOUR

LILLIAN

illian glanced around her. The waiting area of Centering Mediation looked like one of her wealthy book club friend's living rooms: white leather sectionals flanked by Danish modern tables. She fingered one of the hydrangeas in the opulent arrangement next to her. Silk. *Everything elegant but artificial*, she thought. While Dahlia Crenshaw-Bates spoke quietly to the receptionist, Lillian tried to remember why she and her lawyer were there. Above the reception counter, framed in silver, was a quotation in poster-scale type: "We cannot solve our problems with the same thinking that we used to create them. -Albert Einstein."

Amen, she thought. In the same moment, Nina entered with a woman Lillian didn't recognize.

"Nina!" Lillian attempted to rise.

"Mom." Nina reached for her.

Dahlia and the other woman glanced at each other; Dahlia shifted toward Lillian.

"We'll have a chance to talk soon," she said. "Once all of us are here."

"All of us?" Lillian turned to Nina, who had taken a seat next to the unknown woman. "Who else is coming?" When Nina shrugged, Lillian asked the woman who she was.

"I'm Marla Sevorian," she said. "Nina's attorney."

"Attorney?"

The door opened.

"Nat!" Lillian exclaimed. "What are you doing here?" She wasn't accustomed to seeing him without a protest sign.

An interior door opened from behind the reception area. A man in his mid-fifties walked toward them, tortoise-shell framing thick lenses. He first bent to shake Lillian's hand.

"Mrs. Nearing, I'm Lewis Anderson," he said. "I will be the mediator today."

"Call me Lillian, please," she smiled fleetingly. "I just don't understand what we're all doing here."

"Our goal is to clear that up," he said before straightening to acknowledge everyone else. "Shall we?" He pointed to the door he'd come from. Lillian allowed Dahlia to help her stand and reached for her hand as they followed Lewis down the hall to a glassed-in conference room.

When Dahlia pulled a chair out for her, Lillian asked to sit by Nina. Dahlia urged her to stay where she was. "It'll be fine," she said.

When all parties were seated and introduced, everyone faced Lewis at the head of the lustrous table.

"Welcome to everyone. I'll repeat what you already know from our outreach team's phone call: we are here to have a conversation. My role is to be sure everyone is heard. I am not here to solve your problem…"

Lillian interrupted. "What problem?"

"...I am here," Lewis continued, "to help *you* solve said problem. To clarify, Lillian, your lawyer has indicated that you are concerned that your daughter, Nina Visser, has been taking advantage of you. Financially."

Lillian swerved in Nina's direction. "You have?"

Nina's expression froze, but she shook her head. Her lawyer, Marla, placed a hand over hers.

Lewis directed his attention to Nat. "Nat, you are here with supporting evidence for Lillian's accusation. This would be a good time for you to talk."

Nat, grim, looked at Lillian, then faced the group seated around the table. "Lilly has been sharing with the vigil group how her independence has been jerked away from her. Her driver's license. Her car. And we have proof of checks that have been made out to Nina, in Nina's handwriting. Large sums. One for over twenty thousand dollars."

Lillian gasped. "Nina, what?"

Lewis cleared his throat. "Lillian, can you share with us the concern you shared with your friends from the vigil?"

"I don't think I said anything to them about any of this." She glared at Nat.

Both of Nat's fists pounded the table. "What are you talking about? Lilly, you've been coming on Fridays by Lyft because you don't have your own car! You told us Nina took your car and sold it. Have you ever seen the money? I'm here because I'm your friend!"

"You don't seem like a friend right now," Lillian said. "Nina, what is he talking about?"

"Mom," Nina started, but Lewis stopped her.

"Lillian, what is your understanding of the concern your friend Nat has presented?"

"He's saying my daughter has been taking advantage of me. Why is he saying this? Nina is taking care of me. She takes care of everything. The house. The bills. The tenant. I wish she lived closer. I know it's hard for her."

"Do you have any response to the charge that she is writing checks to herself from your accounts?"

"She reimburses herself for things she's paid for—on my behalf."

"Let's focus on the single large sum Nat brought to our attention," Lewis said. "The check made out to Nina for over twenty thousand dollars. Do you remember what this expense was?"

Lillian shook her head. "I have no idea."

"It was for the American Airlines tickets, Mom." Nina's voice was shaking. "You charged them on your credit card for a…" Nina looked at Nat. "…future tour you thought you'd lead to Cuba. Remember?"

Lillian did not remember.

"When the credit union used your checking account to pay your credit card bill, all of the other automatic payments continued to be withdrawn, and overdraft charges alerts came in fast and furious. I had to cover some of it myself as," Nina's eyes watered, "damage control."

Again, Marla placed her hand over Nina's. "We have bank statements here from both Lillian's accounts and Nina's," she said. She looked around the table. "This is easy to reconcile." She handed a file to the mediator, who pulled out his reading glasses.

"You see?" Lillian smiled at Lewis. "Nina is protecting me. Nat, I think you are trying to protect me, too. I appreciate that. But this is my daughter. She has my best interests in mind."

Nina rushed from her chair to hug Lillian around her shoulders from behind. "I love you, Mom." Then she turned back to look at Nat.

Nat scowled. "This system," he muttered.

Lewis cleared his throat again, and asked that everyone remain seated while he finished reading the documents. Pulling off his glasses, he looked up. "As we explained previously, this meeting has been recorded for the court. The evidence presented this morning supports Nina Gilbert's intentions to work on her mother's behalf." He looked pointedly at Nat. "To *protect* her financial interests." Turning to Lillian, he smiled gently. "Everyone around this table is here because they are concerned about you. Hopefully our meeting has cleared up any confusion for all parties. If you, Lillian Nearing, agree, I will ask both attorneys for a statement that the charges against Nina Visser of elder abuse be dropped."

Lillian's eyes widened. "Elder abuse? Heavens, no. Are we done? This is… absurd. Nina, can we go?"

All eyes fell on the mediator. He stood. "Thank you, everyone."

Goodbyes were hasty. As people pushed in their chairs, Nat's hit the table edge hard.

Nina held Lillian's left hand to steady her. As she always did. At the exit, Nat came alongside. "You sure you're okay, Lilly?" He said.

Lillian waved him off with her other hand. "We're fine. Thanks for your concern. Let everyone at the vigil know we're—" she cocked her head toward her daughter, "just fine."

He directed his next statement to Nina. "I'm just confused. It's… she doesn't remember any of these things she told us?"

"Maybe you understand now why I asked for your help?" Nina seethed between her teeth. Or so it seemed to Lillian. It had been a long day. She was ready to go home.

Chapter Sixty-Five

Lillian and Nina

New Year's Day 2023. Monterey Bay.

As she leaned back into the Adirondack chair, Lillian watched the gray ocean dissolve into the sky, blurring the horizon. The blanket Myles brought from the hotel room covered most of her. Pulling it tighter, she warmed with gratitude for her son-in-love's thoughtfulness as well as for the length of her down coat. She shivered, but the view was unequaled, and the smell of salt invigorated her senses. It had been a long time since she'd been outside on the coast.

"I wish Jenny could be here."

"Mom, you'll see her next weekend."

Jenny was flying in from Chicago to stay for a week.

Mingus nestled into Nina's lap as she and Myles sat in chairs on either side of Lillian, gazing at the tide as it spilled toward them and then retracted. The ocean always provided perspective, and it was perspective that Nina and Myles sorely needed. Still processing recent events, things seemed surreal.

Reflecting back to the moment after the arrest when Myles contacted their nephew for help, they recalled how Alex's confidence had provided a modicum of relief.

"Aunt Nina's been charged with financial elder abuse because of someone's suspicions," he said, "but you have nothing to worry about, I promise." He'd actually chuckled. "The truth is going to be easy to substantiate. Once she meets with Marla, she'll just need to answer some questions. It might even end up getting resolved in mediation."

It had.

"Let's not relive any of this with Mom," Nina had said to Myles after the judge's decision.

"It's a wonder," he said. "Even after the welfare visit with the social worker, the visit from the attorney, the mediation, she doesn't seem to remember any of it."

"Why should this be any different than any of her other short-term memory lapses? Given time, it will be as if it never happened." For Nina, it was a closed case. "It will only disturb her if we tell her."

The cliff at their backs was a launching point for adventurous hang gliders. Within a few minutes after settling in, a glider rose above them, interrupting the mesmerizing lull of the breakers. Myles gently squeezed Lillian's hand so she was made aware of what was overhead.

"Oh!" she exclaimed. Her white head followed the glider as it caught currents of rising air. Its wing was painted a brilliant scarlet; the color popped against the overcast sky.

"Did you ever try that?" she asked Myles.

He shook his head and pulled his knit hat to cover his ears. "I've gone parasailing with a parachute that's attached to a speedboat," he said. "Nothing like this… although I did once participate in a tasting of a seventeenth-century wine. *That* was an adventure."

Lillian raised her eyebrows, then turned to Nina. "What about you?"

"Jumped out of a plane," she answered. "Not this."

"You jumped out of a plane!?" Lillian sounded shocked. "Why?"

"Youth," Nina smiled at her mother. "You did crazy things, too."

"Really?" Lillian seemed to be digging into her memory. "Like what?"

"You hitchhiked across Europe by yourself," Nina began to list things she knew about her mother's life. "Right after World War II, Mom. You were a Jewish girl teaching English in Bavaria!" Lillian nodded, closing her eyes. "You marched in civil rights marches and risked arrest. You were an election monitor during South Africa's first free elections. That was a scary, violent time."

"But not crazy," Lillian responded. "It didn't seem particularly adventurous. It needed to be done, and I was able to do it," she said. "That's all."

She went quiet. The glider was gone, replaced by a flock of big-jawed pelicans sweeping the surface with their distinctive silhouettes. Gulls' screeches grew fainter, blown away with the wind, and sand filled the folds of the blankets. The sun approached the invisible line dividing the sea and the sky.

Lillian spoke again. "We wanted a family. But…"

Nina and Myles watched and listened. *Where was this coming from?*

"But I wasn't the parent Cal was. He was such a good father. Loving. He enjoyed you and Jenny so much."

"Mom."

"I'm so glad you had Dad. And I see all the time the same kindness in you that he had."

"Mom," Nina flushed, "You influenced us too. And… I really wonder sometimes if you'd been born when I was born… if you'd even chosen to have children."

"Like you chose not to have children?"

"Yes."

Lillian thought for a moment. "Maybe I wouldn't have. But even with all our mistakes with you and Jenny, and even though I wasn't a great mother, I'm so glad we had a family."

Nina smiled. "Well, to state the obvious… I'm glad, too."

Myles squeezed Nina's hand. She often stated the obvious.

"Happy you approve," Lillian pulled the blanket tighter. The wind had picked up.

Nina felt grit in her teeth. "Let's go in!"

Myles helped Lillian up from the wooden chair while Nina took her other side. They made their way through the sand to the accessible unit they'd rented for the long weekend. Once inside, Myles headed to a bedroom to watch the end of a game while, in the diminutive seating area, Nina turned on the gas fireplace.

"Gas?" Lillian frowned. "I hate that we're using fossil fuel."

Nina left to make tea. Lillian gazed into the flames, remembering a fragment of something said while they were on the beach. What had they been talking about? Having children? Cal? She remembered how, toward the end, Cal asked almost daily why he was still here. She remembered clearly what she kept answering: "You have given to others all your life. You're here to receive love, Cal."

Nina returned to the living room and set down two steaming cups. Rooibos. Lillian thanked her daughter for remembering her favorite tea, the tea she and Cal had discovered in South Africa.

"Nina, I'm just so old. Why am I still here?"

"Mom, you ask that a lot. Have you thought about it? Is there something you still need to learn?" Nina asked.

"I can't think of anything."

"Tastes like old socks," Nina said, recoiling.

"What does?"

"Mom, you get that we have blind spots, right?" She skipped over the bitterness of the tea. "Things others may observe about us, but we can't see for ourselves?"

"Like you don't realize how judgmental you can be."

Nina shifted in her seat.

"And how bossy you are."

"Yes, Mom," Nina said. She noticed an unfamiliar lift, an absence of... what? Of... swear words in her head. She laughed. "Like that."

"But there are other things, too, that I don't know if you see in *yourself*. That you are a great friend." Lillian paused. "And you've become *my* friend."

Nina looked directly into Lillian's green eyes. "It's true. We have become friends. We've lived long enough to be grownups together. How lucky is that?"

"We caught up with each other, didn't we?" Lillian said.

"We caught up."

Lillian's eyes filled. She turned toward the flames in the fireplace. "But I have a question."

Nina waited.

"Did I drive here?"

"No, Mom. Myles drove us to the coast."

"I wasn't sure," Lillian smiled. "I thought so."

"The important thing, Mom?"

Lillian faced Nina. "What, dear?"

Nina kissed her mother on the cheek. "We're together. And we're heading in the same direction."

"We're traveling together in love."

"Yes, Mom."

Even with the windows closed, the sound of the ocean lulled and crashed, pulled, and gave way. Night was here. And in the north, a star.

Acknowledgements

Many special people helped with the birthing of this novel. My gratitude goes to:

- My River Rock Writers friends, for their commitment to surprise as we write together on Tuesdays.

- My beta readers: Dane Andrus, Craig Ulmer, Laurie Owens, and Beth Maerten.

- Stephanie Dethlefs, for coaching a habitual pantser-writer to use a map.

- Robert Henry, for his masterful copy-editing and formatting skills, good nature, and quick turnarounds.

- Beth Johnson, for her attention to balancing weight inside a poem.

- JB Maerten, my writing partner and motivator, who showed me that novels really do get published. (Her book, *Of One Mind*, is a fascinating read.)

- Lexi Negin, for walking me through the Sacramento Courthouse and the arrest, booking, and arraignment process.

- Nada Orlic (Erelis Design), for her collaborative openness to sensitively creating a cover to reflect Nina and Lillian's relationship arc.

- My editor, Dr. Mary Rakow, whose gifted sense brought more of my voice to the page.

- Carol Rex, MSW, for sharing her knowledge of Adult Protective Services in California.

- My beloved Dane, who willingly carves out room in our lives for my writing, always tells me the truth, and doesn't complain about eating late.

- My mother, who inspired the story she will never read.

Caregiver Resources

When I found myself slammed by the tsunami of caregiving, I kicked and thrashed to find my way.

Now, I'm a big believer in learning from those who've navigated the waters before us. Friends and family among you are likely to have been caregivers, assuming they aren't currently. Experienced friends who answered my phone calls were my search and rescue team, casting me life preservers on choppy seas.

Guidance for caregiving is also available from organizations and government agencies. An excellent place to start that search is to tap into the vast resources provided by AARP, along with local senior centers and Councils on Aging.

And if you're not sure what to ask, here are some questions, for starters:

- How do we manage a loved one's financial obligations?

- How do we find trusted caregivers for in-home care?

- How do we locate appropriate care homes and facilities?

- How do we connect with formal and informal support groups?

- How do we connect with healthcare professionals skilled in working with the aging?

- How does long-term health insurance work?

- How do we communicate compassionately with someone who is in cognitive decline?

- How do we find ways to restore ourselves when we feel depleted?

The answers you find will likely lead to more questions. Eventually, your knowledge and understanding will broaden and deepen, and when the time comes, you can supply a life preserver for others as they face the unmapped territory of helping the elders and less able in their lives.

BOOK CLUB QUESTIONS

1. Nina feels blindsided when she learns that her father is dying. Does this reaction surprise you? How did you react the first time you faced the death of a primary person in your life?

2. After Cal dies, Nina perceives Lillian's lack of visible grieving as emotional avoidance. Why do you think she worries about her mother's way of responding to her profound loss?

3. As Lillian purposely forges on without Cal, Nina embraces the openings her retirement affords her. After a significant loss, is it possible to normalize life?

4. After COVID shuts down face-to-face connection, Lillian uncharacteristically reaches out to her daughter. Nina is overwhelmed with surprise and unexpected tenderness. Did your relationships change during the pandemic?

5. When it becomes increasingly apparent that Lillian needs help, Nina initially feels resentful. Is this response one of entitlement? Is there a way to interpret her resentment differently?

6. How does one reconcile caregiving for another who did not emotionally connect with the caregiver in the past?

7. How do the caregiving roles of siblings and other family members come into play? What are some ways geographically distant family might provide support to the more local caregiver?

8. How is Lillian a sympathetic character?
How is she unsympathetic?

9. How is Nina a sympathetic character?
How is she unsympathetic?

10. It is not uncommon for elders to be financially exploited by caregivers. What is your understanding of Adult Protective Services?

11. Dementia challenges caregivers on many levels, depending on the stages of cognitive decline. Nina feels protective of her mother's dignity and chooses to keep Lillian's cognitive decline concealed from both Lillian and her circle. How does this act of love complicate Lillian's friends' interpretation of events?

12. Dementia distorts the idea of the person we knew "before," sometimes in disturbing ways far beyond the depiction in this novel. In what ways might dementia bring something essential and enriching to family members and friends?

Karen Andrus is available to attend book club discussions in person and virtually. Contact: karenandrus7@gmail.com